MA

MADAM LYDIA

Philippa Masters

This book is a work of fiction.
In real life, make sure you practise safe sex.

First published in 1996 by
Nexus
332 Ladbroke Grove
London W10 5AH

Typeset by TW Typesetting, Plymouth, Devon

Printed and bound by
BPC Paperbacks Ltd, Aylesbury, Bucks

ISBN 0 352 33115 1

Foreword

The story of my Great Aunt Lydia continued to delight and astonish me as I sat reading the neatly written piles of manuscript. In my mind, visions of the lady I had known, a typical example of a prim Victorian lady, strict, and smelling of lavender, alternated and contrasted wildly with the images of the light-hearted, humorous, and deliciously lascivious girl depicted in her saga.

Could these two really be one and the same person? Could the tiny, silver-haired woman who had always filled me with a kind of respectful awe, who was held in high regard by all who knew her, and who looked as though she could never have committed even the tiniest of sins, really be the girl in the story; the girl who debunked what she disparaged as 'proper society', who reveled in the delights of sex, who knew and joyously indulged in every trick and naughtiness there was?

Hard as it was for me to believe, it had to be true, for other evidence confirmed it, and the manuscript was definitely in her own copperplate handwriting.

I had followed her amazing story from when she had been a trembling, innocent sixteen-year-old girl in South Africa, 'awakened' by the tribe of Africans who had kidnapped her. (Told in *The Awakening of*

Lydia.) I had shared with her the delights of her shipboard adventures when sailing back to England, and her voluptuous experiences when staying with the local Turkish ruler while the ship's engine underwent repairs (*Lydia in the Harem*).

In the third part of her story, *Lydia in the Bordello*, curiosity, bad luck, good luck, and strength in the face of the hypocrisy she scorned, caused wild and dramatic changes in Lydia's life. From the cherished daughter of a British colonial official, she became an outcast, forced to stand on her own two feet in a hostile and predatory society. With a strength of character and sense of humour I found staggering, she not only met the challenge, but built for herself a whole new life using the only qualification society had provided for her – herself.

That the little old lady I had thought so prim and proper could once have been what she called a *fille de joie* – and to judge from her tale an enthusiastic and popular one – astounded me. Now, as I read on, my astonishment, and my admiration too, grew further.

The circles within which she moved, and the aspects of society she reveals, show that the world of late Victorian and early Edwardian times was far from that which history books suggest. 'Sex societies' for the upper classes; live 'performances' for the enjoyment of salacious audiences; 'house parties', 'private engagements' and flourishing brothels; even the 'training' of upper class teenagers, are all described in simple, common sense and non-judgemental terms. And it is a revelation!

Philippa Masters.

One

I was off on my first private engagement as a *fille de joie*, one of Lady Amelia Amberson's 'professional girls'. It had been arranged by Karl, my procurer and Lady Amelia's partner in running her bordello, the *Silken Web*. Karl always arranged these engagements, in which we girls went to the home of our client, or to his hotel, for an evening and night of paid pleasuring. He had already sent Kate out on a couple, and this was my debut, as it were.

As was, apparently, often the case, my unknown punter had particular tastes. I was dressed rather young. My skirts came not much below my knees; the lacy edges of my pantalettes showed underneath, and between them and my little button shoes I had on striped cotton hose. My hair was parted in the middle, and held in bunches over my ears, I wore a floppy felt bonnet like a girl hardly out of school, and no cosmetics.

The only feature that made me look other than a young girl was the way my blouse was fitted tightly to play up my breasts, which bobbed and jiggled about beneath the cotton quite visibly, because Karl had forbidden me a corset. That the effect was as naughty as Karl intended was soon shown.

Albert, Amelia's groom, was to drive me to my assignation. He well knew what business I was about.

Though he had first seen me as Lady Amelia's guest, he now knew I had become one of her girls. The way he looked at me as he handed me into the carriage told me clearly that any reservations he may have had about trying it on with me when I first came to the house had long disappeared.

His eyes took in every bit of me, and especially my unconstrained breasts. I almost giggled, for I was sure that he was tempted to feel me up as I bent to get into the carriage. He did not, though he did keep turning to look at me through the little trap-door used for communication between passenger and driver as the horses clip-clopped steadily along.

I was quite wound up about my engagement, and what the client would want of me, which Karl had left rather vague, and was not really paying attention to the drive or to Albert. Thus, I was somewhat startled when the carriage came to a stop in the deep shadow of a side-street, and bounced as Albert leapt off the driving seat and climbed into the carriage with me.

I could see next to nothing but I did not need to, for his hands were suddenly everywhere!

'Oh heavens no, Albert,' I squealed. 'Don't! You'll mess up my clothes. Oh! Stop it! Get your hand out of there! Oh!'

I was tumbled back across the seat. His hot lips were seeking mine. A hand was scrabbling at my blouse. Another was already under my skirt, pulling at my underwear.

'Oh, Lily, Lily,' he panted, using my professional name. 'I've got to have you! You're a tasty little piece, and I've got to have you or burst!'

I had to fight him off. I even had to give his face a slap before he would desist. I could not do with going to my assignation all hot from Albert. I managed to get him off, and cooled him a bit by promising he

4

could have a nice shag later, but it was a sullen Albert who drove me the rest of the way.

With a final smoothing of my blouse and skirt, and pulling my cape close about me, I gave a pull at the bell-handle. I heard the bell ring some way off, and waited. It was a grand, three-storey house in a curving Nash terrace. I ran over in my head the few things Karl had told me. A rather superior looking footman in a handsome uniform opened the door.

'Good evening,' I said, looking down as though I were shy. 'Pray tell me, is my benefactor Mr John Thomas at home?'

The footman remained impassive, though he obviously knew what business I was about. He stepped back, swung the door wide, and gestured me to enter. At the far end of the palatial, marble-floored lobby, stood my punter. He was a balding man of at least sixty, with a sharp nose upon which were perched brass-framed *pince-nez*. I felt a flush of relief that he was not too unappealing!

He threw his arms wide. 'Fanny!' he called. 'Fanny, my darling! Run to your beloved uncle! Let me see you!'

It was all clear to me now; Karl's advice, my costume, everything. My punter was, clearly, a man who enjoyed fantasy and play-acting, and in this scenario I was to be coy and call him 'uncle' as a young lady might her beloved benefactor. Feeling silly, I scampered with skipping steps across the marble tiles towards him, putting a wide smile on my face, and spreading my arms.

He grabbed me to himself, hugged me tightly and kissed me on my cheek. I noticed that he had been chewing on a *cachou*, so at least his breath would not be off-putting. He put his hands on my shoulders and held me off from him to look at me.

'My, my, but how you have grown,' he said, unbuttoning my cape while looking only at where my breasts jiggled against my thin blouse. 'You are quite the lady now.'

This, I thought, was likely to be an interesting evening. Taking me by the hand, and swinging my arm as though I really were his young friend, 'Uncle John Thomas' led me through into a beautifully furnished parlour. Heavy drapes of blue velvet shrouded the windows. Neat little tables stood beside deeply cushioned armchairs and a vast settee. A fire burned brightly in an iron and marble fireplace. Flowers (Flowers at this time of year! He must be wealthy indeed!) spilled out of vases.

'Uncle John Thomas' sat himself down in an armchair, still holding my hand so that I was obliged to stand close.

There was a brief moment of complicity in which he looked at me with no play-acting, for there was business to be conducted. He drew from an inner pocket the envelope which contained my fee. I took it and stowed it in my reticule before once again becoming the fluttering thing he wanted me to be. It was a game he was obviously experienced in, for with a glance to the envelope as I put it away, and another at the way my breasts strained my blouse, he went back to acting.

'Now, my dear little Fanny,' he said, smiling almost unctuously, his eyes flicking from my face to my bosom. 'Tell your uncle what you have been doing with yourself all this while since I last saw you. Have you been a good girl?'

I guessed straightaway that I was in for a game of verbal battledore and shuttlecock, for he was going to talk as though we had known each other for years, and my job, if I was to please him, was to pick up his hints and respond in the right loving-admirer manner.

'Oh yes, sir. I have been as good as gold.' I beamed down at him wide eyed, and swung my shoulders from side to side, as a shy young girl might.

His face became stern. 'A really good girl? Not naughty at all?'

I was in a bit of a quandary. How was I supposed to respond? I ventured that what he wanted was for me to have been at least a little naughty; why else would he have framed his question thus? Therefore I made myself be all shy and guilty, and looked at the floor, and laced my fingers together below my waist, and swung my shoulders more, but said nothing.

A gleam came into his eye.

'Aha!' The tone of his voice told me I had ventured right. He was pretending to be strict, but was actually getting stirred up. He went on. 'So! My little friend has secrets from her benefactor. Come; sit here. You must confess all.' And he pulled me down on to his lap.

He was keeping his face straight, but his eyes told of his delighted excitement. I knew not where the odd conversation was supposed to go next, so kept silent and pretended to be shy.

He bounced me on his knee a little, incidentally getting me more comfortably settled up against the hardness I could detect within his breeches. One arm was about my waist, and his free hand was on the arm of the chair.

'Have you been out in the woods with those naughty farm labourers again?' he said. 'Have you allowed them liberties?'

I guessed his game. I was to be a naughty girl confessing to a caring elder. He would use the occasion to excuse whatever 'liberties' he was himself about to take with me.

'Yes, sir.' I said, leaning my head against his

7

shoulder as though in repentance. 'But only a little bit, honestly!' It seemed to please him.

'And did you let them do this?' The hand that had been on the arm of the chair was suddenly cupping my left breast.

'Yes, sir,' I whispered, pleased that I had guessed the game correctly.

'And this?' He began to knead my breast, and tease my nipple. 'Did you let them do this?'

'Yes, sir. I'm sorry, sir.'

'Surely you are not going to tell me you let those fellows do this?' And with admirably skillful fingers, he unbuttoned my blouse, and got to my bare breasts.

It became quite hard to play my assigned role. All his questions demanded a positive response, and he used them to get my blouse pulled out of my skirt and flung wide, and my skirt up above my knees, and his hand rummaging inside my pantalettes. And all the time I was having to say that, yes, I had let 'those ruffians' – whoever they were supposed to be – do this, and do that.

There was a considerable element of humour in what he was doing, what *we* were doing, for was I not playing up to him? At the same time, though, the more stirred up he got in playing out his pantomime, the more aroused I was myself becoming.

When his hand became active between my thighs, I parted them for him. When a finger slipped into me, and a thumb teased my cherry, I was hard put to it to respond to his inevitable question with 'Yes, sir, yes! I did, and I am very naughty!'

It was almost a relief to get down to the proper business of the evening; to the real reason he was paying me to be there. He slipped me off his lap to kneel on the rug. My blouse was as much off as on.

My felt bonnet had gone I knew not where. He stood up. Our positions ensured that his hips were close above my face.

'Did those fellows show you this?' he barked, his throat tense as he ripped open his breeches. His cock was of moderate size, but circumcised (which I like) and with a shining, purple bulb.

'Oh no, sir,' I squealed in mock horror. 'Well, they did, but theirs were not near as big as yours!'

'You wicked girl!' he hissed. 'You are too naughty for words! What else did you let them do?'

The game ended up with me admitting that, in the woods I had let them put their 'things' up me, and with 'Uncle John Thomas' telling me that I was a strumpet and should be spanked. Then he walked out of the room!

How strange men are!

He had paid for my services, and could have just shagged me; shagged me as many times as he liked, or had the strength for. Instead, he needed to go through this game of benefactor and grateful beneficiary in order to get stirred up, and had then left me.

How silly! He would not have been a bad shag to look at him, and the cock that had pressed against my bottom when I sat on his lap had not been insignificant. In addition, I was quite ready to stay until morning, as much because I was quite stirred up as because I was being paid for it. He could have had half a dozen shags if he'd liked!

Instead, I was left to gather my rumpled clothes about me, get up off the floor, and seek out the footman. I would need a cab to get me home, for Albert was not due to collect me until morning.

The footman had been very dignified when he had let me in, and his face had borne a hint of disapproval. Now, his expression was very different.

A girl knows instantly when a man's mind is set on being naughty with her. This man had about him that tension, that sort of preening hopefulness, which suggested he was hot for me, and his eyes flicked over my blouse with open salaciousness.

He was quite an imposing figure in his uniform; tall and straight, with broad shoulders and fine legs. Only his complexion, which showed the ravages of acne long cured, detracted from his image.

He stood as tall as he could, and a little closer than strictly necessary. It was obvious what he wanted. I wondered whether being shagged by the footman was included in the fee which was safely tucked into my reticule.

As he led me across the marble floor of the lobby, the footman was edging me towards a large table against the wall and to one side. My mind was working rapidly. He had not said anything, not asked for it. Then again, he knew what sort of girl I was playing; knew what I had come here for. Perhaps he did the same with every girl who came here, for surely I was not the first. Even so, it seemed pretty impertinent of him to assume that he could get a ride, as it were, on the back of his master's money.

Then I suddenly realised what was really afoot. I noticed that a door, just beyond the table towards which the footman was edging me, was a few inches ajar. Through the gap I espied the glint of *pince-nez*!

The game was not over. My punter had a second game to play. He was going to watch! Mentally, I got myself back into the part of 'Little Fanny'. Obviously, the new game was about the footman having his way with me 'against my wishes' on the table there, for the delectation of his watching master. How was the game to be played? Was I to be such a naughty girl that I fancied the servant? Or was I to play at being sweet and reluctant?

A hand suddenly groping my bottom gave me my answer. I squealed and leapt forward, partly in genuine surprise, for the hand had felt me up very thoroughly between my buttocks. I spun round, putting on an expression of outraged innocence, at the same time getting myself neatly between the corner of the table and the wall so that he had me trapped.

'Sir!' I yelped. 'What has come over you?'

What had come over him was unconcealed lust, for his face showed that although this might be a game, he fully intended to play it to the hilt.

A strong arm went about my waist. I was crushed to him. A big hand landed on my breast. Hot kisses cut off my cries of protest. I pretended to be terrified. I pretended to struggle – and did actually struggle a bit when he tore open my blouse, for that was going a bit too far, I thought – but let him get me against the table.

As I was pushed back on to the polished table top, the punter got an excellent view of my breasts through my torn and gaping blouse. My skirts were thrown up to my waist.

'Oh, please don't! Please don't!' I cried, continuing to play my part as an innocent being ravished. 'Oh, sir, you terrify me!'

He got my legs up, and was fumbling inside my pantalettes. He began to tug at the waist of my skirt. Then I had an idea to give my punter an even better view than he might have expected.

'Oh, sir!' I yelped. 'Please don't tear my clothes! You have already ripped my blouse. Don't tear my skirt too! I will get into awful trouble with Uncle John Thomas. Please don't tear my clothes. If you will stop molesting me I'll be a good girl. Honest I will. I'll take them off for you, I really will. Please get up off me.'

For a moment the footman looked puzzled, then he grinned as he realised my ploy. He let up on me. I tugged at the fastenings of my skirt and pushed it down about my hips. He did the rest, pulling it right off me and tossing it aside. I sat up and undid the few remaining buttons of my blouse.

'Do I have to?' I said, all timid and pretending to hesitate. He nodded eagerly, and I slipped the torn garment from my shoulders and held it out to him, looking down shyly, and half covering my exposed breasts with my forearm. 'You will not be rough with me, will you?' I asked, reclining again upon the table top, which was cold and hard against my bare back.

He began to untie the laces of my pantalettes, tugging off first the right leg, then the left.

'Oh no!' I cried. 'Not those too! You will have me naked! Oh no! Oh sir, what are you doing! Oh, you are so wicked!'

What he was doing was lifting my legs wide apart and burying his head between them. I adore it when a man does that! And this man was greedy! It was as if he was trying to bury his whole face within me. And he had such a tongue! It got very difficult to remember that all this was for the benefit of the man peeping through the gap in the door.

The footman got my legs over his shoulders. One arm was around my hips, the hand feeling down for my mound. The other hand was palping my buttocks, spreading and kneading them, even teasing into my bottom-hole.

He rasped his hot tongue the full length of my folds, which were already moist and seeping. He had got his fingers to me by now, and was holding my lips spread. His tongue got to every delicate membrane, even finding and exploring my burning entrance.

I had ceased acting a part. I had already been wound

up by the game with 'Uncle John Thomas', but I had not come off. I did now. The footman's tongue and lips were working on me overwhelmingly. I was rolling my head upon the hard table top, and teasing my own nipples. When, at the same shattering instant, he thrust a finger into both my nether orifices and sucked almost painfully hard on my clitoris, I cried aloud, and shuddered into such a come as set my hips bucking.

He did not let up on me, either. When he withdrew his mouth from me so that he could stand up, letting my trembling legs slide off his shoulders and down his arms, his hands continued to work me. Still teasing and fingering me with one hand, he fumbled at his breeches with the other.

His cock bounced forth. It was handsome and stalwart. And heavens how I wanted it! Somehow I managed to remember who I was supposed to be.

'No! Not that!' I cried in a small voice. 'Do not do that to me! It is too big. You will hurt me! Oh, no, you are up me. You wicked man. Oh, you do shove so! It is in me to my ribs! Oh faster, faster! Oh sir! Please! Oh! Oh!'

He was deliciously vigorous, and thrust at me hard and slow. The words I called out had been half false. My continued coming was very real. It had been as good a shag as I had enjoyed in a while. I only hoped that my watching punter had got as much pleasure out of it as I had.

His duty and me thoroughly done, the footman stepped back from me, put himself away and did up his breeches.

'And let that be a lesson to you for being naughty!' he said – his only words during the whole engagement.

He walked off with surprising dignity, and I was

left to scramble off the table and into my clothes. I guessed that this, too, was part of tonight's strange game. Thus, I made something of a production of it, pretending to be upset, gathering all my garments together and putting them on the table before beginning to get dressed, staying naked save for my striped hose and boots for as long as possible, so that my punter should benefit.

When at last I was ready to depart, the self-same footman who had just fucked me to a finish was at the door, ready to hand me into the hansom cab that had been sent for to take me home. To see the dispassionate, even superior, manner with which he conducted me to the cab, you would have thought I really was just a visitor, and not a hired girl who had just spent two hours or more playing sex games!

The cab driver at least knew I had not been just a visitor. Perhaps cab drivers see enough of London life after dark to know it all. Perhaps this one had taken girls from my client's house before. Or it might have been that he knew, from my saying of Amelia's address, what game I was on.

Whichever it was, my evening ended with him rejecting the idea of the fare, for which I was fumbling in my reticule, and climbing into the cab with me.

'Don't worry about that, ducks,' he said, reaching for his fly. 'Give us a nice little gobble, and we'll call it quits!'

I stared at him in amazement. Had I heard right? I had! The cabby had sat himself down beside me, his trousers agape, and a very stiff cock was staring up at me. I stared from the single eye of his ruby plum to the two twinkling eyes in his grinning face. Suddenly the ridiculousness of it all hit me. I burst into a fit of giggles, and it was some while before I recovered myself enough to shuffle round in my seat and bob my head down.

He tasted surprisingly clean and fresh. Towards the end he got a bit too excited and I had to push him back lest he choke me, but I 'paid my fare' to his satisfaction – a great deal of satisfaction, to judge from the amount I had to swallow! – and at last I wended my tired way through the front door of what was now my home.

I compensated Albert, who was meant to collect me, later that afternoon, by the way, and it was rather nice for he is a vigorous chap, although Kate got a little jealous for a while.

With seeming inevitability, Karl was on hand to welcome me. He regarded me quizzically as I entered, but relaxed at my smile and weary shrug.

I found that I had developed a warmth of feeling for Karl. True, he was now what can only be called my procurer. True also that he had arranged this evening's work and knew, if not in detail, what I had been about and what I had done, and had done to me. But his attitude was so different from that of most men I had known.

Not for him the secretive little attempts to get in with a girl. Not for him the treating of a girl as a silly thing who could be conned into a tumble, or if not could be boasted about as if she had. He was perfectly comfortable with the fact that I was now, to all intents and purposes, a whore, a girl who shagged for money, and did not look down on me for it.

We were friends and business partners. More than that, he treated me with a companionable good humour I had rarely come across in a man before.

Now, as I smiled and smoothed a weary hand across my brow, he handed me a glass of brandy as a restorative, and told me that a hot bath was this very minute being drawn for me. Knowing our arrangement, and determined to act professionally, I rummaged in my pocket and pulled out the envelope containing my fee.

It was twenty pounds; four crisp, white fivers. Karl took one, as per my arrangement with Amelia, and smiled as he folded the others back into my hand. He did not say it, but I could see regard and admiration in his face. I had become a 'professional girl', and had come back from my first private engagement with the money, and paid up my dues, and all was well.

I felt almost smug at my success in this new world as I lowered myself into the wonderful, scented bath. This life, I thought, might not be too bad at all.

It was indeed not a bad life, except by the moral standards of so-called proper society, of course. Amelia and Karl were relaxed employers, and stuck to their bargains, and neither Karl nor Paul were over-demanding with regard to sharing my bed. They did visit me at night, of course, and they were welcomed. They were, after all, excellent and sensitive lovers, and always made sure I had at least one come before they left me.

Another sign of their sensitivity and understanding was that they never tried it on if I had spent the evening at the *Silken Web*, Amelia's bordello, or had been out to a private engagement. I was especially grateful for this on my bordello nights, for after a girl has sucked or shagged a dozen men in the course of one short evening, she needs to rest a little.

I became positively happy in my new life, and I know that Emily and Kate did too. We spent a great deal of time together, for our days were pretty well our own.

We would meet for breakfast at about ten in the morning. We would drift down to our meal clad in those self-same Chinese silk robes Amelia had given us, not caring that they slipped about quite a lot, and knowing that those who saw the parts of us which were thus exposed – a breast here, a thigh there – did not care, nor judge, either.

Indeed, one of the most noticeable things about the whole of Amelia's establishment was that everything and anything seemed to be taken in stride. Not the butler, not the footman, not the maid, nor the housekeeper, seemed to care a jot that there were three young women about the place who habitually went around in the most shocking state of undress, whispering and giggling together and generally acting the fool.

And we did indeed act the fool. It was as though we were schoolgirls together. We laughed and whispered and gossiped. We snorted over silly comments about dear old Bailey, the butler, and his slow walk, or some punter with an oddity we had shagged last night. We played tricks on each other, like the time Kate had gone to answer the doorbell, the maid being busy, and just as she threw the door wide, Emily – hiding behind the hall stand – tugged her robe and made it fall right off. Oh how she squealed as she was suddenly naked in front of complete strangers!

It was not all silliness and laughter, of course. Karl made sure of that. Although friendly and as relaxed as could be, he was ever the businessman. After all, he had three new and popular girls on his hands and he made sure we were profitable by arranging private engagements for us whenever he could; they never paid less than twenty pounds, and even a busy night at the bordello might not net more than fifteen.

Even girls as ready for sex as we three were appreciated that twenty pounds for a night with usually just one man was better business, and much less tiring, than fifteen pounds for a dozen quickies – no matter how odd the desires of that one man were!

And some were odd indeed, as you shall learn.

Karl also began to arrange afternoon engagements for us, in hotels or at business or diplomatic premises. These were shorter than our evening engagements, seldom more than a couple of hours, but paid just as well. One met an odd assortment of punters on such occasions; furtive little men, extravagantly carefree men, men who got you to meet them in a public area before they took you off, so that they could later boast about giving you a good fucking.

The two things they had in common were that they demanded of their girl the most extravagant and noisy comes (pretty well always faked), and most of them avoided her eyes when handing her the envelope with the cash in it before business began.

Let me hasten to add, lest you think me too disparaging of my clients, that most of them were actually rather likeable. As the months passed I found myself, like Kate and Emily, building up a nice clientele of regulars, and developing a pleasant pattern of living.

We always rose late, as I have said, and took our time over breakfast and our preparations for the day. If one or another of us had a client booked for luncheon and the afternoon, she would bathe and dress early, and depart for her assignation, while the others would still drift about half undressed until it was time for them to prepare for their own engagements.

We pretty well decided our own routines, except in

so far as Karl arranged our private assignations. We all knew that we owed him a debt, and never refused such engagements. We went decreasingly to Amelia's bordello, though sometimes all three of us felt the need for a night of simple shagging, especially if we had just had a series of odd clients who required acting or other little performances.

Two

The first months of the year 1900 were momentous ones. The newly titled and rapturously happy Mrs Felicity Nasseri went off to Egypt with her husband. Somehow, Karl arranged for the solicitor who was my guardian to get papers that gave Tiliu's presence in England legality, and she straight away married her beloved Sharpe, and joined him on his sea voyages. The war in South Africa was on the turn, with Kimberley and Ladysmith, and later on Mafeking, all having their sieges raised.

Not least momentous were the developments in my own life, and what I began to learn about myself.

The party to celebrate my eighteenth birthday, or rather the parties, for there were two of them, were what began to set me off.

On my actual birthday – February 14th, as though St Valentine had chosen it on purpose – I travelled down to Portsmouth. It was lovely to see Alice and Tiliu again, even though I had seen them only a couple of weeks earlier at Felicity's wedding. It was all the more delightful because Captain Prendergast's ship was in port, so Alice had her husband back for a while, Tiliu had her Sharpe, and of course dear William and First Officer Donaldson were also on hand.

We had a splendid supper party, which led to rather naughty revels, and at last to me getting yet another insight into the kind of person I really am.

The thing actually began with Alice's interest in my clothes. They were in the latest London mode, and she enthused about my narrow waist, bell skirt, and leg-o'-mutton sleeves. Being in the flush of excited friendship and, I have to confess, a little on the tipsy side, the conversation soon got around to my under-things, and it was not long before I was showing them how neat and diaphanous my silk stockings were, and demonstrating how cunning the idea of suspenders rather than garters was.

The face of Alice's husband showed me how universal is the fascination men have for that little gap between the tops of a girl's stockings and the hems of her knickers, especially when it is set off by the line of a lacy black suspender. I found myself oddly thrilled as he dragged his eyes away from what I was displaying to glance meaningfully at his wife. He at least would not be going straight to sleep this night!

Soon, and with no active discouragement from our four male companions you may be sure, I was taking off my frock, and as I did so I found myself becoming more and more stirred up. I was down to my very revealing underthings in the company of people fully dressed. I liked their eyes on me, and especially the way the men were getting hot. I willingly paraded up and down, emphasising the sway of my hips and pulling my shoulders back so that my breasts were prominent.

Even though these were all old friends and lovers, and we knew each other's bodies intimately, I was getting excited by parading for them half naked. Obviously, there is a strong element of the exhibitionist in me!

* * *

By the time Alice went off with her husband, and Tiliu with Sharpe, I was as aroused as anybody. Just like old times I was left alone with William and Donaldson. The three of us had spent so many delectable times together aboard ship that there was no urgency, except that I was as randy as my two men obviously were.

We did not bother to go upstairs. After taking one more turn about the room just to enjoy the increasing sexual tension and the feeling of their eyes on me, I stopped in front of the fire, stepped out of my flimsy knickers, and posed before them.

Donaldson and William knew me as well as I knew them. Soon, in concert as though they had rehearsed it – and who knows, but they might have done just that on their womanless nights at sea, while wanking and reminiscing about me – they began working on me.

Lips found my neck, just where it makes me shiver so. The top of my basque was pulled down and my breasts bounced free. Teasing lips and tongues found my earlobes and nipples, and the backs of my knees and my inner thighs, above my stocking tops and inside my suspenders.

As I stood upright, the warmth of the fire on the backs of my legs competed with that of the hands and mouths moving all over me. The sensation of two hard male bodies pressing against mine, was wonderfully exciting. Soon, as knowing fingers slipped between my legs and began to toy with my clitoris, I was panting and weak kneed.

I was lifted up and swung round on to the settee so that I reclined on my back. Donaldson came with me, still kissing me, his hand inside the top of my basque and teasing my nipple beautifully. Gentle hands lifted my knees, and nudged them apart. Warm breath wafted at my centre. A mouth touched.

Heaven!

William knew so well what to do. Had I not taught him myself, those few months ago on the high seas? He did it now, his fingers delicately easing apart my folds, his mouth finding my nerve-ends, his hot tongue moving, slowly at first, then with growing rapidity, the length of my crease and then circling my cherry. Oh, he knows how to lick a girl to paradise does William!

At exactly the moment my loins took me over, and I began to writhe into my first lovely come, Donaldson's cock touched against my lips. My mouth opened to him exactly as my vagina opened to William's tongue; eagerly, and urgent for satisfaction.

They did not satisfy me yet, though. They knew, now, how a girl likes to be built up towards it, to be teased and toyed with, and excited and delayed, so that when she does come it is volcanic. That they did now.

Donaldson would not let me get my mouth fully on his cock. He touched my lips with his gorgeous plum. He let me suck a little in, then pulled back to smooth its musky satin over my cheeks and nose before letting me have another little taste.

William used his tongue like the devil incarnate, flicking at my straining cherry, exploring my folds, dipping into my cramping entrance, only to flick away again to kiss my navel and thighs.

I churned up into that appalling, wonderful, staggering, glorious agony in which every nerve-end screams and screams for release, and waves of convulsive, electric heaven pulse out from, and back to the centre of one's womanhood, in ever increasing, overwhelming surges.

I gasped for joy as William's lovely cock thrust into me. And again as Donaldson's slipped into the valley of my bosom and his firm hands folded my hot breasts over its throbbing length.

I was so happy that night that anything William and Donaldson wanted of me was joyously given. I went on to all fours on the rug, so that Donaldson could take me from behind while William probed for my tonsils. I knelt astride William's lovely cock while sucking the standing Donaldson.

I was on my back. On my knees. Between them, as they took me front and back. They had me – no, I had them – in every way our stamina allowed, until at last all of us collapsed into delicious exhaustion. And all the while, the gas-mantles had been lighting the scene as brilliantly as if we had been on a stage!

This exhibitionistic side to me was brought out again by one of my birthday presents. Alice had made for me, with her own hands, what she called a house-dress. One could certainly have worn it only indoors, for it was far too suggestive to be worn outdoors.

It was made of fine cream silk, very soft in texture, and closely fitting from the hips upwards. It buttoned high to the neck, and had long sleeves with little puffs at the shoulders. The skirt was long enough to suit the most modest young lady, but the way it was cut and sewed, on the bias, ensured that it lay close down over my hips, and clung to my legs as I walked about. Though covering me from neck to floor, it was actually the most revealing dress one could possibly imagine, especially when, as I did for my second birthday party two evenings later at Amelia's, I went naked underneath; the softness of the material clung to every part of me it touched.

I wore it that way because, to be perfectly honest, the idea excited me, and I was thrilled by the appreciative looks it drew from the party guests.

I sat in the place of honour at the head of a table groaning with food and wine. Opposite me, at the far end, sat Amelia, looking positively regal with her hair swept up. She was wearing a deeply cut gown of satin figured in a paisley pattern.

Kate and Emily, too, had taken the occasion to dress enticingly. Emily looked soft and delicious in a frock of red and gold regency stripes, with a frill of fine lace at the square neckline drawing the eye to the swell of her soft breasts. Bolder than Emily, Kate had on a black gown, so tight and low in the bodice that her breasts were revealed almost to her nipples, their charms emphasised by the black chiffon insert that rose from her daring neckline to a neat frilled collar high at her throat; it was so transparent it was a mere shadow over her luscious curves.

But it was I who caught the attention of the four men present. I say this not out of a spirit of competition, for how can one think of competing with women one loved as much as I loved these three. No; I say it out of simple delight at the effect of my superficially modest frock upon my audience – and at Alice's cunning in the making of it.

Covered from my neck to my heels, I was nevertheless more revealed than even Kate, whose lovely breasts threatened at any moment to spill out of her frock. I wore nothing at all underneath my house-dress, not even stockings. It felt as though my body was sheathed in warm kisses, the silk was so soft and clinging. My breasts were outlined as though in a coat of soft paint. Even as I had entered, I was deliciously aware of how all eyes had fixed on the way the silk clung to my hips and thighs as I walked to the table, and how each of the four male guests registered that I was naked beneath the clinging material.

25

As their eyes moved over me, and you may be sure they did so very busily as each bowed and kissed my hand in greeting, I was already becoming well stirred up. Amelia – perceptive Amelia! – half concealed a little smile as I sat down, and instantly adjusted my position to lean back in the chair. Sitting upright, as I had, had brought my sensitive skin into sudden contact with the moquette of the seat cover, which actually prickled right through the silk of my dress. The sudden, unexpected stimulation to my already excited parts was quite a shock.

Amelia seemed to know exactly what had happened, and what I was on upon, and I blushed as she caught my eye with another smile. Later, as my birthday party progressed, I began to sit more upright on the chair, with my back curved a little and my knees parted.

I was in a very strange state, and when I thought about it later realised what new aspects of licentiousness in myself were being revealed. I had deliberately chosen to wear a frock that was titillating in the extreme. Now, I was working myself off on the seat in front of anyone who cared to look; Amelia at least looked and understood.

By the time we had reached the hour to blow out the candles on my cake, I had been rubbing myself against the chair so long I hardly had the breath to puff at the flames. Part of me was acutely aware that everybody around the table knew what I had been doing, and the thought excited me even more.

There were eight of us at the table. Karl and Paul, of course, as well as we four females. The others were new to me. On Amelia's either side sat two men I had not met. One, a balding man with a flushed complexion and a whinnying laugh, turned out to be the solicitor who was my legal guardian. He was, by virtue of our peculiar English laws of majority and gender, to all intents and purposes my owner, since he had power of disposal over my person.

The other man, was handsome in an odd, foreboding sort of way. He had a veritable mane of raven black hair which was left loose and flowing, a dark complexion, and eyes so black and piercing they chilled one. He was apparently a long term friend of Amelia, and hailed from France. It turned out that he was of middle age, though his lithe figure belied the fact. He looked nearer to thirty than fifty.

This person distracted me greatly, for though he spoke only to Amelia, his eyes seemed to convey to me that he was aware of why I had worn that particular frock, and to be both tolerant of and amused by my desire to display myself. On those occasions his eyes caught mine, it was as if he saw and knew, and I had the feeling that he would figure large in my life at some time.

I was dragged back from my odd reflections to the celebration of my birthday by the cheerfulness of Kate and Emily and the charm of Paul and Karl, my two neighbours at the table. We ate lightly, and all about me chaffed and laughed a great deal. Toasts were proposed and drunk.

I did not join in with the easy freedom of my companions, for I confess I was inordinately conscious of the sensations of my body, and the way my nipples throbbed against the silk of my frock. I had an almost irresistible desire to take Karl or Paul, or indeed any other man for that matter, aside for the shag I very much needed. Or perhaps not even take them aside! I only know that in my tizzy, I drank rather more wine than was sensible!

* * *

At the end of the meal, as the gentlemen lit their cigars and Amelia her cheroot, my birthday presents were brought in. As you might have expected from the company I was in, each box and parcel I opened contained a present as naughty as it was delightful. From Emily I had stockings; half a dozen pairs, all black, all very delicate and diaphanous, all with lacy tops. From Kate, I had some matching knickers and bodices often referred to as camisoles. They were all of silken lace and almost too delicate ever to be worn. Karl gave me a gorgeous robe of silk so soft it ran through the hands like warm water. From Paul I got a set of hair brushes beautifully inlaid with ivory. The handles were of a rather suggestive shape that fitted the hand familiarly.

By the time I had opened all the presents and kissed their donors, the atmosphere was quite warm, and decidedly naughty. I noticed that the Frenchman was already paying close attention to Emily, and when I kissed the solicitor who was my guardian (and whose name I did not even know yet) he let his hand slip casually over the side-swell of my breast.

I smiled up at him as he held my shoulders after kissing me, and pushed my hips just a little forward. The mingled surprise and delight in his eyes as my pubis pressed against his loins almost made me giggle. Through the silk of my frock I felt him twitch alert, and smiled inwardly. He would not be getting any tonight, but who knew what delights might arise at some future time?

Then came the crowning shock of the evening, and the crowning embarrassment. Kate suddenly called out that Amelia had not made me a gift. To be honest, in my distraction I had not realised it. In a second, everyone was calling to Amelia. Where was her present to Lydia? Where was her gift?

Amelia, always with a sense of theatre, paused a long minute, a smile of cunning triumph lighting her features. When all had fallen silent, she clapped her hands. A footman, an African one, entered the room with great dignity, his features a mask of impassivity. He came up close beside my seat, and stopped. He was not carrying any tray or parcel that might have held a present. At first we were all puzzled.

There was a moment of silence then, as one, the company burst into howls of laughter. A second more and the connotations of the scene hit me too, and I felt myself blush to my toes.

I could not believe it! Amelia was beaming at me, her whole face alight with amusement and not a little archness. Kate and Emily were looking from me to the African open mouthed, their eyes brimming with excited laughter.

He was my present! This tall African, impassive, almost intimidating in his footman's uniform, was Amelia's gift to me. I was staggered. I knew that the company I kept these days was wickedly naughty, but this!

I became confused and lapsed into a whirl of emotions, which was not helped by the effects of the wine and my earlier arousal.

It was shocking that Amelia should offer me such an outrageous present, yet I had felt a lurch in my depths at the very sight of him. Memories of my beloved Talesi, bodily as well as mental, flooded me.

It was shocking, too, that all the company were nodding, smiling and giggling in the knowledge of what he had been given to me for. Yet that self-same knowledge was already tightening my breasts, and I had not been able to prevent my eyes taking in the shape of his breeches and the manhood outlined by them.

With a trembling hand I lifted my glass yet again to my lips. I could think of nothing to say, and nothing to do save try to steady my nerves with more wine.

Amelia suggested that we remove ourselves to the sitting room, where we could be more relaxed. At once everybody agreed, and began to bustle about. When I too stood, I learned I had not drunk wisely, for I swayed on my feet. My footman grabbed my arm to steady me, and I felt a shock in my tummy at the touch of his hand.

I looked up at his face for the first time. That, too, was a shock. He was still impassive, but there was in his deep eyes a surprising gentleness, as though he fully understood my confusion. His features were fine and chiselled, his forehead high, his nose narrow and his lips full. He reminded me so much of Talesi I wanted to touch him to prove I was not dreaming, but I held myself back, still embarrassed at the situation.

As I followed the others into the sitting room he moved close behind me, and I could almost feel his presence. I was in a very strange state, knowing that this silent, statuesque man had been presented to me for the purposes of sex. I was aware from his eyes that he knew it too, and I felt deeply shy and embarrassed, for all the world as though I were some little virgin on her first encounter, and not a woman of experience, what society would have called 'a woman of easy virtue'.

It was ridiculous, but the wine and my confusion had driven common sense out of my head. I sat a little way away from the others, in a vast wing-chair that was turned sideways to them. I hoped, I suppose, to become unnoticed. My footman (whose name I later learned was Ashoko, and who hailed originally from what is now called Nigeria) followed, and stood close.

I was becoming rather fuddled with the wine and with my awareness of his presence. Even though I tried, I could not get out of my head – and the corner of my eye – the image of his tall figure so close by, and the whiteness of his breeches, and the shape of his legs.

I leant back in the chair and closed my eyes, determined to gather myself. After all, I was no shrinking violet, and had to regain my composure.

Suddenly, I felt a fingertip touch upon my neck. It moved to trace the shape of my earlobe, the curve down towards my shoulder, and along the edge of my high collar. In my already over-stimulated condition, the touch jangled my nerve-ends. I knew whose fingertip it was and tried to deny it to myself. I failed.

When his hand slid down to cup my breast, with such lightness it could hardly be felt except in the hardening of my nipple, I knew I ought to come alive and protest. But I did not.

A strange mood was on me. In my heart I was back among the Tukanna tribe, once again the willing slave of Talesi and the others, obliged to obey their sexual demands upon me, yet eager to accept them. Ashoko's hand as it oh, so softly caressed my breasts through the silk of my dress, was Talesi's. Ashoko's subtle, cinnamon-and-cloves aroma was that which I had learnt to love back in Africa.

At a slowly swirling distance, I was aware that he was fondling me, was undoing the buttons that held my dress closed, was slipping his lovely hand in to soothe the throbbing in my breasts. It was happening at two removes, as it were. I felt my pleasure at his touches; then I felt his touches; then I saw how he was undoing me and moving me.

I had slipped down in the chair so that I was more reclining than sitting. My dress had come open to my waist. Ashoko's mouth had found my breasts, while his hands smoothed further down.

Then, somehow, my frock was off me, and I was lying on the chair naked while Ashoko caressed me from my ankles to my shoulders, his kisses and touches everywhere lighting flames in me.

Through a mist I became aware of faces watching. It did not matter that we were being observed, for somehow Ashoko was out of his footman's uniform and was warm and naked as he entwined with me. Everything was moving slowly; everything, that is, except the responses within my body.

I knew that I was naked, and Ashoko too. I knew that eager eyes formed a circle about us. It did not matter. Or rather, in a way new to me, it added to the thrill of it all. I was being swept away by the combination of this beautiful reminder of my time in Africa and the exhibition we were making.

Ashoko's body was close to me. My eyes swam open to see his beautiful loins. His cock was oh, so close. I moved my face towards it, sought to lick the glossy plum at its head. He moved away from me, denied me the delight I sought.

In a dream, I was lifted up, moved, lowered on to a vast sofa. Ashoko was above me, smiling gently. My body was afire, my heart pounding, my very toes curling with desire. He kissed me softly with the touch of a butterfly. His gentle lips moved over me, over my forehead, my neck, my ribs, my arms. His tongue dipped into my navel, traced the curve of my inner thighs. I was in a dream of mounting sensation. My arms had moved themselves above my head; my legs had bent themselves and parted wide. I had absolutely abandoned myself to whatever he wished to do with me.

His mouth found my centre, and I whimpered at the excruciating, wonderful touch of his tongue on my weeping labia. He knew well the way to stir me! A hand reached up to find my breast. Another smoothed over the undercurve of my thigh. His wicked, ravishing tongue drove me on.

As though he could read my mind, at the very moment the overwhelming sensations he was causing in me began to turn towards agony, he clamped his hot mouth upon my aching clitoris and sucked and licked.

Every atom of breath burst from me in a great gasp as my come pounded me like breakers on rocks. I was lost, gone, churning and writhing and sobbing in such waves of orgasm as made me want to die.

He eased off then, but did not release me from his voluptuous torments. He lifted his mouth off me, yet continued to torment me with butterfly touches of hands and lips on every part of me, always returning to my quim.

Can an orgasm be continuous? Can those swelling and ebbing waves of sensation be called part of one long, helpless come? Or is each excruciating, wonderful peak an orgasm in its own right? I do not know, and it does not matter. All I do know is that Ashoko tormented me into peak after peak of glorious agony until I did at last feel I was dying. Ashoko then took my quim full in his hand, pressed the heel of his palm against my mound and rocked it. As he did so he sank several fingers deep into my writhing vagina, and set off such cramps and explosions in my wracked body that I fainted.

When I regained conciousness, I was in a bed. I knew instantly that I was not alone. In the very faint light seeping through the window I saw that Ashoko was there with me, not reclining but sitting propped on pillows looking down at me. His hand was touching my hair. His face was gentle and reflective. When he saw my eyes flicker open he smiled and stroked my hair.

'You are too beautiful for me, mistress,' he said. His voice was honey and bass notes and velvet. 'I hope I have not disappointed you.'

Disappointed me? I was almost startled from my languor by the ridiculousness of such an idea. I could not reply, except to shuffle around beneath the blankets which covered me and kiss his warm chest. His hand, the one that was not stroking my hair, traced my cheek and the line of my lips. Oh, he felt so warm, smelt so good!

I nestled myself against him, drinking in his warmth and scent. He slid down from his sitting position so that we lay body against body, thigh against thigh. I touched him, my palms almost sparking with rapture as they ran over his hard stomach and the muscles of his chest. I kissed him again and again. He let my hands roam over him while his own gentled my brow and neck.

I found his delta, and cupped in my hand the ripe fruit that lay among his crinkly hairs. His penis pressed up against the blankets. I wriggled around. He had not let me kiss it before. Now I was not to be denied.

Oh, he tasted of the gods! Talesi where are you? He kept still and slid his fingers through my hair as I sucked him. I was in a state. I wanted to eat him alive! Wanted this glorious cock in every part of me. Loved its being in my mouth. Longed for it to be in my vagina. Wanted both at once. One fabulous cock in both places.

I was mad.

He reached down and gently lifted my face off his wonderful member. I resisted, but he was not to be denied. I was somehow on my back now, and he was between my thighs. He entered me. Oh heaven, how he entered me!

I was more ready than ready can possibly be. He was slow. Knowing. In control. Not for him the sudden thrust, and pump, and come. He came into me a little at a time, push and pause, push and pause, push and pause, so that my whole being was enthralled and empassioned by his movements.

It was not so much a shag as a transportation. What with the way I was straining for more, and the way my sheath was writhing upon him, any other man would have rammed in and done his business. But Ashoko was my present. He held himself back, for my pleasure was his only desire.

My hips had a life of their own as they bucked to get more of him. Then, glory of glories, his hands were under my knees and my legs were lifted as he surged into me. I burst into the come that he had been building in me, my transports so violent he had to hold me down I bucked so much.

Naturally, Ashoko had not really been given to me – that would have been unthinkable. He did, though, become a regular feature of the establishment. He was not really a footman either, but something far naughtier.

He was, to state it squarely, a male equivalent of one of Amelia's girls! The notion that men would pay girls for sex was by now perfectly normal to me, but that women should do so had never entered my head. Why it hadn't I do not know, but when it did it seemed entirely sensible. If a man can hire a woman, why not a woman a man? And especially a man such as Ashoko. Any woman hiring his services would be getting quite a bargain.

You may be sure that Emily and Kate availed themselves of Ashoko's services as soon as may be though not, of course, for payment. Payment was only for outsiders. Between us sex was free both in terms of money and of lack of the usual mealy-mouthed rules of society.

That is not to say that we went around all the time shagging each other silly. It is just that, if two of us felt the urge to engage, we did so, and just for the gentle pleasure of it. Simple, friendly fucking, with no urgency and no subterfuge. Delicious!

Three

The life I was now living afforded me leisure and a healthy income. One night spent at the bordello would get me as much as fifteen guineas. I will not say it was easy work, though. Putting on and taking off one's clothes a dozen times; faking polite conversation while negotiating the price and the particular requirement; performing whatever it was the punter desired; pretending to be sent wild by him; all of this added up to tiring work. Often, I would have to drag myself up the stairs to the bathroom, and then collapse on to my bed too tired and too stiff-hipped from a dozen shags to even don my nightgown.

A bonus, apart from the money that is, was that as time went on I developed a clientele of regulars, whom I got to know and (mostly) like. They told me their names, though I was sure they were mostly false. More particularly, they talked to me and told me of their problems and difficulties. I learnt early that, once a man is assured of his shag and does not need to work for it, once he is released from the desperate need to impress by his vigour or the size of his cock or whatever, he relaxes and talks and – once the girl has accommodated herself to his particular want – becomes almost smugly confiding.

Take 'Mr Hacker' for example. The first time he picked me out at the *Silken Web* he was rather stiff and grandiose in his manner, as though he were as concerned to impress me as he was to shag me. Early on in my career I used to think this sort of thing rather silly. They were paying for me, so why did they not just fuck me and get it over with? I soon realised that my thinking was shallow. Yes indeed, they wanted a fuck, wanted a pretty girl who would spread and swoon for them. More than that, though, and actually far more fundamental, was that they wanted, no needed, reassurance and a warm welcome.

That first time 'Mr Hacker' was almost brusque in his treatment of me. He bought the regulation bottle of champagne, on which I was paid commission, but hustled me upstairs pretty quickly. He said not a word (it was not until our third engagement that he actually spoke to me) and so I just stripped off my skirt and knickers and lay down for him.

The shag was over in a couple of minutes. He got out a fairly standard-sized cock without even taking off his jacket. He did not look at me, or at least not into my eyes. I held him and guided him in, and bucked my hips for him as I had long ago learnt to do to make a man think I was transported. He pumped a few times, and spasmed into his come, and put himself away.

What made him different from the successful quickie I was learning to work for – get the punter upstairs, get him to come off as fast as possible, and get back downstairs to attract the next punter – was that, as he reached the door to leave he turned and looked at me. It was not the look of a punter, nor the guilty look of a man who is ashamed of what he has done, but something else. He did not speak, but in his eyes there was something not far off from thanks and hope and, oddly, something like respect.

The third time he picked me out, he startled me.

We were in the bedroom and I had already got my frock and knickers off. I was just about to lie down on the bed when he spoke for the first time. He was almost apologetic in tone, and he stumbled over his words. The gist was, though, that he wanted to see my breasts.

I learnt, during subsequent engagements, that the only breasts he had ever seen were those in classical paintings in galleries, or statues in graveyards! Yet he was a married man! I knew, that very first time I peeled down my *chemise* and showed my breasts to him, that here was an unhappy man.

As I knelt on the bed and pulled down my *chemise*, and cupped my breasts up over the top of my corset, his eyes grew huge. He asked if he could touch me. Did so with trembling fingers. I was amazed.

How on earth could such a simple thing as seeing or touching a girl's breasts be so important to him? Yet it clearly was. He touched me, and stared at me, as though I had given him the forbidden fruit of Eden. How could it be that a thirty-year-old married man was so wild for bare breasts?

It turned out later, as he talked to me on his fourth, fifth and subsequent visits, that his wife always insisted on going to her room well before he did; that on the twice weekly occasions he was permitted into her bed, she was always buried under the covers, and allowed him only ever to pull her nightgown up to her hips before 'doing it' and showing him she was ashamed at his animality.

How can a woman be so stupid? I saw an image of his wife in my mind, tightly coiffeured and corseted, strict with her servants, lines of tension already growing around her mouth. Poor woman. She, like so many in our hypocritical society, did not know what she was doing, or missing.

39

Both of these people were victims, 'Mr Hacker' of his shyness, his wife of her stifled upbringing. I could only help one of them directly, but perhaps could help the other from a distance, as it were. I am quietly satisfied that, in response to my encouragement to be bolder, after perhaps ten engagements together, 'Mr Hacker' proudly confessed to me that his wife had let him suck her nipples.

Let him? The poor woman did not know where she was at! Mind you, after a while he stopped coming to the *Silken Web* altogether, so I guess his wife might have found his boldness pleasurable.

Another regular was 'Cecil'; he gave no other name. He was a short, thick-set man, dark complexioned and very hairy. He liked to have me from behind, bending over the foot-rail of the bed, and wearing only my stockings.

He was a jocular, rough diamond sort of chap, and made no bones that watching me strip off to my stockings was a large part of his pleasure. Since he always paid over the odds, I used to drag out my stripping for him so that he got a good show.

It is interesting that so many of my customers like me to exhibit myself for them – and interesting, too, how much I enjoyed doing so.

'Cecil' liked crudeness. He was crude himself, and noisy, calling out all sorts of things once he had me bent over the end of the bed. He always wanted me from behind, for he found the sight of a naked girl bending over with her feet apart wildly exciting.

He would run his hands all over me, and not too gently either, though it was a pleasant kind of roughness. He would press up close behind me, merely opening but not removing his trousers, and fondle and finger me before gripping my hip-bones and thrusting in.

'Take my meat! Take it up your tight little twat!' he would bellow. 'What an arse! God, what a hot little cunt! I'm going to fuck you cross-eyed, you lucky little bint! I'm going to come so hard you'll burst!'

He was actually only moderate in the 'meat' department, but to hear him talk of the women he had shagged, and how he'd driven them mad with lust, and fucked them over and over again, one would have thought he was a veritable Hercules. His delusions were all in his words, and so I gave him words back.

In my poshest and most demure accent, as I stripped for him, I would ask whether he was going to fuck me now, and beg him not to be too rough on me. This always made his eyes light up with lust. Once I had bent over and I felt his hands on me, I would wriggle my bottom and beg him to, 'Get it up me! Get it up me now! Fuck me! Fuck me hard! Oh God, I'm coming! Harder! Harder!'

He never gave me a come, but he was always so delighted by my pretended excitement that when he had spurted into his own come (which was usually surprisingly copious) he would stay inside me a while, withdraw, caress me lingeringly on my buttocks and leave a generous gratuity behind him as he departed.

Perhaps the loveliest of my bordello regulars, though, was 'Andrew'. He was a slight, nervous looking chap of about thirty. His hair was always cut badly, and his clothes seemed not to fit him very well. Had you seen him in the street you would have dismissed him as insignificant.

And insignificant was the way he saw himself. How he ever plucked up the courage to enter Amelia's bordello I will never know. I do know that it was I who picked him, rather than the normal way, where a girl 'hovered' – as Amelia called it – and a punter picked her out.

I had already had half a dozen punters the first evening 'Andrew' appeared, and so was not exactly anxious to find another for a while. As I sat close to the musicians, scanning the crowd and enjoying the way my fellows manipulated their potential clients, I became aware of an odd little figure off to the side of the room.

He was sitting alone. His collar was too large, and his jacket too tight, and his whole body seemed tied in a knot of nervousness as his eyes flicked about the place. He looked from the girls to the punters and back again, with a sort of rabbit-like terror. My heart went out to him. It was obvious what he was here for, and just as obvious that he was too nervous to actually approach one of us girls. Had I not done something about it, the poor boy might have sat there all evening, desperate and shy, and got nothing.

Rejecting the champagne, as it was always insipid stuff, I got the waiter to supply me with two large measures of brandy. I carried them across to where 'Andrew' was sitting. He looked startled and very nervous when I stopped at his table and offered him a glass. He was clearly very disconcerted.

It was I who had to talk to him. As I chatted with feigned casualness about this and that, I began to feel almost sisterly, he was so tongue tied and tense. It was obvious, from the way he could hardly drag his eyes up from my neckline, that he was terribly excited by my presence, and the suggestive ambience of the club, and most of all by the possibility of sex. But, it seemed, he could not bring himself to make the proposal.

He tried several times. I watched him as he drew in

a breath, his eyes boring into the cleft between my breasts, and attempted to solicit me. He could not. In the end it was I who took him by the hand, I who smiled reassuringly, I who led him towards the stairs.

I knew already he was a virgin. I felt rising in me that same hotness I had felt with William when I had seduced him on the ship. What woman would not feel a churn of excitement in her womb at the thought of giving a man his first experience of the glories of the bed?

I almost kissed him, he was so excited as I opened the door of my allotted room. I resisted, though, because kissing punters is unprofessional, and I was determined to be very professional with my nervous virgin.

The bedrooms at the *Silken Web* were not large, being places for business rather than repose. The rooms were furnished with a bed, of course, a wardrobe for hanging one's clothes, a washstand and a straight-backed chair. Most noticeable, though, was the abundance of mirrors.

Someone should write a treatise on the function of mirrors in sex. Perhaps they have. Their function now was to give the still twitchingly nervous 'Andrew' half a dozen views of me as I slowly stripped for him.

I adore the way men get so tense and excited as they watch a woman slowly remove one garment after another for their delectation. There is an art to this sort of undressing, and 'Andrew' was almost vibrating like a tuning fork as I practised it for him.

I unbuttoned my bodice slowly, turning away as though from modesty, but still giving him good views in the mirrors. I untied my waist-sash, then slipped first one sleeve, then the other, off my shoulders. I allowed the dress to slide slowly down towards the floor, and smiled inwardly at the way his face reddened and his eyes flicked all over me.

He could hardly see any more of me when my dress was off than when it was on, for my petticoats and *chemisette* covered almost as much as my dress did. It did not matter with Andrew, though, for he was as excited as if I was already nude.

As I slipped my petticoats down over my hips and let them fall to the floor, he gasped. He gasped again when I bent to pick them up, for my loose *chemise* gaped forward and he got an excellent view of the way my corset pushed my breasts up. His eyes almost fell out when I pulled my *chemise* off over my head and stood before him in only my black corset and stockings, little button boots, and a pair of the flimsiest knickers.

On a whim, I ordered him to take off my boots for me. To my delight, he dropped instantly to his knees and began to fumble at my ankles. I was already pretty stirred up by my stripping for him, and the sight of him kneeling at my feet, fumbling with trembling fingers at the little buttons on my boots gave me a strange extra thrill.

When he stood up after carrying out his task, panting as though he had run a race, I moved closer to him. He looked so tense and terrified I had to resist giving him a hug of reassurance.

Instead, I smiled, and unbuttoned his jacket. I hung it on the chair, where it was soon joined by his waistcoat and necktie. As I proceeded to remove his shirt and undervest, and then knelt down to take off his boots and hose, a mood of gentleness, almost motherliness, came over me, for I could feel him actually trembling with nerves.

He even flinched a little and held his breath when I made to unbuckle the belt at his waist, and to unbutton his fly. My mood became very unmotherly when I tugged down his trousers and underpants together, for what bounced out was a delight.

44

His figure may well have been slight, almost skinny, but his cock was not! It was still asleep – from his nervousness I supposed – and nestled amidst a bed of soft brown curls.

I told him to lie down on the bed. I stood above him, smiling at the eager nervousness in his eyes and, I confess, enjoying the way they roved over me. Slowly, I pulled down my knickers and kicked them aside. His eyes locked on to what was now revealed to him. It was clear that he had never seen a girl's honeypot before, and was fascinated.

I parted my knees to give him a better view, and slid my hands down over my waist and thighs. I could feel myself moisten as his eyes virtually devoured my cunny.

I moved to lie beside him, and smiled reassuringly as he actually flinched when I reached down to cup his balls. They were tight and warm. My fingers moved to circle his cock, which was already thickening deliciously.

Suddenly he grabbed at me, and was rough and clumsy from over-eagerness and lack of experience. I pushed him off, and told him to relax, for I would do it all. I stroked his cock, and was gratified to feel it stiffen handsomely. Although he had not asked for it, and probably did not know it was possible, I bent my head down and sucked him a little. Only a little, even though he tasted delicious, for it was my intention to give 'Andrew' his first ever fuck, and I didn't want him to come off too soon.

He grew like a pole, a handspan or more in length and nicely thick. I took my mouth off him and moved to get astride him. He was staring up into my eyes and hardly breathing as I grasped his cock and manoeuvred it along my already moist folds. I got him to my entrance and sank down on him. Even as my swirling sheath engulfed him he burst into a massive come, bucking beneath me as though electrified.

'I'm sorry! I'm sorry!' he almost whimpered when his come had subsided. He looked as though he might actually become tearful, he was so distressed.

I coaxed him, and told him not to be upset. 'It is all right. Don't worry,' I told him, stroking his cheek and squeezing my cunny against him. 'Stay there. Stay there, and all will be well.'

I moved my pelvis gently, my sheath clinging to his softening cock. I got him to caress my breasts, showed him how to fondle a girl, and tease her nipples to delight. I wriggled on him, pressing my thighs tight against his bony hips. He began to grow inside me. Soon his eyes were wide with surprise and delight as I began to ride him.

It is wonderful to be astride a man. It is wonderful to feel him grow and stiffen when he is already inside. It is wonderful to roll and circle one's throbbing cunt against a man's hard pelvis so that one is in control of the glorious surges of sensation that pulse from one's cherry to one's heart and back again. It is wonderful when a man takes a long time because he has already had his first come. It is wonderful to give a man his first ever shag.

To have all these things at once, as I now did, is glorious beyond wonder. Soon, I was in a come of my own that had me arching and bucking, and grinding on his lovely cock like a wild thing.

I went home after that lovely shag with 'Andrew'. I was in such a languorous glow that I could not contemplate serving another punter. I was also rather embarrassed, for my delight at finding him in the first place, and the glory of taking his virginity, had driven from my head the fact that it had been a professional engagement, and I forgot to charge him!

I charged him all the other times, of course, though not as much as usual, for as an office clerk he was not well paid. Also he was, in a sense, a student rather than a punter, and our engagements were more in the way of lessons than straight shags.

He came on well, too, and was soon fucking me as voluptuously as any of them!

The most significant regular, though, was one of Karl's private clients. Unusually, Karl told me nothing of who the client was or what his special requirements would be. That should have put me on guard, I suppose, because Karl always gave me at least some guidance as to what to expect.

That first time, I went off all innocent and unsuspecting, not even perturbed by the closed private carriage that had been sent for me, rather than the groom Albert or a hansom cab. Clearly Karl and Amelia knew me better than I knew myself, for had I been told what to expect I would have shied away from the engagement.

It was probably only half an hour's drive, but in the darkness of a curtained carriage it felt longer. When at last the carriage drew to a halt and the door was thrown open, I found myself standing at the portal of a mansion, its door open, the lobby within brightly lit.

Even as I began to mount the steps towards the door the coach rattled away. All was quiet save for the whispering of the breeze, and I could see no one about. I felt a chill of peril, for I suddenly felt rather vulnerable.

I squared my shoulders and mounted the steps with more boldness than I really felt. I was a professional, I told myself. Karl had arranged this and he would not allow me to be imperiled; to be nervous was silly.

Even as these thoughts ran through my mind, though, the fact that he had told me so little, and that my journey out here had been so secretive, preyed on my mind.

The door was opened by an impassive footman. He ushered me in. All was reassuringly normal. Then he led me aside to a small, unoccupied room, rather than to my client, which was unusual. He left me without a word.

It was a sort of ante-room with a few chairs, a low table and little else. I waited for what seemed ages, but was probably not more than ten minutes. Those minutes before one meets a new private client are always nerve-wracking for a girl. What will he be like? What will he demand? Will it be just a bit of play-acting and a shag, or will he want other things?

When the door suddenly burst open I was so screwed tight I almost leapt with nerves. Then I got confused, for instead of the randy male client I expected, it was a woman who entered the room.

She swept towards me with her hands out and a bright smile on her face. She called me Lily as though we were old friends. For a moment I was nonplussed. There was something familiar about her. Something about her hair, about the set of her figure, the way she held her shoulders. Then it struck me. She had been one of the company at the New Year's house party in Warlington. I could not think who she was, but she was definitely familiar.

As if being greeted at a private assignation by a woman were not strange enough, what now transpired was, in the cold light of day, outlandish in the extreme.

To start with I addressed her deferentially as 'milady' but she smiled and told me to call her Beatrice. Then she sat, and so did I, and she gave me a glass of sherry for all the world as though we were neigh-bours calling on one another. She chatted of this and that, mentioning Warlington, and Amelia, and Karl as merely everyday matters and acquaintances. And amidst all this she outlined to me a proposition that made my eyes widen.

I had to look at her hard. Had I fully taken in what she was suggesting?

I had. It gave me pause, not least because it seemed to touch, as though guided by some cunning mind, upon that exhibitionist part of my nature I had lately been growing increasingly aware of.

Her proposition completed, Beatrice became still and awaited my response. I glanced up into her eyes, unsure. She was smiling gently, and there was a sort of reassuring challenge in her expression.

I nodded. I would do what she asked, even though I had hardly got beyond listening when she talked of an audience and a performance. I know now that it was my own desire that drove me, but at the time I told myself that I only agreed because I had been hired to perform, and to back out would have reflec-ted badly on Karl.

It was an elaborate arrangement. I was given clothes to wear other than my own. Quite plain things, of cheap materials. I soon learnt why.

A blindfold was placed over my eyes. I had argued over that when she was describing her plan. The idea of being unable to see quite scared me. In the end we compromised: I wore the black blindfold because the audience would find it exciting, but it was made of chiffon so that I could still see through it to some degree.

Beatrice then conducted me to my place in the drama. As she had explained, a gag of black velvet was tied around my mouth so that I could not call out, soft ropes were bound to my wrists, and my arms were raised and tied above my head to the pillar I had been positioned against.

The room was but dimly lit and I could see little. What I could discern suggested that I was in a kind of private theatre, with a half-circle of seats rising in tiers around me. Then I could see nothing, because what light there had been was extinguished, and I was left to wait in the dark.

It seemed a long wait and I grew increasingly nervous, not least when I began to hear scuffling and whispering as though numbers of people were gathering about me, attempting to be silent.

My head began to run with disturbing notions. Supposing the performance went further than Beatrice had said? Supposing there were more to it? I tested the ropes that held my wrists. They were fast; I was indeed bound firmly to the pillar. I was tied up and the gag prevented me from calling out. Only the fact that Beatrice had kept her promise about the chiffon blindfold prevented me from becoming disturbed about my helplessness.

Everything went very quiet. My nerves were by now so screwed tight, I could veritably feel the invisible audience breathing. A drum started, very softly. Then suddenly, everything was brilliantly lit by electric lamps, and for a minute I was even blinder than before.

The drum was growing louder and more insistent. As my vision cleared from the brightness, I could discern through my chiffon blindfold that the half-circle of seats around me was filled with people, at least half of them women, all fashionably dressed and obviously wealthy. Was this one of those societies Amelia had told me about?

Any further thoughts were cut off by a sudden crash of the drums and the advent of an apparition which startled me. There, at the centre of the stage, appeared as if by magic an astonishing figure. He was wild and naked save for a loincloth of leopard's skin, and a chain of animal teeth and bones about his shoulders. He was waving what I knew from my time in Africa is called a machete.

I gasped as loud as the audience, for the figure was terrifying. It was only as he got close up in his wild dance that I realised the figure was actually Ashoko, for his face was outlandishly painted. In an instant my terror turned to amusement. My lovely, gentle Ashoko would never hurt me. Mind you, the savagery of his dance, and the way he waved the machete so close to me, were very convincing at times!

Ashoko is, as I have already related, a disturbingly beautiful man. He had been handsome when I had first seen him in his footman's uniform. Now he was thrilling as he danced athletically about the stage, even though his abbreviated costume was more the product of someone's imagination than actual experience of Africa.

Even so, as Ashoko danced about me to the throbbing of the drums, moving close, backing away, moving close again, part of my mind was aware of the effect his dance must be having on the audience.

I know of those fantasies and excitements our society teases itself with. Now I was enacting one of them. I was to play a fair-haired Englishwoman, bound, gagged and blindfold, at the mercy of an African savage. The audience was here to see me stripped and shagged, even if it was only as an act of theatre. They got their desire.

Ashoko danced up and back, up and back. Then he grabbed the neck of my frock and ripped it open.

I did not need to act, for the force of his action jerked my body about. He moved away and approached again, now waving his great knife. I froze as he slid it down towards my waist, nearly as carried away by his performance as the audience.

He cut through my sash and ripped at my skirt. My outer garment fell to the floor. Ashoko waved his knife close before my eyes. He ripped off my petticoat and danced about me, gyrating his hips. The audience's tension was palpable.

Ashoko's dance now made it plain that his motive was sex. He got himself right up against me, pumped his hips at me, ran his hands over my face and hair, handled my breasts, and thrust a hand between my legs.

Even though I knew I was taking part in a performance, I was nearly carried away by this. It was almost as if I was in reality the helpless victim of this savage.

He grasped the neck of my *chemise*, waved his machete all around my head and shoulders, then suddenly slid it blade first down between my breasts. Had he not given me the tiniest of grins, I might have believed his performance as much as the audience seemed to. The chill of the cold steel went straight to my heart, though I knew the blunt edge was towards my skin.

With a shout, Ashoko slashed through the thin material covering me. He tore the remnants of my *chemise* from me, exposing my breasts to the crowd.

He moved behind me. His hands came round, one on either side, and slid over my ribs, cupping and squeezing me. My role was to be terrified and struggle. But I hardly needed to act, for I was getting as carried away by Ashoko's brilliant performance as was the audience, who were by now hushed and straining forward in their seats. For effect, he was pretending to be pretty rough with my breasts, squeezing and bouncing them, and pretending to pinch my nipples.

He worked on my breasts for quite a long time, and if the sight was arousing for the audience, it was all the more so for me. I like a little roughness as part of the sex game – what girl does not? – and even though the way he was handling me was for the audience's benefit, not mine, it was having its effect!

He let go of me and started his dance again, moving wildly around me, coming close, bouncing my breasts, and thrusting his loins against the thin cotton of my drawers, which was all I wore now, save for my stockings. It was to my drawers that he now turned his attention.

He grabbed the waist and tugged them up hard, so that the material was pulled almost painfully tight up against my cunny. He thrust a hand full between my thighs and squeezed me. Then his machete was waving again.

He slid the flat of the cold blade over my exposed torso, even patting my breasts with it. He gripped my left nipple and pulled it. He gave me another of his reassuring grins and, as he motioned with the gleaming knife, I found it difficult to keep from laughing aloud at the horrified expressions on the faces of the audience. His performance had them so utterly convinced!

He slid the flat of the blade menacingly down over my tummy and thighs, then moved it slowly between them. I had been squirming and struggling, but you may be sure I kept still now! I could feel the steel right up against my quim. Even though Ashoko was amazingly adept with his knife and I knew would never dream of hurting me, I took no chances and remained frozen so as to avoid any accidental injury.

He paused. He slipped the blade back and forth so that its blunt edge was rubbing, not unpleasantly, against my cherry. The audience could hardly breathe from the tension, his acting was so good.

Then he crouched and slid the blade slowly, teasingly up inside the leg of my drawers and grinned broadly at the audience. They were clearly fearing the worst for me as they anticipated his next move.

There came a great gasp of relief when he suddenly whipped the machete up and back, slicing through my drawers from hem to waist in an instant. The garment fell open and slid down my leg to lie around my ankle.

I was now entirely naked save for my stockings. The audience burst into applause which jerked my mind back to reality, for I had been almost as carried away as they were.

Four

If I had been carried away at Ashoko's savage stripping of me, I now began to get carried away in another sense, for he began to work to stir me up. He was still a little rough as he began to feel and fondle me from head to foot, but it was a knowing and pleasurable roughness, a calculated squeezing and probing, and exploring.

He was making sure the audience could see everything he did to me; could see the way he lifted and cupped my breasts; the way he ran his hands over my ribs and flanks; how he traced the shape of my thighs; how he pulled my knees apart to slide his strong hands up between my legs.

He knew exactly how to handle me, and had I really been a captive I might well have found myself becoming aroused as he teased and toyed with me. By the time he finally cupped my quim and began to finger me, I was panting for him behind my gag.

He moved away from me. He began to dance again, but less wildly now, and moved his pelvis very suggestively. He came to a stop facing the silenced audience, and stood for a long moment like some exotic statue. Slowly, he undid the waist of his loincloth, pulled it off and let it drop to the stage. I heard gasps, and some of the women in the audience craned forward, hands to mouths and eyes wide – though certainly not with terror!

Ashoko turned towards me, the cause of the women's excitement standing proud and glorious from his loins. He had, I already knew, a beautiful cock, more than a handspan in length and correspondingly stout. Now, it looked almost savage in its pride, the dark bulb at its head seeming to stare straight at me, the thick veins along its length standing out like snakes.

He approached me slowly, stroking its length with his fingertips. He paused again when he was close before me, then reached down to grasp me between my knees. With a sudden surge, my legs were hoist off the floor, and parted wide. He stepped forward. Unguided, the head of his cock found my eager folds. With a single, awesome thrust, he was in me to the hilt, and I was gasping and writhing with the glorious shock of it.

He fucked me slowly, his body flexing like some fabulous beast's as he thrust and eased, thrust and eased, grinding my spine against the post I was tied to, lifting and lowering me by the power of his hips. My knees were hooked over his arms. I was so splayed that he was in me to his pelvis, the grinding of his hard body against my labia and clitoris making me groan aloud as spasms built within me.

My arms had begun to ache earlier from being tied above my head. Now the ache vanished. I became unconscious of the audience, of the lights, of my gag and blindfold; I became unconscious of everything save the wonderful man ploughing me, spearing me to my grateful heart.

I was coming long before he was, writhing and groaning as I hung there, my hips pumping against Ashoko's as though they had taken on a life of their own. He held back so long, so long! When at last he did come, ramming into me, lifting me up with the

56

sheer power of his cock, and pumping his heat into me, I felt as though my very head would burst! I am sure I would have screamed had my gag not prevented me. I know I bucked and churned like a fish on a spear, and actually bumped my head against the post in my transports.

I was conscious of little after that. I know the audience applauded wildly, that Ashoko lifted me off and lowered my feet gently to the floor, that I was untied, and that I was lifted in his strong arms and carried off the stage.

I recovered myself in a small parlour, where Beatrice herself gave me a restorative glass of brandy and thanked both Ashoko and I effusively. My clothes were already there and I dressed, a little unsteadily you may be sure.

To my amusement, as I put my envelope into my reticule, from the corner of my eye I noticed that as Beatrice handed Ashoko his envelope with one hand she was stroking his bottom with the other. I am sure that lovely man began earning a second fee as soon as I left to go home!

'You seem to be a little pensive, my dear,' said Amelia. I had returned home after my theatrical performance with Ashoko, and was indeed somewhat thoughtful. Kate and Emily were both out on engagements and Karl and Paul were at the club, so Amelia and I were alone in her parlour.

'Come along, Lydia. A penny for your thoughts.'

I hesitated, not quite sure how to express my thoughts. 'Tonight –' I said at last. 'Do you know what my engagement this evening entailed?'

Amelia had not known who my client had been, but when I told her it had been Beatrice she nodded and looked at me shrewdly.

'Hmm. I suppose, since it was her, some kind of display was involved?'

I nodded in response.

'And were you shocked?'

'Well,' I replied, 'I was surprised, yes. Shocked too, I suppose. I know that sometimes our work involves onlookers, and I remember that back in Warlington at New Year things were pretty public, but I did not know that people actually put on performances like tonight's.'

Clearly, I still had much to learn about the world I had become part of. Beatrice, it transpired, was well known among a certain circle for the theatrical performances she arranged. Usually they were held at her place in Kent, and only occasionally here in London.

Amelia reminded me about the conversation we had had months ago about what she called 'societies'. Beatrice led one such, and there were many others. Perhaps, she suggested, I might get to learn about some of the others as time went on. What she was more concerned about, though, was what my feelings were about such exhibitions as the one I had taken part in tonight.

It was this that I was most unsure about.

Part of me thought the whole idea rather vulgar. To have groups of wealthy people buying the services of such as myself and Ashoko to put on public displays for their entertainment seemed somewhat tasteless. It was as though they were making objects of us, treating us, if you will, as circus animals.

On the other hand, those very doubts struck me as hypocritical. Who was I to judge? I who had displayed myself to friends and lovers many times, and who had taken naughty pleasure in watching others at their love games.

And I had no choice but to admit that I had responded to Ashoko's sensuous dance, and indeed to the very fact that there was an audience. Also the shag at the end had been stupendous!

After my rather rambling description of my feelings, Amelia, with her usual shrewdness, went straight to the heart of the matter. She surprised me by asking whether I had looked in my envelope yet.

I hadn't. I had not even thought about it. At Amelia's behest, I drew the envelope out of my reticule. Now that my attention had been drawn to it, I realised that it felt rather thicker than usual. I tore it open. Instead of the usual four white five-pound notes, there were a dozen. Sixty pounds! As I looked at Amelia in astonishment, she smiled.

'Yes, child,' she said, her voice soft and reflective. 'In this world, as you well know, pretty well anything can be bought and sold, and if a person has enough money almost any taste can be catered for. Beatrice and her circle get stimulation by watching younger, more beautiful people than themselves make love, and they pay very well for the privilege.'

She sat back in her armchair and took a sip of her brandy.

'Ask yourself, Lydia,' she continued after a moment, 'what really is the difference for people of our profession between selling pleasure to one person in private, and selling pleasure to an audience?'

And indeed, I thought a little ruefully, what difference was there? Apart, that is, from the huge fee and – I had to admit it – the delight my own senses got from being watched.

I was not myself hired again by Beatrice for some months, though I gather that Ashoko became pretty well a weekly visitor to her. And not for exhibition purposes you may be sure! The person who was hired, and whose engagement caused me concern, was Emily.

In the months since she had joined Kate and me in our life as 'professional girls', sweet Emily had truly awoken to her femininity. She had become limpidly sensuous, revelling in the sensations of her body, at least among our little family at Amelia's house, and eager to explore the arts of sex. More than that, her charms were multiplied by a manner that was always softly hinting rather than demanding; there was always an underlying glow of satisfaction and an eager, questioning need for confirmation that she was loved, especially after she had spent an evening at work in the *Silken Web*.

So soft and lovely had her new life made her that of the three of us now living in the house, it was she who got most attention. And she never seemed to refuse the request of any member of the household. To see such a delicately lovely creature smile gently, and go aside at a nod from Albert the groom, or John, the senior footman, was both ravishing and moving. To see her delicate little blush as she excused herself from our company, and glanced almost shyly at whichever fellow it was had sought her, was enchanting. To see the delicate softness which imbued her whole manner when she returned from her tryst warmed the heart. Oh, if I had been a man I would myself have fucked her to a frazzle!

Indeed, on those few occasions she slipped into my bed, I found myself revelling in her eagerness to please, and in the skill she was developing in her fingers and tongue. Were there no longer any men around, I thought one night when she had taken me to heaven, Emily would suffice to keep me more than satisfied.

What was most glorious of all was the way she built up to her comes. For me, it is an eager build to beauty, and to tension, and at last to the welcoming of glorious release. With Emily, it was as though she struggled against it.

I would work on her, and tease every nerve-end I knew of, and lick and nibble and fondle and finger, and I would feel her building and building, and resisting and resisting, until at last she could bear no more, and would sob and pulse and spasm, almost in tears as her body had its voluptuous way with her. Oh, making Emily come was glorious!

I will never forget the evening of her first private engagement. She was in a positive tizzy of fright and excitement, and I could not help hugging her with what felt uncomfortably like motherliness. She rushed up to me, blurted out her news, hugged me, and rushed off to prepare. What tore at my heart was that uppermost in her mind, it seemed, was the desire for approval.

When she had gone upstairs, Karl came to me. It seemed that her client was the very same one I had been to on my own first engagement. I protested that it should have been me going, for I knew the client, and I berated Karl that it was unfair to send such an innocent as Emily. How would such a naive girl be able to play the games her client required?

That was precisely why he had come to me, Karl said. I knew what was required, and he wanted me to have a word with Emily before she went off; to inform her as to what to expect. It was moving that he too cared for her defencelessness, and I loved him a little at that moment.

As I spoke to her, feeling like some old maid Sunday school teacher preparing a pupil for her catechism, Emily's eyes grew wide, and her face lit with amazement; finally she collapsed in helpless giggles. We rocked and cried with laughter in each other's arms, it was so ridiculous.

As she went towards the door to depart, having tidied herself, Emily turned. She gave me an arch look. 'That footman. Is he really –?' she said, and made a very obvious, and very graphic, gesture with her arm. I fell about, my ribs hurting. She may have been an innocent in so many ways, but she was certainly a ribald minx when it came to business matters!

In the early hours of the morning, she slipped into my bed and awoke me from a dreamless sleep. She kissed me softly, and thanked me for loving her, which I knew by now I did, and kissed and licked me to paradise. And as though she had plotted to make me love her more, when I awoke next morning, she was lying cuddled against my side, her face as open as a cherub's, with her thumb planted between her lips like a child.

Only the fact that her hair was still in its bunches, and she was naked, with little fingertip-sized bruises about her nipples, and that her lips were plump and flushed, betrayed what she had been up to last night.

But to return to Emily's engagement with Beatrice.

Over the months, I had become almost a big sister to Emily. Though she was, in fact, a couple of years older than me I still felt protective towards her. Surely, I said to Amelia, a girl as timid as Emily would find performing before an audience frightening. And anyway, what would the performance entail?

Amelia reassured me as best she could, but it was Emily herself who tipped the balance. To my consternation, she positively insisted on fulfilling the engagement. I think it was, at least partly, because she knew I had myself performed at Beatrice's theatre, and if I had done a thing Emily was always eager to do it too.

Nevertheless I still had reservations, and I insisted that Karl and Amelia should arrange that I attend the performance, unpaid and as part of the audience. This they managed somehow, and it proved both very enlightening and the source of interesting possibilities.

I had not really seen the theatre when I performed there because of the lights and my blindfold. Now I did, and was most impressed. It was situated in a large, handsome house set in its own grounds near Hampstead Heath. Beatrice, as beautifully dressed and coiffeured as the last time I had seen her, greeted me when Albert drove me up in the carriage, and treated me quite as though I were a normal guest rather than the 'working girl' she had hired to perform that erotic pantomime of terrified virgin and African savage with Ashoko.

Indeed, I had proof that her attitude towards me was something other than 'lady and hired creature' when she took my elbow as we entered the lobby of her mansion and, speaking low and smiling archly, she told me that my performance had met with universal approbation. She also hinted that Ashoko and I might be invited to perform an encore. The mention of Ashoko's name reminded me of my suspicions about her fancy for that glorious Nigerian, but I was careful not to mention it. To do so would have been far from professional.

There was a large number of people present, one or two of whom I recognised as clients. Naturally, however, nothing was said or otherwise indicated, for discretion's sake. Most of the people were wealthy-looking men, generally of mature years. The sprinkling of women present were also mostly in their thirties or more, and I began to feel a little out of place until, to my surprise and delight, a party of younger people bubbled into the reception room. Among them was Lady Veronica, whom I had first encountered at the New Year's party in Warlington all those months ago.

The image of that strange tableau, when I had knelt to shave her virgin love-lips, and watched as she had been released from that virginity so voluptuously on the leather couch, sprang into my head and I felt my nipples harden.

She looked very different now from how she had appeared when I first met her. Then, she had been all softness and eager submission. Now, there was still eagerness, and softness too, in her manner. However, there was also a sort of joyful confidence, an open happiness in her demeanour, that lent her a glow of loveliness which was like gilding the lily, for she was undeniably beautiful.

Her hair, rich corn gold in colour and so glossy it seemed to have its own light, was set with a soft fringe that danced on her lovely brow and, flounced out by the band of black satin that encircled her crown, soft ringlets that fell down past her bare shoulders.

Her frock was of deep blue taffeta, cunningly cut to show off her pert breasts and the curve of her back. A vast bow emphasised the swell of her hips, and the front of her skirt was cut straight to show off the movement of her long legs. She looked ravishing. Had she been a member of my profession rather than a lady of the nobility, she would have had no difficulties in making a very comfortable living.

She seemed as delighted to see me as I was her, and soon we were chattering away like old friends. Naturally, our conversation centred upon our respective adventures since the house party, and Veronica was deeply curious about my work. She, of course, had no need to earn a living – as I hardly did these days, having already a very healthy bank balance – but betrayed great curiosity about the life of, let us be plain, a prostitute such as I.

How did I regard my clients, she wanted to know. How did I feel if they were ugly? What if they were 'kinky'? This was a new term for me, and one that seemed to mean someone who likes rather more than simple shagging, which covers pretty well everybody as far as I can see!

Veronica certainly fell into whatever class it was she categorised as 'kinky'; she told me early on that she was still shaved 'down there' where I had first shaved her, and that her bum was still a little sore from the weekend, when her master (that was the term she used) had gone a bit hard with the crop. I drew a breath and held back at that, being averse then to some of the things I had heard concerning riding crops and women's backsides.

We had no time to continue our conversation, for a bell rang and a footman's stentorian voice invited us to enter the theatre; the performance was about to begin.

It was indeed a real theatre, though shaped as a half-circle rather than being rectangular. The half-round stage upon which I had performed my delicious play with Ashoko was empty and in darkness, but the tiers of seats which faced it were rapidly filling with excited, whispering spectators. I managed to find a seat in the front row, slightly to one side, and to my delight was soon joined by both Beatrice and Veronica, who apparently knew each other.

The theatre took perhaps five minutes to fill, and when the electric lights dimmed and a sort of spotlight lit up the stage, Beatrice left her seat. Very elegantly she mounted the little flight of steps which led up to the stage, turned when she was fully in the spotlight, and faced the audience.

'Friends,' she said, her voice clear and filling the room, 'the entertainment we have for you this evening will be a little different from our usual fare.' There came a murmur, as of disappointment, from the audience, but Beatrice raised her hand imperiously.

'Yes, I say, a little different.' A grin, a wicked grin, spread across her handsome features. 'For example, those of my lady friends who have come to see some healthy cocks will not do so!'

Another roar of disappointment, this time higher pitched for it came from the females among us. Beatrice clapped her hands for silence.

'You will, however, be more than satisfied I can assure you. This evening's performance will not be the mere acting out of delightful gymnasticals, but something wholly more interesting.'

I was beginning to become curious. I had visualised Emily taking part in a performance like mine; some kind of playlet ending with Emily being stripped and shagged for the delectation of the audience. If it was not to be that, what had Beatrice cooked up for my pliant, gentle little friend?

'What we have for you,' she continued, 'is more in the way of a competition. We have found a very lovely young woman for you, and one who is as shy as she is beautiful.'

If she was referring to Emily, I thought, it was ironic. Although Emily always did seem a little shy, the adjective was incongruous applied to a *fille de joie* such as she. My thoughts were cut off as Beatrice continued, and what she said nearly made me laugh aloud.

'What makes this young lady special, my friends, is that her modesty is such that she positively struggles against the excitements of sensuality. Indeed, for this sweet creature orgasm is something to be fought against! Just imagine a woman who does not want to come!' Even a moment's thought would have told the audience this was ridiculous. I knew Emily very intimately, and knew that Beatrice was exaggerating quite wildly. It was not the case that Emily did not like to come, it was that she enjoyed the building so much that she always fought to delay her climax. What Beatrice said next told me that sweet Emily was in for a wonderful time.

'Therefore,' our hostess continued, 'our little contest will be between this sweet creature and several others, whose task it will be to bring her off as quickly as they can. We have set a target time of one hour. To add interest, our young lady will be rewarded. In addition to your usual contribution, of course, she will be given the sum of one guinea for each minute she can hold out. On the other hand, her teasers will each be rewarded with one guinea for every minute under an hour they manage to make her come.

Oh, and to add a little piquancy, dear Emily must obey any instruction they give her as to the disposition of her limbs and body. Ladies and gentlemen, friends, I give you Emily and the Naughties!'

As Beatrice raised her arms and stepped aside, a gasp rose from the audience, to be overtaken by cheers and loud applause. On to the stage came three beautiful girls, naked save for tiny translucent skirts.

They each had lush dark hair brushed down over their backs and shoulders, and their eyes were heavily kohled to make them even more exotic. Between them they were hauling a contraption that was part bed, part frame, and part I know not what.

On it, or hanging from it – both were true in part – was Emily, naked save for a huge veil of chiffon draped across her, which had the effect of making her look even more erotic.

The contraption upon which Emily was held was as ingenious as it was strange. Emily's torso was supported by a leather upholstered section, like an abbreviated couch, which supported her from her shoulders to the small of her back, leaving the soft peach of her buttocks overhanging deliciously. Her ankles were held in some stirrup-type affairs, attached to metal uprights. These were themselves attached to horizontal metal rods which also supported the couch. Emily's wrists were fixed beside her head to the frame which supported it, and the way she kept her elbows close in an unsuccessful attempt to cover her breasts was typical of my lovely, shy friend. Naked to the world, about to take part in a sex contest for the entertainment of an audience of strangers, she still tried to hide her breasts and to keep her knees together. So sweet!

The sight of the bound Emily and the three naked maidens who were about to minister to her was alone enough to entertain the audience. The performance itself held them hushed with excitement.

The veil of chiffon was slowly drawn from Emily's body. One girl stood by Emily's head, and the others on either side of the frame by her waist. Grasping the metal rods, they slowly turned the frame so that we in the audience could view Emily's loveliness from every angle. Then they positioned it in the centre of the stage, where it and its beautiful cargo were brilliantly lit by several spotlights.

A case-clock with a face at least eighteen inches across was wheeled on to the stage by a burly footman, and positioned at the back of the stage, so that the time could be seen while hardly moving one's eyes from the delicious tableau. The footman set the hands at one minute to the hour, and pulled the winding chain.

For that long, single minute, the audience was hushed; the three girls who were going to work on Emily, and Emily herself, were motionless. Only the loud tick of the clock disturbed the total silence. When the clock struck the hour, it seemed so loud and so sudden we were all shocked.

The three girls then turned towards their prey.

Emily's wide eyes flicked from girl to girl as they leant towards her, and she licked her sweet lips in nervous anticipation of the contest which was about to begin. The first thing the girls did was to change Emily's position in the frame to one that was more open.

She had been trying to cover her breasts with her elbows. The girl by Emily's head calmly unfixed her wrists and pulled her arms up above her head. Then she fixed the straps that had held her wrists around her upper arms, so that her elbows were held on either side of her head.

The effect was to pull Emily's breasts to a more prominent position, and it was to these lovely orbs that the girl now turned her attention. She did not touch Emily with her hands yet, but bent forward and shook out her long, dark hair, and began to trail it slowly across Emily's milk-white skin. She teased around and over the firm swell of Emily's breasts and nipples, and the effect was instant and obvious as

Emily gasped and shut her eyes; her sweet nipples at once stood proud.

I well know how sensitive Emily is in her nipples, and have often taken advantage of the fact by kissing and sucking them until she is gasping. I knew that what was happening to her now must have been the sweetest of torments. What the other two girls now began to do must have been the same redoubled!

Manipulating the frame to which Emily's ankles were fixed, they moved the uprights outwards and up towards the top of the contraption. Thus, Emily's feet were pulled apart and her knees, which she still kept clamped together out of modesty, were bent near double.

The ripe hemispheres of her pale bottom looked ravishing, as did her wriggles as the girls began to scratch very softly around her cheeks, along her cleft, and over that part of her inner thighs that they could get to. I well knew the delicious tingling the tracing of delicate fingernails over the skin can bring, knew too that Emily loved having it done to her. Lucky girl indeed, to have two pairs of cunning hands teasing her in a manner she revelled in!

The first girl was now licking Emily's breasts. While the second girl moved to slide her hand back and forth along Emily's cleft, each time drumming a single fingertip against the little pucker of her rosehole, the third took Emily's knees and slowly pulled them wide apart.

She looked absolutely wonderful lying there, and the whole audience could see that she was already moist from her tormentors' teasing. Only five minutes had elapsed!

Standing on each side, the girls now began to caress the length of Emily's splayed thighs, moving up from her knees. They gently scratched at her delicate skin; caressed the swell of her buttocks; pressed fingertips against her rosehole and slid them up to caress the length of her cunny-lips. They pressed gently on her tummy just above her pubic bone, then moved up to her knees to begin again.

Emily had her eyes screwed tight as she sought to resist these insidious caresses, but the fact that her lips were already parted in that half-smile of arousal I knew so well, and that her breathing was quick and shallow, betrayed the effect they were having on her. The effect upon me was pretty well as strong, for my own breasts felt swollen, and my cunny distinctly warm! From the corner of my eye, I noticed that Veronica's hand was very busy in the trousers of the gentleman sitting beside her, so clearly I was not the only one to find this exhibition exciting.

On the stage, the girls had changed their tactics. While two were now kissing and licking Emily's breasts and running their hands over her thighs and torso, the third was busy between her legs. She had knelt and placed her hands flat on the join of Emily's thighs and pudenda. With her fingertips she pressed rhythmically against the swell of Emily's mound, while her thumbs parted the swollen love-lips and foraged insidiously between them.

Emily has the loveliest of cunnies; plump and dusted with a down of fair curls. Now, as the girl teased her, and her loins began to move to the irresistible sensations being roused in her, it looked positively beautiful.

The girl's hands moved. Emily's love-lips were fully parted, and her folds glistened red and swollen. As the girl eased a fingertip into her entrance, her clitoris roused and stood proud. The girl lowered her head, and began to tease it with little flicks of her tongue. Emily gave a groan, and the muscles of her thighs and tummy tensed as she reacted to the voluptuous sensations.

One girl was kissing Emily's mouth, and licking and caressing her neck and ears and underarms. The second was caressing her torso and dipping her tongue teasingly into her navel. The third was sliding several fingers in and out of her oozing vagina and smoothing the slick juices along her cleft and around her pert rosehole, all the while moving her writhing tongue along Emily's seeping folds and lapping at her straining cherry.

Emily's mouth was slack, her eyebrows were arched as she struggled in vain against the pleasure that was overtaking her; her breathing was quick and ragged. A deep flush had suffused her breasts. The muscles of her tummy were flexing and trembling, and she was clearly having a hard time keeping her hips from moving.

I knew the signs well. Emily was near her climax. I glanced up at the clock. Heavens! Over half an hour had passed, yet it had seemed only minutes.

Still Emily held out. She always resisted orgasm, I knew, and to her instinctive resistance was added the terms of the contest, but even so! The way these girls' hands and mouths were moving over her would have driven anyone else mad. I knew I would have come a dozen times at least, had they been doing it to me.

Between Emily's legs, the girl's head was bobbing more rapidly and her hands were moving more insidiously. Emily's thighs were trembling. I was holding my breath as the girl's tongue lapped at Emily's clitoris and teased around her entrance; I knew she was very close now.

The climax came very suddenly. As the girl closed her lips upon Emily's clitoris and sucked hard, she pressed a juice-slicked fingertip into her rosehole and several others into her vagina. Emily went rigid, then groaned aloud and shuddered into her release as her hips bucked wildly. Every muscle in her lovely body seemed to spasm at the same instant. Her head rolled from side to side, and her features were overwhelmed with a smile of ecstatic torment.

Every face in the audience lifted to scan the clock, and there rose a gasp of admiration and a storm of applause. Emily had lasted forty-two minutes!

She had put on a magnificent performance, but I well knew that the longer she held back the more overwhelming were her comes. She had held back for forty-two minutes, and her come had been volcanic. I wanted to make sure that she was being loved and cared for after such a shattering performance, and not just left to her own devices.

I excused myself, and made my way behind the stage. I found her being more than cared for – positively cosseted, in fact. She was lying up to her breasts in a steaming, scented bath, with the three girls who had so seduced her. The girls were chattering and giggling, and kissing Emily and each other while they sponged her and washed her hair. When she saw me, her eyes grew huge and her face was bathed in a smile of contentment. She said only two words – 'Oh, Lydia!' – but they spoke volumes in terms of pride and happiness. I returned to the drinks party well contented that my lovely friend was, literally, in good hands.

Five

The drinks party after Emily's performance was rather lively. I took no more than two small glasses of sherry myself, for as you know wine goes to my head rather. I received propositions from a couple of gentlemen, but turned them down even though I was still somewhat stirred up.

I was, in fact, more interested in looking for Lady Veronica to continue our conversation. She was not in the dining room, where the main body of the party was, but since the erstwhile audience seemed to have the run of the house I decided to wander off in order to find her.

The house was huge. I looked first in the library but backed out hurriedly, stammering my apologies at having disturbed Beatrice, or rather, her companion. The lady herself was kneeling on the floor, too busily sucking the gentleman's glistening member to notice me.

The next place I tried, some kind of cloakroom I believe, was also in salacious occupation. I began to mount the wide, curving staircase, but I heard giggles and some rather more suggestive noises coming from above my head, so I returned to the dining room. I would await Veronica there, rather than stumble in on any other couples working off their excitations.

Veronica entered the dining room after about half an hour. The only signs that she might have been 'up to something', as the saying goes, were that her hair was a little tousled, her eyes were sparkling, and her cheeks and lips were flushed. She kissed me enthusiastically, and once again began to quiz me about my work. Really, it was almost as though she envied me!

It ended somewhat unsatisfactorily, at least as far as I was concerned, for I wanted to find out more about Veronica's own life, and about the society she belonged to, but a message came that Emily was waiting, and I had to leave. I was delighted, therefore, to receive a letter through the post only two days later, inviting me to spend a weekend at her place in Buckinghamshire.

I rushed at once to Amelia, of course. She was as pleased as I, but rather more cautious. Was I aware that Lady Veronica moved with a rather special society, she asked. Did I really understand that she would try to tempt me into that society, to make me one of its playthings, as she was herself?

I am ashamed to say that I poured scorn on her concern. Was I not an intelligent woman, experienced in the ways of the world? Had I not looked after myself when I was the slave of the Tukanna, and afterwards here in England when thrown out of my home by stupid Aunt Maud? Why, I demanded to know, was she trying to put a blanket over my enjoyment?

To my astonishment and, I confess, chagrin, she put her arms about me, and kissed me, and told me that she was afraid of losing me! A sudden swell of tenderness so filled me as to bring tears to my eyes. How could she lose me? Was she not my deep friend, my helper and advisor in my time of difficulty? Was she not now my guide and protector as a young woman in a masculine world?

I hugged her, my dear Amelia, and told her I would never leave her. We kissed and clung to one another, warmed by what we both knew then was our mutual love; a love deeper than one feels for a man. A feeling of such closeness, such depth of oneness, swept over me that all I could do was bury my face in her bosom and hug her.

I promised Amelia that I would be careful, and even that I would take Kate or Emily with me as a sort of chaperone. At last she reluctantly agreed. Thus it was that, on a Friday several weeks later Kate and I were waved off at the railway station by Karl and Amelia, having promised to be back on Tuesday safe and well. 'And,' my wicked Kate whispered as we rolled up the carriage window and took our seats, 'with any luck, thoroughly shagged!'

A very pretty dog-cart was awaiting us at the little railway station not many miles from Aylesbury. We had, rather foolishly perhaps, brought more suitcases than could be fitted easily into the cart, so we kept our hat boxes on our laps as the smartly uniformed young driver wedged the last of our cases around our feet.

Kate had been thinking, and indeed expressing, decidedly naughty thoughts all through the train journey, and I was obliged to tap her sternly on her knee to stop her eyeing the young servant too openly. We had been invited by a member of the upper classes: it would not do to start our visit by getting off with one of the servants! And anyway, we should at least have the good manners to wait until we reached the house!

The house was everything I had imagined and more. A vast Palladian pile set in rolling acres of park land, it positively took our breath away. As we mounted the wide steps to the terrace where Lady Veronica waited to greet us, Kate was staring about her and actually hurting my hand, she was gripping my fingers so tightly. Neither of us had ever been in a place so palatial.

If Veronica noticed how awed we were, and I am sure she did, she made nothing of it. Indeed, it was as though I were her oldest and dearest friend as she threw her arms about me and kissed me on both cheeks in enthusiastic welcome.

Veronica swept us into a vast, panelled hall chattering happily, though I confess I was too awed by the surroundings to take in much of what she said. Footmen scurried up the wide, sweeping staircase with our cases. An under-butler appeared in order to take our capes and hats. A plump and immaculately turned out maid hurried off to fetch the tea Veronica ordered, and we found ourselves in the loveliest of sitting rooms, with French windows opening out on to a wide brick-paved terrace overlooking the park. It was all rather overwhelming.

When I introduced Kate, whom Veronica had not met before, she was welcomed almost as enthusiastically as I myself was, and Veronica illustrated straightaway that this might not be exactly a decorous weekend.

'And you are of the same profession as dear Lydia,' she said with a beaming smile. 'How lovely! You must tell me all about it if we have time. And –' she leant forward, pressing a hand on Kate's knee whilst smiling archly '– it makes one more beauty for our revels!'

Kate glanced at me with surprise, but all I could do by way of elucidation was to shrug my shoulders.

The revels to which Veronica had referred began that very evening. After taking tea in the spacious sitting room, Kate and I were shown up to the rooms which, since Kate had not been expected, we were to share. There was not just a bedroom either, but a dressing room and even a little sitting room. And more, there was a huge and luxuriously appointed bathroom and lavatory just along the corridor.

Kate was positively bubbling with excitement as she rushed from room to room, exclaiming at the richness and beauty of everything. We had been told that dinner would be at eight, and that we would be summoned by a gong just beforehand. Since we had several hours until then, we set to it to bathe and prepare ourselves.

The bath was so big that both of us could climb in together, and you can be sure there was much giggling and foolishness as first I washed Kate, and then she washed me. Kate is a naughty minx, and I had to pretend to be very stern with her to stop her concentrating her attentions on certain of my parts which did not need *that* much washing – if you could call what she was doing washing!

Mind you, she was just as naughty when we were towelling each other, and I have to confess that half an hour or so was spent doing things other than getting ready for dinner when we returned to our bedroom. Still, a woman seldom looks lovelier than after she has had a slow and satisfying orgasm, so we probably improved our appearance by that delicious delay!

We were both nervous when the gong sounded, and descended the stairs hand in hand.

The dining room was as large and opulent as the rest of the house had led me to expect. A long mahogany table, set for a dozen guests, dominated the room. On it, silver cutlery and cut-crystal goblets and decanters gleamed among candelabra and bowls of flowers and damask napkins. A big, carved sideboard was almost overloaded with dishes and tureens. Beside it stood a silent butler, looking as dignified and impassive as any butler you could read about in a novel.

To my surprise, Beatrice was among those present, looking quite regal with her hair up in a glossy chignon. She wore a gown of mauve taffeta, although the neckline was perhaps rather too low for it to be truly regal. Beatrice took me around to make the introductions, while Veronica took Kate.

I was somewhat overwhelmed by the rank of the gentlemen to whom I was introduced, for none was less than a baronet, and several were from the very topmost levels of our nobility. I began to get in a bit of a tizzy about whom to address as 'your grace', and whom 'my lord' or simply 'sir', but Beatrice put me at my ease by whispering that I should call them by their given names.

Apart from Beatrice and Lady Veronica, Kate and I were the only females present, until I got another surprise. There was a little flurry at the door and, apologising profusely for being tardy, in hurried the girl who had been with Veronica at the house party in Warlington; the girl who looked so like Veronica she could have been her sister, and who had gone through the same lascivious ceremony as had Veronica.

Was this, I wondered, a meeting of the society Amelia had cautioned me about, rather than simply a weekend gathering? We would see.

Dinner was a much more dignified affair than I had suspected in the light of what I knew about at least some of the company's predilections.

Silent footmen, supervised by the butler, served

mulligatawny soup, followed by delicious poached trout. For the meat course, there was both beef and mutton, each superbly roast. Next came a delicious upside-down pudding, and by the time we moved on to the cheese course I felt stuffed to the gills.

I also felt somewhat tipsy, for each course had been accompanied by a different wine; each one was delicious, though I cannot remember any names, and I had drunk rather more than was perhaps wise. Thus, when we ladies retired so that the gentlemen could indulge in their port and cigars – a foolish outdated custom, in my opinion – I made straight for a large sofa. Veronica and the other girl, whose name I learnt was Phoebe, placed themselves down beside me; both of them were also a little giggly from the wine.

Since Beatrice, Veronica and Phoebe were members of a society dedicated to licentiousness, and Kate and I were known to be *filles de joie*, you may be sure the conversation turned to matters lascivious. Quite what the gentlemen were discussing over their port I naturally cannot say. I am sure, though, that they would have been surprised had they overheard us.

Healthy-minded women, in a group, are at the very least irreverent about men and sex. Our group was so now, and indeed we were more ribald than simply irreverent. The capacities of various men, whose names meant nothing to Kate and I, were discussed and giggled over. First I, and then Kate, were teased into telling stories about our more amusing punters. Giggles grew to chuckles, and soon to open laughter, with each of us setting the others off with our snorts and cackles.

Quite what the gentlemen thought when at last they joined us I cannot say, but they did look rather askance, especially since our attempts to suppress our laughter only made matters worse and the next ten minutes were punctuated with muffled snorts and giggles whenever two females caught each other's eye.

The gentleman I had been introduced to as Bertie proved the calming influence by seating himself at the pianoforte; he played most beautifully, and sang in a splendid baritone voice. Then somebody suggested a game of blind tig-tag, and I at once suspected that we were getting towards the business of the evening.

The group had clearly done this before, for at once they decamped for the large sitting room by the terrace that Kate and I had first been shown into. I had not noticed it before, but I now realised that the chairs and sofas formed a half-circle, and that by moving a single table a wide area of floor between the seats and the French windows could be cleared. This, it transpired, was to be the stage upon which the game would be played.

With ineffable tact, Beatrice suggested that, since Kate and I were new here, we might prefer not to join in because the game might become a little unconstrained. Since she well knew how we made our living, this struck me as marvellously sensitive.

I glanced at Kate. She looked a little doubtful, but when I raised an eyebrow enquiringly she suddenly grinned and nodded her head eagerly. Beatrice was so delighted that we wished to join in that she kissed us both, and the game began.

Bertie was the first tig, and he was smiling broadly as the blindfold was tied about his head. It was a very thick and broad one to ensure that he could see nothing. Beatrice turned him around three times, and the rest of us dispersed ourselves about the room. The object of the exercise was very simple. The tig was required to catch, or tag, one of us, who thereupon had to stand still while the tig tried to identify him or her by touch alone.

If the identification was successful, that person then became the tig.

It might have seemed rather ordinary had there not been the 'variations' Beatrice had introduced. If a person was caught and successfully identified, he or she was required to remove a garment before donning the blindfold and becoming tig. If the identification was wrong, the tig had to take something off. This rule certainly promised to make the game more interesting.

Bertie began to move about, his arms outstretched, as the rest of us tried to avoid him. The space between the ring of seats and the French windows was quite large, but with a dozen of us moving about in it, being caught was pretty well inevitable. There was, too, an unstated twist to it which made me grin. All five of us females were wearing full-skirted gowns, which meant we took up much more space than the gentlemen. Also, we rustled when we moved, and the tig's ears were not covered by the blindfold.

Bertie clearly took advantage of this, for when he came close to Veronica and she made to move away, his head cocked and he took a quick pace forward and captured her. She stood stock still as Bertie tried to identify her using only his hands, and you may be sure that those hands explored rather more than just her facial features.

'Off with your frock!' cried Bertie in triumph, when he had successfully named Veronica, and off it came before she donned the blindfold. She looked very fetching in a white cambric *chemise* and lace-edged drawers, for to my surprise she wore no petticoats. She wore no corset either, on purpose I suspected, and her breasts jiggled enticingly as she searched blindly about her.

She quickly caught a tall gentleman called Charles,

and made everybody laugh by placing her hand straightaway on his crotch. She rubbed him quite vigorously, and possibly for a little longer than was strictly necessary for the purpose of identification, for there was a very obvious bulge in his breeches when at last she called out his name.

Soon, everyone was laughing and excited, and clothes were strewn all about the place. Several of the gentlemen had lost their breeches and more, and of the females only I still had all my clothes. It was Kate who caught me, and at her first attempt. This was luck for her as it transpired, in view of what then happened to me.

Kate squealed with pleasure when she identified me and ordered my frock off. The blindfold was very effective, and I was in pitch darkness as I began my search. I found somebody quite soon, a gentleman, and at once realised my quandary. I had only met these men at dinner. Even with my faculties unencumbered I had to think hard to remember whose name was whose, but by touch alone the task seemed impossible.

I reached up to find how tall he was. I felt the breadth of his shoulders. I touched his hair, and felt the size of his nose. I essayed a name. I was wrong. Off came my first petticoat. By the time, with enormous relief, I caught and identified Beatrice I was down to my stockings and *chemisette*, and was becoming convinced that I would soon be stark naked!

To cut a long story short, by the time Bertie suggested a night-cap of brandy and champagne at around midnight, the game of blind tig-tag had achieved its desired conclusion. Like me, Veronica and Phoebe had on only their stockings, Kate only her stockings, *chemise* and knickers, and Beatrice nothing at all.

None of the gentlemen had on any breeches, and the one called Charles had on only his undershirt and hose.

Inevitably, the real business of the evening soon began. Veronica was quite blatant about it. With her glass of champagne in one hand, she went straight up to Charles and reached up beneath his undershirt. Leading him by his cock, and grinning wickedly, she took him across to a plush sofa and pushed him down on to it. Neither Beatrice nor Phoebe were much behind her, either, and soon three sofas were in active use.

Even girls as experienced as Kate and I were rather surprised at how blatant these people were. Veronica was on her back being ridden by Charles, with another man's cock in her mouth. Beatrice was astride the man of her choice, squirming on him and squeezing her own breasts. Phoebe was on her hands and knees with her companion pounding at her from the rear, her head tossing with pleasure. That Kate and I were not to be left out soon became apparent.

Suddenly, Bertie was standing in front of me, looking a little ridiculous in just his hose and shirt tails. He made me a solemn bow and intoned, with great dignity, 'Excuse me, *mademoiselle*, it would give me great pleasure –'

I did not hear the rest, for I burst into giggles. Bertie was not in the least put out, and soon he too was laughing as we made our way across the carpet to a large, thickly cushioned settee. I was delighted to discover that he possessed a stalwart cock and was an excellent lover. Also, joy of joys, he began by licking me to arousal before attempting to shag me.

He proved to be a skilled and sensitive lover and, though well into his middle age, had plenty of stamina. I adore it when a man is as concerned for his partner's pleasure as he is for his own, for so many are not. He made sure he got me well stirred up with his hands and his mouth before getting between my legs. He entered me slowly and went deep.

His weight was on his elbows, and his hands were rolling my breasts, whilst his lips and teeth were nibbling at my neck; his cock was up me to the hilt. He stayed good and deep, pressing his pubic bone against my stretched love-lips and cherry, and circling in me deliciously. He varied his movements, sometimes adopting a slow, voluptuous thrusting, moving his whole length in me, sometimes staying in deep and giving little jerking movements which sent shivers of hot sensation through me. He was playing me like a musical instrument, and soon I forgot what was going on around me as he built me towards my come.

He read me well, and built me and built me with his lovely weapon until I was panting and rolling my head, my sheath writhing on him in greedy spasms. Sensing his moment to perfection, he started thrusting hard at the very instant the first wave of my orgasm crashed through my insides. Then, glory! he too began to come, pushing so deep into me that spurt after spurt of his hot jism seemed to flood my very soul.

When, centuries of swirling ecstasy later, I was able to open my eyes, Bertie was smiling down at me.

'Excellent, my dear,' he said, giving me a kiss on my brow. 'You are every bit as lovely and fuckable as dear Beatrice told me you'd be!'

Had I not been drifting down from a beautiful come, and had Bertie not been slipping deliciously out of me, I might have been chagrined at the idea of Beatrice describing me as 'fuckable' to a perfect stranger, but at that moment nothing much seemed to matter, save the gentling swells of my afterglow.

To my surprise, though I was lolling on the settee looking, I was sure, as thoroughly available as I felt, nobody else came for me. I had expected something of an orgy. There were, after all, seven men at the party, and long experience told me that the sight of naked girls writhing under thrusting loins gave men the energy to move from girl to girl. There was certainly a lot of writhing going on, for Kate was still being had by her partner, Beatrice was bent over with one man taking her from the rear and a second ploughing for her tonsils, and both Veronica and Phoebe were astride recumbent gentlemen and riding wildly, their full breasts bouncing with their efforts.

I watched for a while, expecting Bertie or the remaining gentleman, whose name I could not remember, to move to me when they had finished their drinks. But no, I was left undisturbed, which was actually a little disappointing, and at last I gathered up my scattered clothes, and made my way up the stairs to where I remembered my room was. I became a bit embarrassed when I encountered two uniformed footmen, but they appeared to ignore my state of near nudity. I supposed they must have been used to such sights.

After my ablutions, I returned to my bedroom and searched out my nightgown then changed my mind, smiling to myself. Surely, in this house, some gentleman or another would make his way to my bed and I would only have to take it off again. Naked, I slipped between the sheets and blew out the lamp.

After some time I was indeed joined in the bed, but it was Kate rather than some randy gentleman. In fact, no gentlemen at all tried to join us which we both found surprising and a little disappointing. Eventually we at last drifted off to sleep in each other's arms.

* * *

Since Kate and I seemed to be the first ones up and about on that bright Saturday morning, we decided to go for a stroll in Veronica's park. The weather was lovely, a perfect September day, and we did not need coats, or even shawls.

The view from the terrace revealed a beautiful, rolling park dotted with copses of mature trees. At some distance was a high wall of old bricks, and nearer to us was what looked like a sort of Greek temple. It was obviously one of those follies wealthy landowners used to erect years and years ago, and we decided to inspect it first.

We were correct as to its nature; it was a folly, and a very nicely built one too, of Portland stone, with half a dozen stout pillars supporting a domed roof. A statue stood on a pedestal at its centre. It was of a very beautiful nymph or naiad clutching at a draped garment that was obviously falling off her and, as seems always the case with such classical statuary, hiding none of her charms.

Looking closely, the nymph seemed to bear a strong facial resemblance to Beatrice at a younger age, and Kate grinned when I wondered aloud whether that lady had in fact posed for the sculptor. Kate remarked upon a number of iron rings that were set into the floor and high up on each pillar, but since we could not work out a function for them we dismissed them, and continued our stroll.

The grounds were even more extensive than we had thought, and revealed further surprises. There were two more follies, one a Greek temple like the first but housing a statue of a handsome young man, perfect in every detail and in an obvious state of excitement. The other was a pyramid. It had a wooden door, but since it seemed to be locked we could not explore it further.

Further on, and out of sight of the house, we came across a haha about twelve feet wide and the same deep. At its bottom there was a perfectly clipped hedge of beech, so thick that no animal could possibly have broken through it. On the other side we could descry other hedges, just as neatly clipped, which seemed to have been planted in some kind of pattern. It was rather too far separated to form a maze, but it was not totally un-maze-like, if you will excuse my clumsy attempt at description. Our curiosity was struck, too, by a conical roof rising from among these hedges.

We decided to follow the edge of the haha to see if there was a bridge over the ditch somewhere, so that we could examine these odd features and find out what the building was. The haha appeared to enclose a surprisingly large area, little of which could be seen because of the hedges. At last we came to a very pretty little structure like one of those drawbridges one sees in paintings of Dutch canals. It was down, and so we walked across.

The hedges we had descried were even odder than they had at first appeared to be, describing sweeping curves, and enclosing wide spaces with narrow gaps dotted about. I could not really figure what purpose they served, for most of the semi-enclosures did not even have benches in them to sit on while taking the air.

The principal effect they seemed to have was to prevent us from taking a direct path to the conical structure we could still see ahead of us. When at last we rounded one last hedge, what greeted us was well worth the wait. It was yet another folly, but one that went straight to my heart, for it was an excellent imitation of an African hut!

Memories of my time with the Tukanna, and my

beloved Talesi and Motallo flooded over me, and I rushed forward with a cry of joy. My squeal was clearly not loud enough to be heard inside the folly, for as I hurried through the doorway I came upon a young couple in the middle of a very hearty shag!

The girl, a housemaid, to judge by the top half of her clothes, which was all she now had on, saw me and gave a little squeal. The young man who had her up against the wall was clearly much too far gone in his passion to notice, for he just kept on thrusting at the girl, almost lifting her off the ground in his excitement.

Instantly, I backed out of the hut mouthing apologies. Obviously in this household everybody was at it!

Six

The formal reason for this weekend gathering began that very evening.

There had been seven gentlemen and five females last night. During the Saturday afternoon and early evening several more people arrived. As dusk was beginning to fall on a warm balmy evening a gong was heard, and everybody moved to the ballroom, which I had not seen before. There was quite a crowd, mostly young, with males and females in roughly equal numbers.

Bertie, who seemed to have the role of master of ceremonies, clapped his hands loudly and quiet fell across the group. He announced that a buffet supper would be served, and at nine o'clock the society would convene here in the ballroom to welcome some new members. Until then, we were free to follow our own pursuits and make our preparations.

I looked, startled, to Veronica. Did she intend that these new members should be Kate and I?

'Oh, no, darling!' She laughed. 'No such thing. Just a couple of debutantes and one of Beatrice's nephews. He's a very pretty lad, and I can't wait to get my hands on him! No, no, you have to be formally nominated and tutored before you can join our little group. But I'm sure you would have no difficulty. Are you interested then?'

I quickly shook my head, noticing that Kate, who I knew was game for almost anything, was about to say yes. Amelia's warning about caution was in my mind.

'Thank you, dear. It is a kind invitation, but I think we need time to consider,' I said. 'We have, as you know, other duties.'

Veronica laughed and tapped my hand playfully. 'Yes, and entertaining ones too, I do not doubt! Still, I'll ask Bertie if you may watch from the minstrel gallery tonight, so that you will have a better idea of what we are about.'

She managed it, and a couple of hours later Kate and I were ushered by a footman to comfortable seats in the minstrel gallery overlooking the ballroom.

We were kept waiting only a few minutes, and just as a clock struck nine the double doors at the end of the ballroom swung open, and the members of the society began to enter in procession.

At the head, looking very dignified but even fatter than I remembered, came the elderly man who had conducted that erotic shaving and deflowering cere-mony all those months ago in Warlington. Behind him, still in clerical garb, came the man who had assisted him then, walking side by side with Bertie. I looked quickly over the dozen or so men who trooped in behind them, but could not recognise the two young men who had actually 'done the deed' with Veronica and Phoebe.

The fat old man took his seat almost immediately beneath where Kate and I watched, and the other men ranged themselves on the straight-backed chairs which ringed the dance floor. There was a pause of perhaps a minute and the old man, who seemed to be the chairman, clapped his hands loudly. At this signal, processing just as solemnly as the men, came the females – and what a vision they made!

Every one was wearing a sort of satin highwayman's mask, but of gold rather than black. Each had her hair flowing long and loose about her shoulders and down her back, her curls or waves gleaming in the light of the chandeliers. Each wore tiny gold slippers which made no noise on the polished wood of the floor.

Each was draped from shoulder to floor in a loose robe of gold-coloured taffeta which floated with every movement and clung like paint to the skin where it touched their bodies. They looked absolutely stunning, for the masks and voluminous robes gave them an air of mystery; whilst they were entirely concealed, at the same time the imagination was drawn to what lay beneath.

Each woman went and stood beside one of the seated men, and remained as still and silent as enigmatic statues. I thought I recognised the figure standing beside Bertie as Beatrice, for she has distinctive hair. I cast my eyes around the assembly, but could pick out neither Veronica nor Phoebe.

After the silence that had attended the entry of these women, I was startled when the chairman rapped his cane upon the floor.

'First business!' he called in a firm, clear voice. At once, a figure I recognised as Veronica floated through the door. She went up to the fat chairman, the soft silk of her robe clinging deliciously to her lovely form. To my surprise, she knelt and touched her forehead to his foot in the humblest of obeisances. Then she knelt back, placed her hands palms upward on her knees and, head bowed, said something so quietly I could not catch it.

'By all manner of means,' said the chairman, and Veronica at once touched her brow to his foot again, then rose and floated out of the ballroom again. 'Second business!' cried the Chairman.

Before this could commence there came a rustle, and Veronica slipped into the seat beside me. Whispering, she told us that she had been given permission to sit with us and relate the ceremonies that were about to unfold before us.

The first of these was an exchange. It seemed that girls who had been inducted into the society were given to its male members until a marriage was arranged for them. At my expression of shock at such a barbaric sounding practice, Veronica assured me that it was no such thing. Rather, it gave the girl in question a place of abode and financial security, and in any case the girl herself had a strong influence over any arrangements affecting her.

In this particular case, for example, two couples had been together for a number of months, and had applied to the society for consent to exchange. This was the ceremony that had already begun down below us, and so distracting was it that I had to get Veronica to repeat to me later much of what I have written above.

As Veronica's voice whispered in my ear, two of the female statues began to move. They both floated up to the chairman and gave the same obeisance as had Veronica. Meanwhile, the men by whom they had been standing had risen, picked up their chairs, and moved them to the middle of the floor.

The two females now rose and moved to where the men sat. Together, as if rehearsed in a stately dance, they sank to their knees before their partners. Both girls now proceeded to undo the gentlemen's trousers, haul out their slumbering cocks, and bow their heads to suck them!

In her amazement, Kate had taken my hand, and was squeezing it almost painfully. The ballroom was absolutely silent as every eye was fixed upon the bobbing heads of the two kneeling figures. Soon, the men were full and erect, and had slid their hips towards the front edges of their chairs. The girls knelt back, then moved forward to place a single kiss on the plum they had just excited. Gracefully, they rose to their feet, and each moved to stand in front of the other's erstwhile partner.

There came the briefest of pauses while everybody, including myself, held their breath, then the girls raised the fronts of their robes, moved forward as one, and planted themselves astride their new partner's lap. A moment's fumbling followed and they sank themselves down, and began the voluptuous writhings of a girl impaled on a rampant cock.

So this was how an exchange was affected. A girl simply kissed her old partner goodbye, and rode off with her new one. How excellently naughty!

The two men remained very still, their eyes closed, and on their faces appeared expressions of intense concentration. It must indeed have taken great power of the will to remain motionless as their delicious burdens writhed and wriggled towards their transports, their mouths slack, their backs arching, their hips circling and pumping.

The fairer haired of the two girls reached her climax first. She placed her hands on her partner's shoulders, bucked her hips convulsively, and curved her back like a bow. Finally she burst into a series of rapid gasps before sinking her head down upon her partner's chest. Then she relaxed as though unstrung. Her face was the very picture of satisfied delight.

Only when she had finished did her partner allow himself to move. As he burst instantly into his own come, he groaned and jerked her about like a puppet. He must have been holding himself back all through her climax; a marvellous feat of self control.

The performance was repeated by the other couple after only two or three more minutes, except that this time the girl burst out with a series of cries which rose in pitch and volume until she was almost screaming; her partner began his come while she was still shuddering with hers.

When I whispered my admiration for the men's performances, Veronica explained to me that it was a requirement that the man allow the girl to climax first, and that if he failed the exchange was null and void. A demanding rule indeed and, I thought, very favourable to the ladies.

Having finished their labours, and I am sure warmed up the senses of their audience – they had certainly warmed up my own – the girls climbed off their steeds, tucked their deflated partners away, and buttoned up their trousers. Thereupon, both couples approached the chairman. The men bowed and the girls curtseyed low.

'Is it agreed?' asked the chairman, addressing not the gentlemen but the girls.

'It is agreed, master,' they replied together. The chairman banged his cane upon the floor; the couples turned and, hand in hand, returned to their places among the circle of their audience, the gentlemen having retrieved the two chairs.

There now ensued a flurry of activity as two footmen entered carrying trays loaded with brimming glasses. These were distributed around the room, and several more footmen followed bearing a large, Chinese silk carpet, which they unrolled on the centre of the floor. The carpet may have been Chinese, but the pattern woven upon it certainly was not. If anything, it was inspired by some Roman bacchanalia, and featured naked couples cavorting in every position imaginable around its edge, and at its centre was an excellent representation of a naked nymph, legs flung wide, being pleasured by the tongue of a goat-headed satyr. This society of Veronica's certainly did not do things by halves!

The drinks were soon finished and the footmen withdrew. Silence once again fell, a silence at last broken by a bang from the chairman's cane, and his voice intoning 'And now to the third and final business!'

Once again the double doors at the end of the room swung open and a procession entered. This one, though, was composed of only six persons. Two were gentlemen dressed as the others were. The third was a woman, masked and robed like the other women. Behind each of these came another figure, entirely hidden beneath drapes which covered them from head to foot.

These drapes were of pure white silk, and put me instantly in mind of bridal gowns. That this was not a false illusion soon became apparent, for what ensued resembled nothing so much as a pagan marriage ceremony.

The newcomers drew up in a line across the carpet, each white draped figure standing next to the person it had followed in. The clerically garbed gentleman came forward bearing a large, black-bound tome for all the world as if it were a Bible, which it clearly was not.

In a high, sing-song voice, he told the assembly that it was gathered to consider the pleas of three supplicants. He asked whether they were prepared to so consider. Assent given, he turned to the first couple.

'Who giveth this supplicant?'

'I do!' replied the gentleman.

'And has the supplicant been properly prepared?'

'She has.'

'Under whose tutelage has the supplicant been prepared?'

'My own, sir, and that of my consort.'

'And is the supplicant willing and able to obey the rules and precepts of this learned and ancient society and to conform to its standards and practices?'

'She is, sir.'

These exchanges, so solemn in their tone, nearly gave me the giggles, for I was well aware of the very unsolemn ends towards which they were aimed. Kate, too, was finding it hard to stifle her mirth, but when we saw how seriously Veronica was taking it all, we controlled ourselves out of deference to her feelings.

The cleric now repeated his questions to the other two couples, getting the same responses save that the woman said 'he' rather than 'she'. I remembered that Veronica had told us that the supplicants were two females and Beatrice's nephew – a very pretty boy, she had said.

The verbal part of the ceremony being over, the cleric slapped his book shut, whereupon the two gentlemen and the woman turned to their charges and began to pull off the silk with which they were swathed.

The figures that were revealed were young, perhaps my own age or a little less. The one in the middle was the lad Veronica had mentioned, and he was not at all pretty. Magnificent is a much more appropriate description!

Naked save for the obligatory mask, his hair was a mane of dark curls, his shoulders were broad, and his limbs long and athletic. His lips were full and red and his jaw was already becoming strong and manly. His chest was bereft of hair and well muscled, as was his flat stomach. But what drew the eye was the mat of black curls below his navel, from which lolled, half erect, a pale, hooded penis of handsome proportions with a pouch of full, tight balls beneath.

I heard Kate whisper, 'Oh! He's beautiful!' and could not but agree with my whole heart. Like us, Veronica was craning forward, her tongue flicking over her parted lips lasciviously. Her words earlier – 'I can't wait to get my hands on him!' – came back to me, and I had to smile. I confess I felt just like that myself!

The two female supplicants were as beautiful as the youth, each in her own way. The girl on the left was almost as tall as the lad, with a shawl of auburn hair falling down her back and to the swell of her pert, uptilted breasts. Her skin was fair and freckled, and she was slender and long limbed. Like the other supplicants, she was standing as if to attention, and one could sense an element of lithe strength in her.

The other girl, in contrast, was shorter than the other two and promised, when she was older, to become positively voluptuous. Her breasts were full, though not pendulous, with large pink aureolae surrounding nipples that stood out proudly. Her waist was quite small, her navel was a deep dimple in a pertly rounded tummy, and her hips curved roundly above shapely legs. Like the first girl, she had been shaven, though the youth had not.

After a long pause during which every eye in the place drank in the beauty of these three naked supplicants, the gentleman on the left took the hand of the girl he was presenting and led her up to the cleric. Silently, the lovely maiden curtseyed, placed a kiss upon the book he held, and returned alone to her place, her presenter moving to one side.

The youth and then the second girl repeated the process, and soon just these three naked visions occupied the centre of the room. Veronica had obviously become quite enthralled by the sight of the handsome youth, for she had stopped giving us her whispered elucidation.

When the trio below us turned and began to walk slowly towards where Bertie sat, to the right of the chairman, Veronica suddenly recovered herself. Grabbing my hand and that of Kate, she stood and began pulling us.

'Come!' she whispered urgently. 'Come, you are not permitted to witness any more!'

I whispered a protest and pulled back, anxious to see more of this exotic and erotic ceremony. Veronica, though, was adamant, the expression on her face becoming nervous and concerned as she pulled us harder. In deference to her anxiety, though with great reluctance you may be sure, we allowed ourselves to be pulled out of the minstrel gallery.

Once outside, Veronica became a little calmer, and apologised profusely. It seemed that the actual induction to the society of new members could only be observed or attended by members, but that she had got so excited at the prospect of seeing Billy (clearly the youth) that she had forgotten herself. We should not even have been allowed to see the unveiling!

She was not allowed, either, to tell us what would now be happening, though you may be sure that we plagued her with questions. All she would tell us was that the ceremony would go on for at least several more hours, that she was dreadfully sorry that she had not forewarned us, and that a little supper had been prepared for us in the drawing room, towards which she now led us.

Both Kate and I were too disappointed to feel much like eating, but she perked us up a bit with her parting, cryptic remark, spoken with an arch smile.

'I'll see what I can do about a little compensation!' she said.

Veronica returned to us after about half an hour, during which Kate and I picked at the supper and drank a little of the rather good coffee, but mostly speculated on what was transpiring in the ballroom. We speculated in a rather desultory manner, to be honest, because our spirits were somewhat downcast. Apart from the game of blind tig-tag last night, this weekend was turning out to be very different from what we had anticipated. On the journey down, we had giggled about enjoying lots of shagging; in fact, shagging seemed to be in short supply so far as we two were concerned!

Upon Veronica's return, prospects improved considerably. First, she told us that our sleeping arrangements had been changed, and that Kate had now been given her own room, to which she, Veronica, would conduct her shortly. Then, her grin already lending significance to her words, she told us that 'attendants' would be available in both our rooms, and she begged that we should avail ourselves of them freely.

She would say no more, and when I caught Kate's glance she made that round-eyed, arch expression of hers I knew so well. She had taken the same inference from Veronica's words as had I. It would have been unseemly to have hurried off immediately and so we fiddled somewhat with our supposed supper before Kate feigned a yawn. Veronica instantly insisted on conducting her to her new bedroom, thus freeing me to go to mine. As I went to my room I ruminated upon the strangeness of our society's manners that two girls dedicated to enthusiastic sex had to pretend not to be eager for a shag!

* * *

He was a distinctly handsome man who looked to be in his mid-twenties. He wore a smart footman's uniform, with a braided blue jacket and very nicely cut white knee-breeches. His finely chiselled face was impassive, and even his deep blue eyes remained unmoved as I hurried into the room.

Only when I got several paces in, almost to the bed in fact, did he move, giving me a deep bow; his dark hair, tied in a cue by a neat black bow, glistened in the lamplight.

'Good evening, miss,' he said, his voice light and musical. 'How may I be of service to you?'

That imp of humour which has plagued me all my life almost swept me away. Service me, rather than be of service, was my first irreverent thought, and it struck me that here was a nice reversal if ever there was one. I had spent the last ten months of my life as a 'professional girl', dedicated to servicing the whims of male customers. Now, here I was being offered exactly the same delights by this handsome young footman as I was used to offering to my own punters. How deliciously ironic!

Then straightaway I found myself in something of a quandary. How to begin? I was used to finding out my punter's preferences, getting my clothes off, and then performing. I sat down on the bed, at a loss for a moment. He certainly was a very nice looking young man.

Then I heard myself saying 'Take your clothes off, please.'

At once, and without demur, he removed his jacket and hung it on the back of a chair. Next came his shoes and his hose, then his white cravat. He looked delicious as he began to blush a little under my gaze, and I found myself turning away out of an odd sense of delicacy. When I looked back, he was pulling his shirt off over his head.

101

His torso was beautiful. Pale and entirely absent of hair except for a dusting on his forearms, his smooth chest was well muscled, and tapered to a flat stomach, set off perfectly by the prettiest of navels. As he began to work on the buttons of his tight knee-breeches, I felt my breasts tighten and my nipples stir.

He turned away to push down his breeches, at the same time peeling off his underpants to reveal a tight, firm bottom that cried out for a hand or teeth. When he turned back to face me, I was hard put to it to stop myself giving a little gasp of delight, for his legs were long and his thighs shapely, and at their join was the sweetest of cocks a girl could wish for.

Still drowsing, it was not what one would call large, but was nicely thick and had been circumcised, which always pleases me. The balls which nestled in his mat of tight curls looked nice and large, and were already tightening.

Veronica's compensation was certainly looking very promising!

I gazed at this delicious figure for long moments, intrigued that he was again blushing, and blushed deeper when his cock began to stir. To break the spell the sight had cast over me, I stood and began to work on my buttons.

'Excuse me, miss.' His voice actually startled me, so rapt had I become. 'Would you please allow me?'

My frock was held by twenty-four small buttons down the front, in eight groups of three passing through silk cord frogging. This handsome, nude young man managed to undo them with great delicacy, and avoided touching me or tugging excessively. His hands, I noticed, were fine but strong looking, and his nails were perfectly manicured. I do so like good hands; ragged nails can be so uncomfortable at certain times!

He eased my frock off my shoulders, and slowly lowered it to the floor.

'What is your name?' I asked as I stepped out of the pile of cloth. He began to unbutton my left shoe.

'Peters, miss.' His touch on my ankle as he slipped the shoe off sent a tremour of delight through my calf.

'No, no. I mean your given name,' I said, lifting my right foot. 'In these circumstances formality seems a bit silly.'

'Yes, miss. It's Peter, miss.'

Peter Peters! Oh dear! I am sorry to say that I giggled. I regretted it instantly, for Peter blushed even more deeply than before. How the poor darling must have been teased over the years. And how thoughtless of his parents to christen him thus.

I reached down and touched his shoulder, blurting my apologies. His skin was smooth and warm. I reached down and got him to stand up. His eyes were so deep and soft I could have swum in them. I slipped my arms about him and reached up to kiss him to prove I was sorry. His mouth was at first tentative, then softened as he returned my kiss, his own arms going around me in a strong yet gentle hug. Oh, his body was so firm and warm, and soon I felt something very interesting pressing against my tummy.

He finished undressing me with a slow, concentrated delicacy which set my pulse beating faster and harder. By the time I stepped out of my knickers, and reached down to touch his hair where he knelt, my breasts already felt hard and swollen, and my quim was moist.

He lifted me bodily, and lay me gently on the bed. I reached up to pull him down with me, but he had other things in mind. He moved to my feet, and began to kiss and caress them.

I am sure there is a direct and electric connection between the soles of the feet and the vagina. As Peter's tongue and lips moved over my instep and the undersides of my toes, his warm breath wafting over me and his fingers gently massaging, I felt my love-lips swelling and unfolding.

After an age, during which Peter kissed and licked and caressed every part of my tingling skin, I became incapable of thinking. But not of feeling though, for what Peter was doing to me was wonderful.

In moving to caress me he had come close, and I was able to touch and kiss him, and drink in the warm scent of his body. Oh, he was beautiful! When his mouth eased between my slack thighs everything in the universe became beautiful. His tongue was gentle on my throbbing folds. His breath was a rapturous zephyr.

Somehow, my eyes drifted open. He was close to me, his manhood now proud and lovely. As his knowing tongue found the centre of my being and sent swelling waves of sensation to my every nerve-end, I moved my head, and parted my lips, and he slipped deliciously into my mouth.

He gave me my first come with his tongue as I sucked him, and caressed his tight balls and buttocks with trembling fingers. Or perhaps I should not call it my first, for in reality it was the beginning of one long, swelling and declining, pulsing and cramping orgasm that in the end had me almost begging him to release me.

Somehow, he was out of my mouth and lying full length upon me, his manhood in me to the hilt, thick and glorious, stretching me as the muscles of my vagina cramped and sucked at him, and my pelvis bucked helplessly.

Somehow, after an age of sunbursts, he was in me

from the rear, his hands grasping my breasts, his breath hot on my neck.

Somehow, he was on his back and I was full-length on his hard body, writhing ecstatically as his strong hands grasped my buttocks and a fingertip drummed on my rosehole.

I kissed his mouth, his neck, his hands. I bit his ears and his nipples. I gasped and writhed, and cried out each time he came in me and thus drove my own comes on deeper and higher, until I felt I must die of it.

It was a long, wonderful night. Sometimes I dozed, or perhaps merely drifted into a trance of exhausted contentment. Each time, I awoke to his voluptuous touch, to suck and be sucked, to fuck and be fucked. He was perfect, as wonderful a lover as a woman could dream of.

At last, I sank into a proper sleep, or rather a stupor of over-stimulation. He was gone when I awoke to full daylight. My clothes, which had been strewn about the floor when he undressed me, were neatly put away. Peter's clothes were nowhere to be seen. Only the chaotic state of the bed was evidence of the shattering night that had passed.

Before I could climb off the bed, Veronica burst into the room, all smiles.

'Well, well, Lydia my darling!' she laughed. 'Clearly, my compensation met with your approval. It is nearly noon, and you are still abed!'

She was dressed in a simple but elegant dress of pale blue cotton, and her hair was in loose ringlets. Still smiling and chatting, she handed me a silk dressing gown whilst looking me over shrewdly as I clambered off the bed. My pubic curls were matted from all my effusions during that energetic night, and

Veronica grinned as I blushed at the way she raised an eyebrow on noticing it.

'So, my darling Lydia,' she said, holding out the gown for me to slip my arms in. 'Did you find my pretty Peter to your satisfaction?'

She was so artless in her tone that I found myself answering her. Soon we were giggling together at the young footman's talents, and comments about having to feed him 'good red meat and plenty of it' to keep his strength up. Veronica had, she told me, trained him herself – what delicious images flashed into my mind at that revelation – and often made use of him during quiet periods.

'And not so quiet periods if I am feeling especially randy!' She laughed as we entered the bathroom for my ablutions. The maid who had been running my bath bobbed a curtsey and left, but it seemed entirely natural for Veronica to remain and continue our chat as I bathed.

And to judge from the way she looked at me as I soaped my breasts and legs, and flannelled myself all over, her interest was not entirely impersonal. Was she as interested in her female guests as she was in her footmen, I wondered?

Seven

It was another of those warm, soft September days and after a light lunch, during which it became clear that Kate had enjoyed her compensation every bit as much as I had enjoyed my own, we went for a very pleasant drive in the nearby countryside. There was a moment of suppressed hilarity when Kate recognised the driver of our little carriage as her compensation from last night, but the man in question – a well-made chap of perhaps thirty summers – remained impassive, and it soon passed.

The countryside around Veronica's estate was well wooded and dotted about with prosperous looking farms. We passed through a couple of very pretty villages, where people obviously recognised Veronica and Phoebe, and doffed their caps or curtseyed in cheerful greeting. I found myself wondering whether they would have been so respectful had they known what games these two ladies got up to back at the mansion house!

These games started up again immediately after a light but delicious dinner.

This time, Kate and I were cordially invited to take part should we wish to. Needless to say, we accepted without hesitation! Although she had been given her own separate bedroom last night, Kate's luggage was still in my room, and so we returned there in order to sort out what we were to wear.

We did not know quite what the tone of the evening would be, apart from promising plentiful sex that is, and had spread out any number of frocks upon the bed when Phoebe came in and made all clear. Frocks would obviously not be needed!

She had on a pair of pure white silk stockings, the skimpiest white lace basque you could ever imagine, and a pair of lacy knickers so fine they were no more than a mist around her nether parts. Elbow-length lace gloves and pretty button-boots with two-inch heels, also in white, completed her costume.

Though the colour of her brief costume may have been virginal, the figure they decorated certainly was not! Her lovely breasts were lifted and offered up by the basque like two pink-nosed puppies eager to frolic. Her cunny was still shaven, and peeped like a pouting tulip through the diaphanous veil of her knickers, and the white line of her suspenders beautifully set off the long curves of her thighs. The shawl of her loose hair, and the wicked smile on her face, completed a picture which was no more and no less than an invitation to shag.

'Come along, girls,' she said. 'You are missing all the fun! There is much to do down at Aphrodite's!'

It took Kate and me less than ten minutes to prepare ourselves. We were already down to our underthings, and had only to whip off the remainder, put on basques, stockings and boots, and we were ready. Soon, three eager, giggling and scantily clad girls were skipping down the wide stairs seeking adventure.

Phoebe's mention of Aphrodite turned out to be a reference to the folly temple with the female statue in it. As we approached, I could see figures lit by what seemed to be several oil lamps.

'It is our new member,' said Phoebe as we began to draw near. 'He performed rather poorly last night, and is now being punished for it. I thought you might like to watch, or perhaps even join in.'

It was indeed the lad from last night, and I recognised him even though he had worn a mask then. I also recognised, with a lurch of shock, what those strange iron rings were for. The young man was fixed to them, his arms pulled tight above his head and bound to a pillar ring with leather straps. His ankles were similarly bound to widely separated floor rings. He looked positively pagan, trussed there naked in the flickering yellow light of the lamps.

What looked even more pagan was the bevy of girls and women about him, some naked, some clad merely in scanty underthings. I was a little puzzled to see that one of the women was holding a large pocket watch and a handbell.

For a moment, I thought that being trussed helpless like that was the lad's punishment, and was a little perturbed. As we got closer, though, and Phoebe whispered in explanation, any qualms I might have had turned to smiles – and salacious ones at that.

His poor performance of last night had been that he had come too soon; it was his duty, and what he had been trained for, to hold back until his partner enjoyed her come, and he had failed. His punishment was to be strung up as he was now in the temple of Aphrodite and stimulated; he was forbidden to come at all until a time limit was reached, hence the watch and bell. Such a punishment!

Even as we approached it became clear through the crowd of females, that several naked girls were working on him. Phoebe eased our way to the front of the crowd, and I stared open mouthed at the scene.

Two giggling girls were moving bunches of feathers

very softly up and down the insides of the lad's splayed thighs. The third was teasing his nipples and his armpits. The lad's teeth were gritted with effort as he sought to deny the stimulation he was experiencing; his beautiful body was rigid and his cock, the most rigid part of all, was straining for the ceiling.

'How long has this been going on?' I whispered to Phoebe.

'Oh, only about twenty minutes, so far.'

'Twenty minutes!'

'Of course, there's a while to go yet,' said Phoebe casually.

To judge from the lad's tension, and the perspiration which dewed his forehead and upper lip, twenty minutes had been a long time.

The girls with the feathers ceased their teasing and moved away. They were replaced by another, this one wearing a short tabard of frilled chiffon, apart from which she was entirely naked. She approached the young man smiling archly, her eyes sweeping up and down his handsome body. He too smiled, though whether it was in welcome, or in relief from the cessation of the feathers' stimulation I cannot say. She moved close, stood between the youth's spread legs, and pressed herself against him. She wrapped her arms around him and stretched up to place a slow, passionate kiss on his mouth; a kiss he tried to pull back from but could not.

Holding his head and kissing him all the while, the woman began to move her body sinuously against his, her breasts squashed against his chest, her tummy tracing lascivious side-to-side motions against his. With his engorged cock trapped between her belly and his, the youth must have been in the most excruciating torment, for she was almost fucking him, but not quite.

Even the sight of what was happening had got me worked up, so heaven knows how the young man must have felt.

'That is cheating a little,' whispered Phoebe. 'Really, they are not allowed to actually touch his tackle. Still, it is of his own choosing!'

'His choosing?' I asked. 'Do you mean he set his own punishment?'

'Of course!' she replied, looking surprised. Then her expression changed as she remembered that I knew nothing of the practices of her society. 'Let me explain.'

Phoebe cast a glance back to where the lad was being teased, then led me down the steps. It was by way of a game, she told me. The society liked to spice things up with little games. Anybody could just shag; anybody did, in fact. One became flat and jaded, though, if that was all one did, no matter how able one's partner. Therefore, she and her friends, the society, added games and teases and dares to lend matters a little more spice.

Last night, after the induction ceremony, young Billy had boasted that he could make even Arabella come. This turned out to be a wild and foolish boast, for Arabella, whom I had not heard of before, was a very experienced woman and something of a mistress of ceremonies in the society. He had failed, of course, for Arabella, in Phoebe's rather graphic words, could 'out-fuck a regiment'.

He had probably known he would fail. He was a clever and licentious lad. In failing, though, he had enjoyed what he had apparently announced as the finest fuck a man could have – I suddenly wanted to meet this Arabella – and got to choose his own punishment.

So, he had chosen to undergo what had seemed to

me a pretty strenuous procedure. And how long, I wanted to know, had he said he could last for? An hour? He would never make it! And what happened to him, I asked, when he failed?

'Oh,' said Phoebe with a grin, 'he gets to choose another punishment!'

I burst into laughter. How incredibly naughty! There I had been, feeling a touch of pity for a lad who was being tormented, albeit in the most delightful ways imaginable, when all the while he had chosen it, and was obviously receiving the most intense possible pleasure!

I stood and began to remount the steps, intent on seeing how this wickedly salacious lad was bearing up. At the moment I did so a bellow went up from the lad, and the women squealed and giggled and ducked aside. Through the gap they made, I saw the young man's body flexing and shuddering, his hips pulsing as gout after gout of white jism shot into the air and splashed on to the laughing females.

When his explosive orgasm had finished, the lad's body went limp and sagged, and his cock began slowly to subside. Then his face became suffused with the happiest grin you can imagine.

Women rushed to kiss him and release him from his bonds. He too was laughing as they virtually carried him out of the temple, and placed him on the grass. They rubbed his wrists and ankles where they had been tied.

'Well,' said Phoebe, with a naughty grin. 'What do you think of our system of discipline?'

What I thought, as Phoebe gathered up Kate and began to lead us off across the grass, was that such a system must positively encourage transgression! I might well like it myself if one got to choose one's punishment. A contest with Beatrice's nephew, for example, to see which of us could out-shag the other, would be a rather interesting penalty!

Phoebe now led Kate and I to Dionysius, the second Greek folly, featuring the male statue. The scene here was very different from that at Aphrodite, but just as bacchanalian. I recognised the two young women who had been inducted last night, and with them half a dozen or more men. All were naked.

The dark-haired girl, the shorter, plumper one, was astride a recumbent man and riding him with slow, lecherous writhings. Her head was turned to the side, and her mouth was moving on the engorged cock of a second man to just the same rhythm as her cunny. Her hands had cupped and lifted her full, soft breasts, and she was kneading and fondling herself lasciviously. On her face was an expression of rapture, and the way her soft buttocks moved as she alternately rose and sank on the cock inside her was voluptuousness itself.

She was clearly having a wonderful time. So too was the other girl, to judge by the way she hissed, 'Yes! Yes! God, yes!' and tossed her head. She was standing bent over at the hips, supporting herself on the plinth of the statue. Behind her, gripping her hips and pumping at her so wildly her breasts were shaking like jellies in an earthquake, was the man I had been introduced to on Friday as Charles. As Kate had told me, he was pretty sturdy in his cock, and had given her a good time.

He was giving this girl a good time now, and as he burst into a very obvious come she gave a positive howl of joy. He veritably lifted her off her feet with his last, frantic thrusts!

When he finished and stepped back, the girl straightened and turned to him, a rapturous smile lighting her flushed features. She threw her arms

113

about him and gave him a long, lascivious kiss. She murmured her thanks as their lips met, and pressed herself full length against him. Breaking the kiss at last, she turned and reached towards a new partner, a young man standing by one of the pillars. Before I could see more I felt a hand on my shoulder. A tall, dark-haired, naked man was smiling down at me, his eyebrows raised questioningly. I smiled in return. I had become pretty aroused by all that I had seen, and was ready for a little fun myself. I glanced at Kate and Phoebe. They were both grinning and making shooing motions.

My new companion and I began to walk away from the temple, and after only a few paces his hand was sliding over my bottom.

Whoever he was, he had a rich, deep speaking voice. As I said, he had dark hair, thick and brushed back to reveal the suggestion of a widow's peak. The bright light of the full moon, however, washed out any other colour, so all I could see of his complexion was paleness. Glancing down as we walked, I espied a weapon which, though soft and swinging as he walked, promised well for what would be happening soon.

Oddly, in view of the fact that here were two people who had only just met, the one in scanty underwear, the other stark naked, both on their way to have a shag, he talked about the weather! Had I not been very eager to relieve my arousal I might have actually giggled, it was so incongruous!

He walked me towards a set of those odd, curved hedges I mentioned earlier. He stopped by a painted wooden chest nestling against one of the hedges and opened it. From inside, he drew a thick, folded item, which I soon learnt was a blanket. This society was well prepared indeed!

With his arm still around me, though this time with

his hand on my waist rather than my bottom, he led me through a gap in the hedge. We came into a very neat little enclosure, elliptical in shape, and with very close cut grass, upon which he spread the blanket. Smiling, he gestured me to lie down and immediately joined me on the blanket beneath the stars.

Irrelevantly, as his face hovered above my own and he moved to kiss my willing lips, I found myself wondering what his name was.

This weekend had roused many questions in my mind. Who were these people, these 'nobs' as Mollie would have put it, who lived lives of luxury compared to my old friends on the game in Brighton? Was it that being freed from economic necessities also made them free from those social conventions of flirtation, pretence, and marriage which I had always found so hypocritical?

Certainly, these people, this society, had cast off the petty rules of comportment clung to as though necessary in our wider society. These quick thoughts that came to me as I reclined on the blanket in the silver light of the moon were soon driven off by my man's first kiss. Why philosophise when one can enjoy.

That first kiss was moving in its gentle lack of demand. A pleasant change from what is usually the case in my line of work. The moonlight made everything silver and black. His body was warm against the cooling of the night air. His breath was sweet and tasted of mint. His mouth was full and seeking on mine.

He was very gentle, and as his mouth and hands moved to rouse me all thought save pleasure at what he was doing, and how good it was to be among people who were so relaxed about our social taboos, left me.

115

He did not hurry. Indeed, he seemed intent on playing me, stirring me up, melting me, rather than upon just 'getting it up' – which is another of Mollie's graphic phrases. If anything, it was I who wanted him to get it up, for I had been already well worked up by what I had witnessed this evening, and what he was doing to my breasts and between my legs was wickedly knowing.

As he kissed and fondled me, quick but soft, my hand reached down and found his manhood. It was warm and firm, and silky. I wanted him in me; needed to relieve my arousal; squirmed to get my leg beneath him, and to get him above me, ready. He teased me.

I rubbed him rapidly, his cock hot in my hand. I wriggled against him, trying to manoeuvre him above me and between my thighs that were desperately spreading for him. He resisted me, and instead played with me, kissed my lips and neck and ears, teased my inner thighs and my engorged labia with his clever fingers.

Only when I could resist no longer, and gasped, 'Oh, fuck me! Fuck me now! Please!' did he move to mount me. He moved lithely to plant his warm body between my splayed thighs and entered me oh, so gloriously!

I started coming even as he penetrated me, and he knew it. He was thick, and stretched me, the ridge between his bulb and his shaft teasing my membranes. He moved like some magical porpoise, his body flexing, his loins driving at me, his breath burning my neck.

His hands were wrapped under and around my shoulders to pull me on. His mouth swept over me and demanded. His whole body demanded.

How long it was until he had his own come I cannot even dream. All I know is that I had started coming as he entered me, continued coming while he moved in me, and felt as if I would die when at last he jerked and spasmed, and I shuddered and moaned with joyous acceptance.

He stayed in me after his come, softening a little but not shrinking much. As we rested, I realised that our energetic shag had actually moved me along so that I was now half off the blanket. The cool, dewy grass felt delicious against my warm skin.

My partner began kissing me again, with the kind of quick, soft kisses I adore. With his hands locked beneath my shoulders, he rolled us over so that now I was on top. With his face now bathed in moonlight I saw, and kissed, the lovable little wrinkles at the corners of his eyes. I moved down to kiss and nibble his soft lower lip. He smiled, and kissed me back, and began to move his hips a little.

One of the loveliest sensations I know is to feel a man who is already in me, but soft, grow stiffer and harder. I began to move myself on him, gently at first, but with growing intensity as he grew inside me. Soon, I had levered myself up on to my arms, and was riding him into a second voluptuous fuck, this time with me in the driving seat, as it were.

My partner kept absolutely still, letting me ride him how I wished. And ride him I did; now slow and deep and circling; now rapidly pulling up until he was almost out of me before sliding down hard upon him. My love-lips felt hot and turgid, and my juices were flowing so freely that there were veritable squelching noises as I rode him.

It was glorious. He was glorious. I had been in one long series of swelling comes ever since he had rolled us over. Every sensation in the universe was centred upon my squirming, clinging sheath, so beautifully filled with his manhood. I could have gone on all night and might well have done so had he not, at last, tensed, and flexed his pelvis against me, and jerked into his second come, causing a final cresting spasm to shake my own body. Delicious!

Back at the house at last, and shivering a little from the cool night air and the dew we had gathered on our bodies, we drank a restorative glass of brandy each. He turned out to be as agreeable in conversation and flattery as he was in shagging, though I never did find out his name, and we spent a good half an hour or more in banter and flirtation before he bade me *adieu* with a little kiss, and went on his way.

Feeling nicely relaxed, I drank a second glass of brandy before deciding to go up to my room to change, for my basque was still a little damp from the dew. Looking down at myself I got the giggles, for I suddenly realised that I had no knickers on. They must have been lying somewhere near that blanket, I thought, and I did not even remember them coming off me!

Still smiling, and relaxed now by the brandy as well as the sex, I went through the door to go to my room. If the scenes I had witnessed earlier at those Greek follies had been licentious, what I now witnessed was lascivious indeed!

There were couples and trios wherever I looked. A man sat on a straight-backed chair while a woman sat astride him, her heavy breasts rolling and bouncing as she rode him. A very pretty dark-haired girl lay on her back on the carpet, her feet tucked into the armpits of the man fucking her vigorously, and what she was calling out in her passion would have made a sailor blush. Through an open door on the first landing, I espied Veronica kneeling and slowly sucking off a man who looked like the clerical gentleman who had conducted the induction service last night.

About the latter I could not be sure because I had not seen him naked before.

There were more unusual sights, too. Two naked women, one seemingly in her forties, the other not much older than myself, were astride the curved rosewood rail of a baluster. Their legs were held stiffly and straight down, so that the whole of their weight was on their cunnies. Their hands were on one another's shoulders as they gazed into each other's eyes, and slowly rocked to and fro. The expressions on their faces were blissful, though what they were doing was, I thought, at least uncomfortable. Who knows? Perhaps they enjoyed a little discomfort. There are worse things under the sun!

In one room, I came upon a plump young woman doing a handstand, her bare feet planted wide against the wall. Spreading her love-lips with the fingers of one hand, a man was pouring champagne into her, then bobbing his head down to suck it back out again. I giggled. What an ingenious way to get tipsy!

Reaching my room on the second floor, I took off the few clothes I was wearing, and ran myself a quick bath. Towelled dry and feeling refreshed, I rejected the notion of retiring to bed, even though the clock showed it was almost eleven. I was not tired, and I suspected that there was a lot of naughtiness going on beneath this roof. Besides, I did not know where Kate was, or what she was up to. I did not feel like getting dressed, so I simply put on the Chinese silk robe Amelia had given me.

I drifted down to the first floor again. The two women were no longer astride the baluster rail. Instead, the younger one was lying on her back on the carpet, with the older one kneeling astride her head. Both women were slowly and lasciviously licking between the other's legs, their hands holding apart red and swollen love-lips to ease access for their cunning tongues. Both, too, were emitting soft cooing noises of contentment.

Leaving the couple to their oblivious enjoyment, I moved along the wide corridor. The scene I came upon next, in a large room off to my left, was just the kind of thing I might have expected in view of this society's penchant for games.

A number of gentlemen, armed with pencils and paper, were solemnly regarding the rear ends of an equal number of females. These females were bent over on either side of an elegant four-poster, with the drapes closed over so that only their bare bottoms and legs were visible. Each bottom had a number in red on the left buttock, and the gentlemen were attempting to identify the woman to whom the bottom belonged.

Naturally, they did not only look, they touched and felt and fingered too. What struck me as ridiculous, though, was their solemn silence, and the secretive way they shielded their papers from one another, like children doing a test.

From the doorway I watched entranced and fought down giggles as the men moved from bottom to bottom, perused them, felt them, scratched their foreheads, made decisions, and wrote on their papers, for all the world like buyers at an auction.

Suddenly a voice called, 'Time, gentlemen!' and the drapes were parted. The gentlemen stepped back, putting away their pencils. Beatrice, whose bottom had been one of those on display, rose from the bed clutching what was either a small hourglass or a large egg timer. She was stark naked, and moved among the gentlemen collecting their papers with all the casual dignity of a good schoolmarm.

To my surprise, Kate was among the bevy of naked women now moving, chatting and giggling, away from the bed. I noticed that her number, seven – lucky seven, as she remarked to me later – was marked on her left breast as well as on her bottom. She grinned and hurried over when she saw me, and we hugged.

Before we could exchange more than a little kiss, Beatrice called out again, and couples began to pair off on her instructions. Kate went over to a handsome young man, and immediately dropped to her knees and took his cock in her hands. Several couples began rolling about on the bed as Beatrice read from her list.

Suddenly, out of the blue, I felt a lowering of my spirits. Instead of being excited by the spectacle of these naked couples, or at least being amused by it, I felt a detachment. Somehow, it seemed artificial to me, as though these people were so sated with privilege and sensation that they had to invent games to unlock their pleasures, or perhaps to give themselves excuses for sex.

It was not my style. I enjoy the little games of flirtation and am as eager for sex as the next woman – perhaps more so – but I have never needed excuses to indulge myself. These people, though, seemed to need to turn what should be simple, healthy indulgences into ritualised charades.

Beatrice called to me to join her group, cutting across my reverie, but I declined. Instead, I wandered off alone, and found myself descending the back stairs towards the servants' hall.

If all above stairs was simulated and febrile debauchery, here among the servants a relaxed naturalness reigned. Due to the lateness of the hour, only the butler, a single maid and a couple of footmen – Peter

Peters being one – were still about. For a moment there was a little awkwardness, for the butler greeted me very formally as a guest of the house, and would not at first accept that I did not wish formality. We all relaxed, though, and soon I was sitting at the table with them enjoying a pleasant chat.

Once he had shucked off his mantle of grave dignity the butler, Mr Cutson, turned out to be a charming and amusing chap. He was in his fifties, with a florid complexion and thinning hair, and hailed originally from Exeter though you could not have told from his accent.

As I had always suspected, the servants in large establishments had few qualms about indulging in their master's cellars, and there were a couple of opened bottles of wine on the table as well as half full glasses in front of the four servants. Mr Cutson poured me a glass, and we were all soon laughing happily at his tales about former employers. I suspected that he could have told quite a few about his present one, but he was far too discreet.

As you know by now, my head for alcohol is not especially strong. What with the two quite large brandies I had drunk earlier, and the several glasses of delicious red wine I consumed now, I became giggly and decidedly tipsy. The case-clock on the wall struck midnight, and I decided to retire to my bed. I swayed a little when I stood, and instantly Peter Peters was at my side to assist me.

My low mood of earlier was quite gone and, as he assisted me up the stairs towards my bedroom, I found myself wondering whether dear Peter might like to stay with me when we got there.

Inevitably, my silk robe had been misbehaving, both down in the servants' hall and even more so coming up the stairs. By the time we reached my bedroom door it was actually off one shoulder and only meeting, rather than overlapping, below its waist. I did not mind at all that Peter could see nearly the whole of my left breast and my leg from the hip down. I wanted him to, in fact, for I was feeling naughty again.

I pouted a little when he told me he could not come in with me. I stood close, and gazed up at him beneath my eyelashes, making my wishes very plain. He blushed, stammered something about being still on duty and seeing Mr Cutson, and hurried away.

It was an hour or so later when I was awakened by a warm body sliding into the bed beside me. It became a gentle and delightfully passionate night.

Eight

We returned to London by the eleven-ten train the following morning. My mood was reflective, but fortunately Kate was so happy chattering about the house and the other guests and her various romps that she did not notice how quiet I was.

I found myself wondering why my spirits had become so flat last night. It was most unlike me, I knew. The imp of naughtiness inside me usually reacts with enthusiasm to frolics, and I seek more to join in than withdraw. What, then, had been different?

I had enjoyed the game of blind tig-tag and the lovely shag with Bertie afterwards. I had got pretty randy witnessing the exchange ceremony in the ball-room, and had then spent a deliciously active night with my footman. Even the scenes in the two Greek follies had worked me up a bit, and the fuck on the grass which followed had been very pleasant.

Yet wandering through the house later, I had become oddly jaded. Why? At base, I concluded in the end, it was the artificiality of it all; the way those people seemed to need to deck what, to me, were simple, healthy frolics with rituals, or turn them into games. It all seemed so premeditated.

That my own life, and that of my friends, was pretty well entirely dedicated to sex could not be denied. Neither could the fact that it often involved games of various kinds, played out for the pleasure of the punter. The point was, though, that these were direct, simple transactions; the negotiation of a fee, in return for which we worked to give as much pleasure to our client as we could, finally sending him off satisfied.

It was indeed simple and honest when looked at in that light, for there was no pretence. As Molly put it down in Brighton; we simply took the dosh, did the deed, and moved on. I ended the railway journey actually feeling a little sorry for the members of Veronica's society, and was able to inform a happy Amelia, when we got home, that there was no chance at all of me being tempted to join it.

During the weeks that followed my weekend in Buckinghamshire, I wallowed happily in the simple pleasures of the *Silken Web* and a series of private engagements arranged by dear Karl.

I had not been to the *Silken Web* for several months, more because I was busy elsewhere than from design, and I found the atmosphere there very pleasant. Little had changed, and it was nice to see familiar faces and to gossip with some of the girls.

I had 'sold' half a dozen bottles of champagne, and had enjoyed half a dozen pleasant trips upstairs, when my heart was given a jolt of delight. I was 'hovering', as Amelia calls it, and debating with myself whether to take on another client or call it a night and go home, when a face grinning with pleasure loomed before me. It was 'Andrew'!

Dear 'Andrew', whose virginity I had got rid of early in my career as one of Amelia's girls, and who had been a regular for a while, but whom I had not seen for months. His demeanour now was very different from what it had been then. When I had first picked him up, sitting alone at a table in the *Silken Web*, he had been a bundle of nerves and shyness, and I had nearly had to drag him upstairs. Now, his manner was easy and confident, his smile open, and his clothing much smarter.

We sat at a table and chatted like old friends – very unprofessional I know, but I did not care – and as we did so I was struck by what a difference good sex can make to a person's life. He had been a clerk in a bank when we met, a respectable but not terribly remunerative occupation. Then, he had been gauche, timid and lacking in self-confidence. After our first time together, he told me, he had plucked up the courage to 'try it' with one or two of the other girls.

He had been successful. He had reviewed other aspects of his existence, and realised that he could do better for himself with a little boldness. He had given up his humble but safe post with the bank, and got a job as a traveller for a maker of confectionery. He had been a success. He travelled the whole of England, south of Birmingham. His income was quadruple what it had been. He had a fiancée, a sweet girl but normal in that she would not allow him more than a chaste kiss. His life was happy and fulfilled (except for sex, of course, for which he used facilities such as those at the *Silken Web*), but most of all – and this went straight to my heart – he had missed me!

What a darling man! He made it plain in terms that had I not picked him up that night months ago, he would have still been stuck in the bank, still timid, and probably still a virgin. I felt like hugging him in delight. Instead, I took him upstairs.

He certainly had changed. That first time, he had been all awkwardness and I had needed to take the lead in everything. Now, he took charge.

The moment I led him into the bedroom and the door clicked shut behind us, he spun me round and took me in his arms. His kiss was warm and soft and seeking. His hands moved lightly over me, pressing me to him, finding my breast. His breath was sweet.

He undressed me slowly, not allowing me to do anything for myself, kissing me all the while, and nibbling my earlobes, my eyelids and my neck. Oh, he was good! He even managed to get my corset off with elegance and little fumbling.

When he had me down to only my stockings, he lifted me and lay me on the bed. I was swept along by his new manner, and was very ready for him. Had he parted me and plunged at that instant, he would have found me moist and eager. Instead, he set to it to stir me up even more.

He began at my brow and kissed and stroked my temples, my eyelids, my nose, cheeks and lips. His soft, questing mouth explored my throat, that curve of my neck and shoulder which always sends chills of rapture through me, down over my collar bone to the cleft between my breasts.

Cupping me with warm, dry hands, he kissed and licked the swell of each breast, flicking his tongue over each nipple in turn, then sucking and nibbling at it. Already, those golden bubbles of arousal were swelling in me, and my skin was hot and sensitive.

'Andrew' was now a lover, not a customer, and a wonderfully skillful one at that. I shivered with hot pleasure as his tongue teased around my tummy button and his fingernails began, oh so gently, to scratch over the skin of my thighs.

They parted themselves for him, and I groaned and shuddered as his mouth found my centre. He parted my love-lips with his fingertips, and began to kiss and lick me. Ripples of ecstasy swelled through my tummy and chest. My breasts were soft and full as one of his hands moved to caress them.

As the warmth of his breath wafted over my loins, his tongue teased around my clitoris. I groaned, and my hips moved themselves to get more of him. I was on a swell of the sea, my body wave after wave of sensation. From a million miles away, through a golden mist of pleasure, I heard my voice saying, 'I want you inside me. Please. Please fuck me. Fuck me now!'

He entered me slowly, a little at a time, more and wonderfully more of him, filling me with his hard heat, sending my head spinning. He had not undressed and his clothing was rough against my skin, but it was a delicious roughness, and the worsted of his waistcoat teased my nipples adorably.

He eased out of me and I turned over; planting my knees wide, I arched my back and pressed my head into the mattress. He entered me from the rear, filling my greedy sheath even more than earlier. He held me by my hips and moved with deep, full-length thrusts that had me gasping in time to his rhythm.

He began to quicken, thrusting harder, deeper. My orgasm swelled and swelled, and burst from my squirming, cramping sheath to every last nerve-end of my shuddering body. Suddenly, he too began to come, pulling me on hard and pumping and pumping his glorious heat into me until I wanted to die of pleasure.

He stayed partly in me when I sagged down on to the bed, all strength gone from my quivering limbs. Slowly, slowly, as his warm breath bathed my shoulder, I spiralled down from the red and gold paradise to which he had driven me, my breathing calming, the delirious cramps that had overwhelmed me easing.

He slipped out of me and rolled to lie beside me.

He kissed me softly on my lips and eyes, his arm around me as his hand stroked my spine and buttocks. It was only when he gave me a harder kiss, slapped my bottom, and said, 'Gosh Lily, you're a wonderful fuck!' that I remembered, with a shock that set me off giggling, where and who I was.

How terribly unprofessional!

'Andrew' stared at me in surprise, which set me off even more, but when at last with streaming eyes, I managed to snort out the reason for my fit of laughter, he began laughing too, and soon we were gasping and clutching one another in our paroxysms.

I did not charge 'Andrew'. After all, my mind had been on my own pleasure during that lovely shag, and not on professional matters such as ensuring his satisfaction. Mind you, as I rinsed and dried his softened cock, and gave it a little kiss before tucking it into his trousers, he did express entire contentment, and asked if he might see me again next week.

I did see him again the next week, but this time I remembered to charge him the standard fee, in advance just in case I got carried away again. Well actually, it was the minimum fee – ten bob for a strip and a shag – even though we were upstairs for an hour and a half, and he got two shags, with a blow in between to get him up again.

I had, in reality, only gone to the *Silken Web* that evening because I had promised 'Andrew' I would see him. Somehow I was not, myself, as keen as once I had been to flirt with absolute strangers, con them into buying a bottle of champagne, and then take them upstairs for a quick fuck. Perhaps I was simply jaded. I loved sex, loved the inner sensations, the sparks inside my body, the feeling of a man touching me, penetrating me, coming in me. But there was something missing.

With 'Andrew', with Karl and Paul, and especially with Ashoko, who I still managed to have when he was not busy with his own customers, it was different. Nicer. It was making love rather than mere shagging.

As a 'professional girl', as a whore, prostitute, strumpet, harlot, call me what you will, I knew how to please a punter. How to gasp and wriggle; how to gaze up under my eyelashes as though he were the most handsome creature in the world; how to pump my hips and clench the muscles of my cunt to make him think he was sending me to heaven. How to cool him if he got rough. How to make him think he was wonderful and had me spellbound with his maleness, while all the time I was only getting pleasure from his wallet.

It is a burden of the job. In the business of whoring, a girl has to shag all and any, and a detachment sets in. It had set in on me now. I became, how shall I put it, unenthusiastic, even with most of my private clients. The little games I had to play to please them began to seem silly. I wanted, or perhaps needed, something more.

I did not know it at the time, but that indefinable ingredient was already on the horizon, in the shape of Monsieur le Comte du Fallier. I knew his face at once, but it took me a little longer to recognise him as the man who had talked only with Amelia at the birthday party at which I had been presented with Ashoko.

I was surprised to see him at our little dinner party that evening, for Amelia usually kept me apprised of who would be about at any particular time. Indeed, Amelia these days was keeping me apprised of more and more things, even asking my opinion of new girls, and my advice about arrangements for functions and house parties. In fact lately she was treating me almost as her partner, rather than just one of her 'working girls'.

But to return to Monsieur le Comte.

It was a small party, just Amelia and myself, Karl, and the count. As he had been at my birthday party, the count remained mostly silent, and I found his presence enigmatically disturbing.

He was not what I would call conventionally handsome, having a face that was a little too narrow, a nose that was somewhat too large, and something of a widow's peak. Nevertheless, there was something compelling about him, something that made one inescapably aware of his presence.

On the few occasions he spoke, his voice was a low, warm baritone made all the more attractive by his French accent. I found myself wanting his attention, though somehow I knew that the usual little tricks of flirtation I had in my armoury would be inappropriate. Thus, I contented myself with sitting quietly, and responding only briefly to remarks addressed to me by Amelia or Karl.

It was not until we had finished our meal and retired to the drawing room, and the other three were smoking their cigars and we were all drinking brandy, that the count turned his attention to me. When he did it was with Amelia, to unfold a proposition that both thrilled me and made me nervous.

Amelia began it by explaining to me that, within the next year or so, she planned to retire from the business, at least in so far as active participation in its management was concerned. Karl would, naturally, continue his overall management of the *Silken Web* and of the private clients, but a woman's touch was essential if the business was to continue to prosper. Amelia said she would like me to provide that touch.

I was as astonished as I was flattered. My first

thoughts, though, were that I could not do it; I was
lacking in experience; I was too young; sundry rea-
sons prevented me. My startled protests were cut off
by the count's first words directly to me.

'*Mademoiselle*, before you dismiss this matter,
please allow Lady Amberson and myself to explicate.'

It was, I think, the first time he looked me directly
in the eye, and I confess I was somewhat jolted. I
have known many men, too many you might think.
From the time, nearly three years ago now, I had
been seduced as a virgin captive by Talesi, through
my games with the officers at the garrison in G—, and
on board the ship returning to England, and since
then as a *fille de joie*, I have met and dealt with all
types.

None, not Talesi, not the Bey whose temporary
harem-girl I had been, not Jonathan Andrews, not
any of them, had possessed such eyes. Only Tiliu's
'stranger', perhaps, the man whose 'juju' had so
overwhelmed her, and who had later taken me so
shatteringly at the orgy after the prince's banquet,
had had eyes like that. His, though, had been cold,
chilling me even as they had read my heart.

The count's eyes, too, seemed to read my heart, but
his were kind; inviting rather than commanding me,
if you take my meaning. I found myself fascinated,
listening to him and to Amelia. Or rather I heard
their words with that small part of my being that was
not hypnotised by this man. The result was that I
found myself agreeing to a proposition which, in the
cold light of the next day, scared me greatly.

Amelia wanted me to become her successor in
running the business. I was, they told me, a good
worker – such a banal phrase to describe a woman
who fucked for a living – and had a wise head on
my shoulders. I lacked, though, any breadth of

experience in the variations and management of the business. Monsieur Le Comte du Fallier had generously agreed to take me under his wing in that respect and, should I agree, would take me off for a period of time to the continent, to gain experience and learn the trade.

I did agree, though to tell the truth it was more because I wanted to be with this man than because I really believed in the project. Looking back on it, I do not think I was actually in love. It was more a sort of fascinated infatuation. I was, though, caught in its spell, and would have followed the count then and there if he had wished.

It was most unlike me I know, and I have never been in such a peculiar state before or since.

We were not to leave for several weeks, at the beginning of December, and I have to confess that the time dragged. I could think of little else than the count. I saw his eyes in my sleeping dreams, and my daydreams too. I recalled, though not without shame, the raging jealousy I had felt when he had gone to Amelia's bed rather than mine that night, and how petulant I had been with everybody next day. I did not even feel much enthusiasm for the new clothes Amelia arranged to be made for me, or at least not until the count saw them and expressed approval, especially of my lingerie.

As the day he would arrive to take me off with him drew nearer, my heart lifted and I grew positively tingly with excitement. It goes to show how he had affected me, so much so that all my cherished common sense seemed to have flown out of the window, and I did not sleep a wink on the night before he was due to turn up!

I am not actually proud of any of this, and indeed

have condemned such silliness in other women. It happened, though, and honesty compels me to describe it.

Fortunately, like all women I am a good actress, and so was able to hide my state when I was with him, and pretend not to be besotted, otherwise he would have thought me a complete goose!

The railway journey to Dover and the ferry voyage across to Calais gave me plenty of time to look at the count, who told me to call him Philippe, and to find out somewhat about him.

The brow below his thick black hair was high and straight. His eyebrows were quite thick also, and he had shaded deep-set, almost black eyes so deep you felt you could drown in them. Two deep lines rising vertically from the top of his nose over an otherwise unlined brow betokened a habit of frowning. But these were softened by sets of wrinkles radiating from the corner of each eye such as we call 'laugh lines'. His lips were full, though not fleshy, and well shaped, and his jaw was firm and dark.

He was quite tall, not far off six feet I judged, and of slender build. When he walked he held his shoulders very square and his back straight, though there was no stiffness in his movements. His hands were slender and his fingers long and, though well manicured, there was nothing of the feminine about them.

He came originally, he told me, from somewhere down near the Pyrenean Mountains, but maintained an establishment in Paris when he was not travelling, of which he did a considerable amount, and upon some of which I would accompany him.

He was not the kind of man to engage in idle chatter, and though perfectly charming in his manner gave away very little about himself. Nor did he wish to know much about my own background. It seemed enough that I was, to quote his words, which burned their way into my head and made me blush with pleasure, 'beautiful, spirited and intelligent'. Apparently both Amelia and Karl had heaped similar praise upon me. I did not mind in the slightest if that made me sound like a grape; I just hoped that this fascinating man would soon pluck and eat me!

He did not. Indeed, he seemed impervious to the fact that I was a woman, and the kind of woman unlikely to say no to a little frolicking. He made no advance on me and did not touch me except to take my elbow when helping me up on to the French railway train, and off it again in Paris. In the end, it was I who touched him, for I took a tip from the female half of a couple I saw leaving the railway station, and put my arm through his as we walked the length of the platform to supervise the disposal of our luggage.

He did not respond at all in the manner men usually did to me, even when I went close and pressed the side of my breast against his arm. It was most frustrating! I fancied him very strongly, and he must have known it, yet he tried nothing.

I simply put it down to the fact that we had been travelling all day and hoped that maybe things would change when we got to his establishment.

It was quite late in the evening when the carriage Philippe had hired stopped outside his *petite maison*, though to me there seemed nothing small about it. Part of a long terrace, fully four storeys in height, it had massive double doors opening on to the street, with two large, curtained windows on each side of the portico, a row of five equally large windows on the floor above, and two rows of rather smaller windows on the floors above that. As we approached the building, the doors were swung open by two rather pretty maids, to reveal a spacious and imposing foyer.

Both maids bobbed neat curtseys, and while one went out to supervise the unloading of our luggage, the second led us across the gleaming parquet to another door which, when she swung it open, revealed, of all things, an elevator.

I had only been in an elevator two or three times in my life, when on private engagements in London hotels. To tell you the truth, they make me a little nervous, what with those expanding lattice cage doors you could squash your fingers in, and the way the floors so rapidly recede away from you. Still, the maid entered with no apparent qualms, and so I followed her.

I had expected, nay hoped, that Philippe would crowd in with us, and accompany me to my room, there to do who knew what. Instead, as the maid pulled the lattice door across, he spoke to her in rapid French, bade me a good rest in English, and turned away.

To say that my spirits were low as the maid showed me to my room on the third floor would be to understate the matter grossly. What an infuriating man! To drag me all the way by train and ferry boat to a city I had never seen, where people spoke a language I knew little of, and then just to dump me in the care of this maid – who probably spoke no English into the bargain – was insufferable!

Later on, of course, I realised how foolish and unfair these thoughts were, for he had not dragged me anywhere, nor dumped me on the maid. And indeed, she turned out to speak excellent English. I learnt later, by which time several distractions had occurred, that Philippe had actually been solicitous for my well being after our long journey, and had meant it when he had wished me a good rest.

At the time, though, I was annoyed and petulant, and not my normal self at all. Even the deliciously scented hot bath that was drawn for me within minutes of our arrival, and the excellent light supper that was brought to my room thereafter, did little to lighten me. Philippe was not there, that was the trouble.

All the while, since I had first looked into those beautiful eyes three weeks ago at Amelia's, and increasingly during the day's journey, I had hoped that the first thing he would do when we arrived in Paris would be to carry me off to bed. I really, really, really wanted to feel his lips on mine, to curl my arms around him, to feel him inside me. To put it bluntly, I wanted very much to shag him, and it looked as though he did not fancy me!

I picked at the supper that had been brought up for me, though it was actually delicious. I drank the whole of the carafe of burgundy, a thing I would not normally do, and took myself off to bed alone. Tired as I was from the journey, and helped by the wine, I was soon asleep despite my low spirits.

I am not the kind of woman whose spirits stay down for long. Actually, there had been the beginnings of a smile on my lips as I had drifted off to sleep, for before leaving me the maid – a pretty black-haired girl with thick eyebrows – had asked whether I required anything else, and had done so with a tiny under-the-eyelashes glance. The almost imperceptible swing of her hips told me that she meant exactly that!

The morning was bright and crisp, and already there was a nice fire crackling in the grate. As I climbed out of the bed, which was as wide as it was long, and clearly not intended for a lone sleeper, the same maid entered the room to tell me my bath would soon be ready.

I was wearing a new nightgown of very pale blue cotton with *broderie anglaise* trimming at the neck, sleeves and hem, and she at once cooed in the most relaxed and familiar fashion about how pretty it was. She even fingered the material, but in a manner impossible to take offence at.

She turned out to be a delightfully ebullient and cheerful girl called Natalie, and a native *Parisienne*. Because she spoke very good English, almost as fluently as her master, she had been designated my personal maid for the duration of my stay.

Her rather broad interpretation of her job was demonstrated straightaway, for she not only followed me into the bathroom, but stayed and gave every impression of intending to remain and actually wash me! Since I knew nothing of how different customs in France were from those at home, I felt I could not demur.

It was the first time anyone had bathed me since I was a small child, unless you count when I was first kidnapped by the Tukanna, and it felt most odd. It was most strange because Natalie felt entirely free to wash every part of me, and to comment on my skin, and my figure and even, when she had towelled me dry, to take a comb to my pubic curls!

Of course, before many minutes of this casual and light-hearted treatment, my mood was very easy, and I was as ready as Natalie to coo and sigh over the new clothes that we proceeded to pull from my trunks and cases. They were as much a surprise and delight to me as they were to Natalie, for I had not really paid much attention to them before leaving for France.

It seemed quite natural that we should pick up garment after garment, and hold them against us as we inspected ourselves in the mirror, me stark naked and Natalie in full maid's uniform.

Amelia had provided me with a vast array of clothing, all of it beautiful and perfectly made. There were no less than eight day-dresses, and a dozen evening gowns most with startlingly low necklines. To judge from the number of basques and *chemisettes*, and the whole pile of knickers, Monsieur and Madame Delat had been kept very busy in their lingerie house, and had obviously been inspired to be as imaginatively naughty as they could. There were dozens of pairs of fine silk stockings, and a whole case of footwear.

Natalie laughed aloud, and nudged me roguishly when, near the bottom of the largest trunk, we came upon the really naughty items. The thigh-length boots and black leather basque I had worn at the house party in Warlington were there, as was the red and gold, lace-panelled basque Karl said he liked so much. So, too, was the house-dress Alice had made me for my birthday.

On a whim, I decided to wear it to go downstairs in. Philippe du Fallier had seen me in it at that party, and I knew it had affected him; I knew, too, from Natalie's reaction, that it was just as suggestive now as it had been then. If Monsieur le Comte had decided to remain cold towards me, I would give him a hard time of it!

139

Nine

I had not seen what Philippe called his 'hotel' that night, having gone straight up to my room in that clanking elevator. I had, actually, thought the term somewhat pretentious but now I understood better. It did indeed resemble nothing so much as an hotel, and a palatial one at that.

The stairs from the second floor, where my room was, to the first were fairly narrow, but those from the first to the ground floor were wide and curving. They gleamed with rosewood and brass. Before I descended, I looked along the wide, thickly carpeted corridors that led off to my right and my left. Brass and ebony stands were ranged along the walls, each bearing a large onyx vase in which grew an aspidistra or one of those plants I have heard referred to as mother-in-law's tongue. Between these stands were large, highly polished doors. All were closed, and I felt it would have been impertinent to open any of them to peep in. Philippe was in the same business as Amelia and I, and who knew what I might walk in on!

The lower stair swept down to the huge, parquet-floored foyer, and I descended it slowly. So far, I had not seen another soul, and I was to learn later that this was quite usual during the morning hours. Indeed, business in this house did not really get under way until the early evening.

The first persons I encountered were two stalwart and beautifully uniformed footmen, standing one on each side of the outer doors. They looked like sentries, and I was to learn that that was more or less what they were, for their sole occupation was to guard the doors against intruders, and to control matters if passions rose between clients or, as happened very occasionally it seemed, between a client and a girl.

As I approached, I was pleased at the way their eyes roamed over me, confirming that my house-dress had not lost its effect; I asked where I might find Philippe. Of course, they spoke no English, and I very little French, so at first there was puzzlement. By dint of speaking louder and slower, and repeating that I wished to see Monsieur le Comte du Fallier, I at last got through to them, and with a grin of relief one of them pointed towards a quite modest side door, and gestured and nodded his head encouragingly.

I went to it, turned my head to check that it was the right door, and was pleased to see that the footmen's eyes were riveted to my figure. I knocked and, hearing a voice from within, opened the door.

The room I entered was obviously Philippe's office. The man himself sat behind a large mahogany desk with a black leather insert for the working surface. Philippe was sitting with a huge ledger before him and a fountain pen in his hand.

He smiled warmly and rose to greet me. I sauntered into the room, quite deliberately putting on my 'working girl' walk. As I had intended, his eyes swept over me, taking in the way the material clung to my figure; it made it clear that I had nothing on underneath. His smile showed me that he was appreciative as he gestured me towards a carved and gilded chair, and I felt a little tingle of pleasure as he continued to watch me as I sat.

If I had thought that my rather blatant appearance, pretty well an open invitation, would have got Philippe's hands on me, I was entirely wrong. Although charming, even gallant, he was all business, explaining what our programme was to be for our first day. He told me that luncheon would be sent to my room at one of the clock, and that until then I was free to explore the hotel. We would be leaving to see something of Paris at two.

Then, as if to add insult to injury, as I rose to leave the office he added, 'And by the by, *ma cherie*, I would put a robe over that dress if I were you. The way you look at the moment, any healthy man will jump on you!'

Any healthy man, indeed! Did that mean that Philippe du Fallier was not healthy, or simply that he was perverse?

I did not put on a robe. Instead, I returned to my room and changed into the most modest clothes I could find; a panelled skirt of yellow worsted, with a matching puff-sleeved jacket that buttoned almost to the neck, and a jaconet blouse with a high, frilled collar.

I was not in the mood to explore the house, and so spent the hour or so until the time for luncheon sorting through my clothes and arranging my footwear neatly in the larger of the two wardrobes.

When Natalie brought up my luncheon she was once again lively and cheerful. I asked her to tell me somewhat about her master, remarking that I found him rather cold. She was shocked.

'*Mais non, mademoiselle!*' she said, with a look of disbelief. 'Monsieur is, how do you say, a lovely man! Very educated. Very wise in the world. Very generous.'

I got her to tell me more. Did he have a wife? He did not. How did he treat his servants? At this, she blushed a little, and her eyes twinkled when she said that he was very good to them.

I learnt that, unusually enough to strike my curiosity, all his upstairs household was female. Upstairs meant the top two floors of the house, where monsieur had his own apartments, and where Natalie and her colleagues stayed. With a neat economy that made me smile, it seemed that Natalie and her colleagues doubled up, as it were, by acting as cooks and maids part of the time – especially when their time of the month made other things impractical – and as ladies of the house the rest.

Downstairs was the two lower floors, the business area as it were, and there were indeed male staff there, as I had seen for myself with the footmen by the door. During business hours, their number was increased to half a dozen or more, with the dual purpose of lending an air of dignity and opulence to the house, and ensuring order among the clients and the girls.

Was there often disorder, I asked. It appeared not, though sometimes a young blade would become a little the worse for drink, or there would be a dispute between two clients about the services of a particular girl. Not often, however, and there was very rarely any trouble between the girls during business hours.

Disputes, even fights it seemed, between the girls did occur but only ever upstairs. On these occasions, it was Monsieur le Comte himself who sorted things out and, if necessary, disciplined the girls in question.

'Discipline?' I wondered aloud.

'*Mais oui, mademoiselle. Le maître*, he, how you say –' and to my astonishment, unable to find the words, Natalie graphically mimed bending, as over a knee, and hoisting her skirts. Then she made certain sharp movements with her arm, palm downwards.

'What?' I was amazed. 'You mean he spanks your bottoms? How awful!'

'But no, *mademoiselle*! It is his right, and we do not mind.'

I was flustered. Such ideas, spanking and so forth, had always been anathema to me.

'How can you not mind? Surely it is very painful, not to mention undignified?'

Natalie shrugged her shoulders. 'Yes, it hurts a little; sometimes a lot. But then monsieur is always so, so nice after!' She smiled archly.

A very selfish thought struck me then. Being nice surely meant that Philippe shagged her. He had certainly slept with Amelia. Clearly it was just me he did not fancy! I cast the thought aside in irritation – irritation at myself, that is.

There was no time to pursue the intriguing topic of Philippe and his practices, for it was time to go downstairs for my tour of Paris.

Against my wishes, my tummy gave a lurch when I saw Philippe awaiting me in the foyer, for he looked breathtakingly elegant and handsome. He had on a deep blue frock-coat with velvet lapels, and silver buttons at the front and cuffs. Below, he wore narrow trousers of very pale cream, with a silk stripe down the sides, the cuffs of which folded neatly on black patent leather shoes with slightly raised heels.

The smooth tan of his face was set off by a white silk cravat at his neck, and a high, starched wing collar. He wore no hat, and his hair had been brushed back and shone brilliantly. But, again, it was his eyes and his smile which undid me, and set my knees trembling. If a man can be said to be beautiful, such a man was Philippe du Fallier, and it was a completely masculine beauty, too.

Whether he knew of the fluster he was causing in my chest, I cannot say. I certainly tried to keep it concealed. However much I might fancy him, he did not fancy me, and a woman has her pride!

He was charm and attentiveness personified during our tour. The day was bright and dry, and Philippe had ordered his open carriage; a vehicle somewhat larger and better appointed than a gig. He tucked a rug warmly about my knees without, unfortunately, touching me at all. The driver, so wrapped in coats and scarves he was almost round, flicked the reins, and we were off.

Paris is very beautiful, and very different indeed from London. Philippe's house was in a street called rue Saint Dominique, and as our carriage clip-clopped around its leftward curve to cross a junction with several broader avenues, I saw the most staggering of sights. There, to our right, set in a sort of garden, rose a glittering tower of metal girders laced together. It fair took my breath away. It was so enormously tall and so frail looking it seemed to me that even a gentle breeze must blow it over.

Only when we got close, driving through what Philippe told me was called the Field of Mars, did I realise how huge and strong it really was. It had been built by somebody called Gustave Eiffel a decade earlier, apparently for no other reason than *joie d'esprit*, and to show that it could be done. Philippe was very proud of it, and smiled broadly at my gasps of amazement. Supported on four great legs of yard-thick iron, it curved up and up to the very sky!

Apparently members of the public could actually go up it, right to the very top, from where the whole of Paris could be seen. I wanted to do it straightaway, but Philippe insisted we put that adventure off until another day, for there was much else to see.

The carriage turned right, and we drove along beside the River Seine, which we crossed by means of one of the many bridges, this one called Pont Alexandre III, and thence to a most impressive avenue called the Champs Elysees, which was very wide, and lined with mature trees. Along this, my head turning from side to side in the gawkiest fashion, until we came to a vast open area called the Place de la Concorde. Then we moved on to the gardens of the Tuileries, where so much of French history has taken place, and eventually to the Palace of the Louvre, which is extremely impressive.

Not so impressive, though, as the cathedral of Notre Dame with it soaring steeples, statuary and its fearsome looking gargoyles to carry the rain off. Again, we spent little time there, for the evening was drawing in, and so we went over another bridge, and through another beautifully formal garden called the Luxembourg. We passed yet more handsome avenues, yet more beautiful terraces of buildings, yet another garden with its own palace – this one called the Hotel des Invalides – and we were back at Philippe's in time for dinner.

Over that meal, taken alone with Philippe after a wash and a change of clothing, I began to gather more of what I would be seeing and learning during my time under Philippe's tutelage; Philippe clearly seemed to regard me as something of an apprentice.

Philippe did not probe me about my history as so many others would have. He simply accepted that, despite my youth (I was still not yet nineteen) I was experienced in the business, and sufficiently sensible and open minded to take in what I was to learn.

'There will be the need for some understanding of bookkeeping,' he said when we had reached the coffee and brandy; the latter was a new one to me, called Armagnac, and was simply delicious. 'You will, of course, employ a functionary for the keeping of your accounts, but it is best to have the ability to keep a check of your own.'

'That, though, will be for the mornings, and will be rather dull I am afraid. More important will be your learning of the various needs you will have to cater for. In this respect, Amelia tells me you are very ignorant.'

I was stung. Not only at what he had said, but the superior manner in which he had said it. Very ignorant indeed! I began to splutter a protest, but Philippe cut me off with a wave of his hand, which irritated me even more.

'She tells me, for example, that you know nothing of *ligotage*, nor of some of the more unusual tastes you are likely to encounter.'

He smiled, friendly now rather than condescending, for he guessed that he had me. What on earth was *ligotage*? What was the significance of the stress he had placed upon these unusual tastes? I was beginning to waver when he said that which set me on my mettle.

'Amelia also tells me,' he said, leaning forward to pour himself some more brandy, 'that you have displayed a rather silly fear in the face of certain notions.'

I will not be called silly! It was a neat trap, into which I walked like a ninny. By calling me silly he had thrown up a challenge which both he and Amelia knew I would be incapable of resisting.

'I will have you know, sir, that I will not be called silly!' I spluttered. 'And as for being afraid, sir, I have seen and known that which would send your hair white! Afraid indeed!'

The interview would have ended there, for I was on the point of storming out of the room, he had me so annoyed. I was stopped by his sudden laugh, and the fact that he took my hand and kissed it.

'No, no, my dear Lydia,' he said, looking at me with delight in those overwhelming eyes of his. 'Do not be angry with me. Amelia has asked me to teach you the more extreme aspects of our profession. To do so, it is necessary for me to have your active diligence. There are, Amelia tells me, matters from which you have shied away; aspects of people's seeking of pleasure which are not to your taste.'

I was curious. I thought I had taken, and given, pleasure in most ways possible. I had shagged and been shagged in as many ways and as many places as could be imagined. I had even taken part in displays of sex performed as a public entertainment. What could he mean? Clearly, having got me riled, he had stopped me thinking straight. He began talking again, leaning back in his chair, and concentrating on the glowing tip of his cigar.

'You, my dear, despite all appearances to the contrary, have led a pretty sheltered life.' I gasped in amazement at this, but he continued, not even giving me time to laugh at such a ridiculous assertion. 'There are many aspects of the human spirit and human behaviour of which you can as yet have no comprehension. If you are to manage Amelia's business successfully, you will need to cater to a wide range of tastes. Do you not agree? Good. My task is to open you to these things.'

He was beginning to sound condescending again. If he had not been so very attractive, I might not have become so irritated.

'I can assure you, sir, that I comprehend a great deal more than you imagine.' I was indignant. 'And am up to whatever you presume to teach me.'

'Are you sure?'

Insufferable man! I tossed my head. He was deliberately provoking me.

To cut a long story short, he manipulated me into insisting not only that I must see anything and everything he could show me, but that I would experience it as well. If only I had known.

Our discussion, nay almost our argument, had me in quite a tense and excited condition by the end, and it was with relief and alacrity that I accepted Philippe's suggestion that, since the house would by now be in the full swing of business, we should go down so that I could look things over.

I do not know what I had expected, as we descended the wide stair to the ground floor, but it was certainly not what greeted me. Philippe led me across the foyer and through a door near the little elevator. This door let into a rear corner of a very large room which resembled nothing so much as a plush restaurant, with a stage at one end, in front of which sat a six-piece orchestra.

Its layout bore some resemblance to that at Amelia's *Silken Web*, with a clear area of floor that might be used for dancing. There was, though, no area for girls to hover, and most of the groups at the tables were actually dining, rather than just drinking champagne. They were mostly men, of course, though there was a fair number of women about, some, to my surprise, of quite mature years.

The orchestra was playing quietly. Conversation among the assemblage was quiet also. Nobody was being arch or furtive. It was not at all brothel-like, if you see what I mean. And when a large, red-faced man wearing a white tie and tails came on to the stage and began to sing in an excellent baritone voice, my head began to bubble with questions.

Philippe saw it, smiled and shook his head as he helped me into a seat at a small table in the corner. A strikingly pretty girl hurried up, carrying a tray upon which were tiny cups and coffee things. She smiled at Philippe in the most relaxed manner, and they exchanged a few words. Philippe chuckled and the girl gave a tinkling laugh before moving away with a bold swing of her hips.

Before I could ask, Philippe turned to me, offered me some coffee, and said, 'Clara. An excellent worker, and very popular.' He leant back in his chair and lit a cigar before continuing. 'As you will have guessed, dear Lydia, my restaurant is what you might call our place of assignation. It is a genuine restaurant, of course, and I am very proud of my *chef de cuisine*. We also provide a cabaret, which becomes more interesting as the evening goes on and the married couples have departed.'

He smiled at my surprise that there should be married couples present in a bordello, and told me that some of them – he pointed to a very staid looking gentleman in his middle years accompanied by an equally mature woman – had actually first met here in the restaurant.

'You mean –?'

'Oh yes, she worked here for some years, and very accomplished she was – indeed, probably still is!'

It came as something of a surprise to me that a man might wed a 'working girl' whose punter he had been and, to be honest, put the French up a notch in my estimation. I had never heard of our more mealy-mouthed Englishmen marrying the girls they paid to use.

The cabaret did, as Philippe had said, become more interesting as the evening drew on. The baritone gave way to a female performer, a tiny creature with a

150

great mane of frizzy black hair, wearing a frock of black silk. She had heavily kohled eyes which looked very dramatic against her very pale complexion. She talked and sang in a sharp, almost shrill voice. I did not have enough French to understand her words, but the laughter, and her roguish expressions and bodily gestures, made it plain that her subject matter was not exactly prim.

When this lady finished her performance, to hearty applause and cheering, there was a pause. Then came the high-pitched sound of a flute, and the electric lighting in the body of the restaurant dimmed. The flute continued, to be joined by the quiet tapping of a drum and some cymbals. A bright light lit up the middle of the stage. Into its beam there came the strangest and most exotic figure.

It was a woman, moving in time to the music – and moving in such a way! She was swathed in veils, seemingly dozens of them, but so fine one could still discern her figure and limbs through them even before she began to cast them off. Her arms were waving sinuously about her head, her fingers wriggling like tiny snakes. At each step, as she moved forward and around, she posed and pointed her knee, jigging her hip so that the array of bells on her belt sang.

Her face below the eyes was hidden behind a thick veil, and about her brow was a band of silver mesh with beads dangling from it. Her eyes were black, and flashed as she looked at the audience.

Slowly, one by one, she plucked off her veils and let them drift to the floor. The tempo of the music was slowly increasing. As it did so, the movements of her hips became more emphatic, and the noise of her bells faster. By the time the last of her veils was off, her arms were waving like snakes and the rhythm was wild.

She wore only two garments. The first was a sort of very abbreviated jacket that reached only just below her full breasts, and was open at the front, giving teasing glimpses of her full, red nipples. The second was her belt, a broad swathe of black satin hung with many small bells, that sat low on her hips. It did not cover her sex, which was shaved and rouged and plump, and which she now made the centre of her dance.

It was a repeat of that dance I had seen in the coffee house in Port Said, which Robertson had told me was called a belly dance. This woman certainly danced her belly! She would take a step and then, with knees apart and arms stretched out sideways, pumped her hips wildly, as though in the most frantic sexual transports, before turning and taking another step, and repeating the performance for another part of the room.

The audience was spellbound, and the only sound was the wild music to which the woman moved. Suddenly, as the flute and cymbals rose in crescendo, the woman dropped to her knees. Rolling her arms, she slowly leant backward, her knees apart. Further and further she went, until her head touched the stage. She writhed until she could take her weight on her feet, then raised her hips, and rolled and pumped them, the painted lips of her sex seeming to part and close of their own accord, as though she were in a come. She was magnificent!

When she suddenly dropped her back to the floor, rolled over, and leapt lightly to her feet, the applause was tremendous and rightly so!

When the lights went up again, I saw that during the belly-dancer's spellbinding performance a thick carpet had been spread on the polished floor of the dancing area. At each of its corners there lay what looked like a great bundle of some kind, draped with a sheet. I looked to Philippe for elucidation.

'Ah, the highlight of the evening,' he said. 'It is a little game I saw in a house in Lyons, and have imported. I call it Dolphins. It is very popular, and brings us a great deal of trade. Watch!'

A girl, dressed as all Philippe's girls seemed to be in peasant style, had approached each of the four bundles. They bent and took a corner of the sheet. There was a low and rising drum roll that screwed up the already palpable tension. At a sudden crash of the cymbal, the girls whipped aside the sheets.

I stared in amazement. What I had thought were bundles were in reality people. Four naked people; two male and two female. They lay curled up on their sides, blindfolded, their wrists and ankles bound. Each looked to be an excellent specimen of youth; the men athletic and well muscled, the girls slender and firm breasted. Before my fascinated gaze, they began to move.

I soon understood why Philippe had chosen such an unusual name for this performance. Bound as they were, the figures could only roll and twist and wriggle in sinuous movements.

Slowly, the four writhing figures converged on one another, and it became clear what the object of this exotic exercise was. Rolling, one of the girls bumped against the other. At once, both girls stopped, then began seeking more carefully. They were top to tail, as it were, and began moving their heads, seeking with their lips to ascertain who the other was, and how positioned. It was deliciously amusing to watch one naked girl exploring another's feet with her lips, while that second girl curled her body so that she could move her face up the other's thighs.

Meanwhile, the two men were still wriggling about

153

blindly, their smooth young bodies flexing and curling as they sought contact. The first came as one of them bumped his head into the wriggling bottom of one of the girls. Both froze for a moment, the girl's face close to her companion's belly, the back of the man's head nudging the cleft of her bottom.

The girl must have realised that the person she had been nuzzling was also female, for now she lay still. The man wriggled round so that he was facing her, and began to explore her with his nose and mouth. The girl tried to roll towards him, nearly squashing his head at first, but soon they managed to wriggle into a position where they were facing each other, albeit with the man lower down than the girl, his face level with her tummy.

He began exploring it with his lips, finding her navel, moving down over the little swell of her belly, and nuzzling against the curls of her mound. Now he knew exactly their orientation one with the other, and began to move more purposefully.

Keeping his head in contact with the girl's loins, the man slowly wriggled around. His legs touched the girl's head. He wriggled some more, trying to get his position right. The girl, too, was moving now, raising her head, turning her face from side to side as she sought him, her mouth open now. She found him, nuzzled against him, took him between her full lips. At the same time, she parted her knees and he buried his face in her, his tongue lapping.

They lay like some glorious tableau, their heads moving as they pleasured each other in that voluptuous manner known to the French as *soixante-neuf*, their bodies slowly beginning to flex against the mouth pleasuring them as their excitement built.

Meanwhile, after considerable effort, the other couple had discovered each other, but were proceeding differently. The man had come up behind the girl, and was pressing his full length against her back, and rolling his pelvis against her squirming bottom. The girl was moving too, wriggling herself against him, and drawing her knees up towards her breast.

From my position, with their feet towards me, I got a clear view of the girl's bottom as she curled her legs, and of her cunny too, already plump and glistening in betrayal of her excitement. His rolling and squeezing against the girl's round buttocks had similarly excited the man, and his cock stood out proud and stiff. He moved to seek her.

Without the use of his hands it was awkward, and made the more so by them both being blindfolded. The man's rampant member bumped blindly against the girl's curves, now slipping along the cleft of her buttocks, now pushing against the back of her thighs. It was very tantalising!

They were both eager to conclude, and both as lithe as they were eager. The man kept trying with his straining cock. The girl wriggled herself, the glistening mouth of her cunny seeking him as eagerly as he was seeking her. They met and found each other. The man flexed his body. The girl wriggled just enough, and he was in her. For a long moment they remained absolutely still, then he began to move in her, gently at first as though afraid of slipping out, then, as the girl arched her back and pressed herself on to him, more rapidly, and with longer strokes.

I could see all. The red lips of the girl's quim clung to the shaft moving between them like a mouth working on a lollipop. Had I been my usual self, it is likely I would have found it ravishing to watch their transports grow and grow, and their writhings and wrigglings build in intensity as they swept towards their orgasms. After all, there had been many occasions in the past when I had got very worked up when witnessing similarly flagrant scenes. That I was witnessing it almost dispassionately, was most peculiar.

Ten

I discovered what is meant by the term *ligotage* the evening after that fascinating cabaret, and discovered that I had in fact seen something like it before, at the house party in Warlington. I found it rather disturbing at first, and had I not had positive proof that those who took part did so for their own pleasure, would have been shocked and put off.

I went with Philippe to a large mansion at somewhere called Parc Monceau. We arrived quite early, at about seven o'clock, to find a group of about a dozen people present. It was a very varied group, with a couple of mature women as well as several younger ones, two of them startlingly beautiful. The rest were men, and ranged in age from hardly older than myself to a couple of men in at least their sixties.

There was a party atmosphere as they drank wine and nibbled at various sweetmeats, and they welcomed Philippe and I with open arms and broad smiles. Several of them spoke excellent English, and while they chatted to me I realised that they already knew somewhat of my background. Philippe had not really told me what to expect, so when one of them enquired whether I would be joining in the fun I could only shrug.

Another, one of the very beautiful younger women, puzzled me further by squeezing my arm and saying, with every sign of eager excitement, 'It is my turn tonight! With Melanie and Georges.'

I would at once have asked Philippe what was going on had I not discovered that he had left the room, and had not most of the others then gone away too. It was most puzzling. Since none of those remaining – one of the older women and two gentlemen – spoke English, I had to contain myself as patiently as I could for what was almost an hour.

Then, at last, Philippe returned. After apologising for deserting me, and doing so very gracefully, he took my hand, kissed it, and led me towards a door saying, 'And now, let the education begin!' What a frustrating man he was; handsome and charming, and at the same time infuriatingly enigmatic! Any temptation I had to round upon him, though, was driven off by the scene into which he led me.

It was a large room, panelled in dark oak and with heavy drapes of burgundy red at one end, covering, I supposed, the windows. A large fire burned in a grate in one wall, with a tiled hearth in front of it containing a stand for tongs, shovel and poker. A thick rug with tassled ends lay on the floor by the hearth, with several deep, leather armchairs around it. The rest of the furniture seemed to be composed entirely of *chaises longues*, with but two quite small tables set against the wall. But it was what else was in the room that stunned me.

Hanging from the ceiling, suspended by thick steel chains, was the girl who had told me it was her turn. A thick leather strap was fixed about each of her ankles. These were linked to the chains suspended from the ceiling, so that her feet were held wide apart. Another pair of straps were fixed tightly around the tops of her thighs. From these, chains rose to a wide belt, drawn very tight about her waist. A third steel chain was hooked to the belt, and this one took the main weight of the girl's body. Further chains were linked from the belt to a heavily studded leather collar around her neck, and yet another chain went from the collar to the one that was supporting her. It was quite tight, and held her so that she was obliged to arch her back and hold her head very high.

Her arms were manacled behind her, not wrist to wrist, but wrist to elbow, so that her shoulders were drawn back and her breasts thrust out. Her breasts were made even more prominent by the fact that yet further straps were buckled tightly around them, close to her ribs, squeezing their circumference so that they were pushed out quite startlingly.

Each hard nipple was encircled by a metal ring, held in place by half a dozen steel chains that ran from the rings to the straps, making her breasts look outlandish, yet very erotic.

She wore a black leather blindfold, but what made her face the most startling was that she wore a beatific smile, as though nothing in heaven or earth could possibly make her happier than she was at that moment.

So transfixed was I by the sight of this beautiful girl dangling bound and helpless in the middle of a plush, but essentially ordinary room, that I hardly glanced at the other people, though they too were clad in strange outfits.

I spun round to Philippe, astonished questions bubbling in my head, but before I could articulate even the first one, he raised his fingers to his lips in a quieting gesture. With perfect calm, he poured me a glass of wine from the decanter that stood on one of the tables, and led me to one of the armchairs by the fire. Then, as I was about to begin my questioning, a door swung open and I was stunned into silence.

There, entering the room with a strangely mincing

gait, was another woman. She, too, was dressed most strangely. The main garment was something which resembled a black leather corset, but abbreviated so that it extended only from her waist to just below her breasts. From the top, curving up over the fullness of each breast, and connected to a metal collar, was a strap of leather about an inch wide. I was startled to see that each of these straps had a split in it at the fullest point of the breast, and that the woman's nipples had been pulled through so that they peeped out, swollen and bright pink against the black.

The reason for her mincing walk was that she had a set of black leather straps about her legs, just above her knees, linked by a glittering steel chain only three or four inches long. When she turned, I realised that her mincing was caused by more than the chain at her knees. There, protruding from between her round buttocks, was the wide, round end of a device which had been inserted into her rosehole.

This bizarre, yet strangely fascinating vision approached Philippe and I, smiling as beatifically as the other woman, gave a slow curtsey, then moved to stand against the far wall.

The next person to enter was the youngest of the men, who could not have been more than twenty-one or twenty-two. He too was clad only in straps and chains, but very differently from the women. Like them, he had a heavy collar about his neck, but his hands were shackled to it behind his neck. A single heavy chain descended from the front of the collar.

Below his navel it became two chains. One was fixed to a narrow leather strap that was looped beneath his balls and buckled up over the base of his shaft. It looked rather tight. The second chain ran to a metal ring that sat half way along the length of his cock which, though soft, was held out from his body.

He too walked gingerly, for the strap and ring looked quite tight. I dreaded to think what would become of him if he got excited!

To complete his outlandish costume, each nipple bore a clip, from which a chain rose tightly to his collar and another went up to each elbow. Bizarrely, he too was smiling as he approached, and he even wagged his elbows, thus pulling at his nipple clips, as though the discomfort it must have caused actually pleased him.

These were the three most astonishing costumes, for although all the others were in various outfits – leather basques, thigh boots, masks, capes and so on – nothing came close to these three.

At last, as I turned my astonished eyes towards Philippe, he condescended to enlighten me. Leaning towards me, and pouring me another glass of wine, he began to whisper.

He told me that we were witnessing what the French call *ligotage*, though he did not know whether there was an English name for it. In *ligotage*, people delight to have themselves bound in the strange costumes I saw before me. But surely, I protested, they are very uncomfortable. That, he assured me, was the main point.

Many and strange are the avenues through which people find their sexual pleasure. These people found theirs in being bound, and in displaying themselves. But there was more and I did not believe him until it actually began.

The young man, who I remembered the woman had called Georges, moved to one of the *chaises longues* and, not without some difficulty I judged, reclined himself upon it, his legs bent over the end, and his knees apart.

At the same time, the woman, the one referred to

161

as Melanie, went to a chair which had been placed to one side of the dangling woman. Very gracefully, she bent herself over its back, her feet apart, the device that had been inserted into her bottom protruding quite lewdly.

Then, two of the men and one of the more mature women stepped forward. Each bore in one hand a device which looked somewhat familiar to me. It was some kind of whip – and then I had it. I had seen its like in Warlington. It was the kind of silk whip the girl on the frame had been receiving.

The handles were perhaps a foot long, and shaped like a silk-clad male member. From the handles dangled several dozen silken threads, perhaps eighteen inches or two feet in length, forming thick, deceptively soft skeins that shone in the lamplight as they swung from their bearers' hands.

I found I could not breathe as the three people positioned themselves, and then could not but squeal as, as if at some signal, all three whips swung through the air and landed upon their targets. I was staggered. The whips rose and fell, landing with a sort of swooshing sound rather than the crack of a proper whip, the two women receiving the strokes on their bottoms, Georges getting his on the fronts of his thighs.

The expressions on all three faces was of nothing else than joy, with only a flicker of the eyelashes registering the actual landing of the lash on their skin. As the whipping went on, with slow, rhythmical strokes, I was astonished to see that these three were reacting as though to direct sexual stimulation. Georges' reaction was the most immediately obvious, for as the silk skein fell across the skin of his thighs, his balls tightened visibly, and his cock began to stiffen and grow thick.

It was only much later I learnt that a blow from one of these whips, unless delivered with the utmost force, was not actually painful; certainly not as painful as a slap from an angry parent. As I witnessed my first ever session of *ligotage*, I did not know this, and was astounded that these people should draw sexual pleasure from what I assumed was agonising.

Had I not been so amazed, I would have realised it was not, for there was hardly even a reddening of their skins from the lashes, much less the weals a real beating would have caused.

Rather than suffering, the three willing victims were showing every sign of rising towards the climax of their lascivious pleasure; their faces betrayed ecstasy, their limbs and bodies moving salaciously, their breathing grew rapid and shallow.

I squealed again when the woman moved her target and began to beat Georges around his genitals. Philippe chose that very moment to kiss me for the first time, very softly on the join of my neck and shoulder. And then, just at the moment Georges began to gasp and buck, and the woman planted her mouth on his straining cock, he kissed me on my lips.

I started, and would have pushed him away, but his arms were about me and his mouth on mine was warm and insistent. I was in a wild confusion. The three beautiful and weirdly garbed people before me were in very obvious sexual transports, yet they were bound and being whipped. I had fancied Philippe madly for several weeks, and been frustrated at his apparent lack of interest in me, yet now he was kissing me and holding me in his arms, and my unruly body was responding to him. The whole thing was completely bewildering!

My continuing bewilderment abated somewhat when Philippe explained to me that the three had actually been eager volunteers, and had indeed reached the pinnacle of voluptuous pleasure, which I had seen for myself. Everything became clearer when, back at his house, he showed me one of the whips. I tested it on my own palm, and then on my thigh, and indeed it left only the softest of stings.

Philippe's gentle explanations about *ligotage* could only go so far towards solving my confusion, for mostly it was about myself. When Philippe had kissed me, my reactions had been overwhelming. The instant his soft lips had brushed my shoulder, bubbles of golden desire had burst in the pit of my tummy. When he had kissed my mouth, my head had spun away and my lungs had felt like bursting. Now, as he undressed me in readiness to make love, I was trembling like some eager virgin entering a new world.

He had kissed me there, in that room full of strange people. He had kissed me, and gently caressed my breasts, in the carriage on the way back home. He had kissed me, and touched my cheek with gentle fingertips, on the way up the stairs. Now, in his palatial room, with its vast four-poster bed with silk drapes, he kissed me as he slowly negotiated my buttons and ribbons, and gently removed one garment after another, until I was tremblingly naked.

He kissed me as he lifted me in strong arms and lay me on the bed. He kissed me as he removed his own clothes. He kissed me as he lay down beside me, pressing his warm, firm body against mine. He kissed me as he made love to me. And it was making love, not just fucking.

He would not let me do anything but lie, and move my limbs at his behest. He explored me; played me like some musical instrument; built me; stirred me; entered me gently at the most perfect moment. He rode me to the sun and back, bringing me to orgasm, then gentling me part way down before riding me to the skies again.

He was, I knew in that part of my mind that was not in a swirl of passion, exerting every atom of long experience in his playing of me, but it did not matter. All that mattered was the wave after voluptuous wave of glorious sensation that swept through me as he moved on and in me; on and on until time itself ceased, and I was lost upon a silken sea of warmth and exhaustion.

I drifted awake the next morning to the tinkle of crockery and the soft shaking of a hand on my shoulder. Natalie, in a silk dressing gown rather than a maid's uniform, was smiling down at me and gesturing me to sit up so that she could give me my breakfast tray.

Breakfast in France, *petit déjeuner* as they call it, is not at all like our English fare. A bowl of strong, sweet coffee, into which one dips a sort of sweet bread-come-pastry the French call a *croissant*. That morning, it tasted like the ambrosia of the gods. I felt soft and relaxed and wonderful, and smiled back at Natalie with perfect contentment.

She in her turn positively twinkled at me with arch delight. 'Ah!' she said, raising her eyes skyward and swinging her hips. '*Le maître, il est merveilleux au lit*, yes?' At my look of slight puzzlement – I had enough of the French to get her gist, but my ear was not yet quick enough – she spoke in English.

'I mean, Monsieur le Comte he, how you say in English, good at the sex. Good in the bed. He fuck you good, eh?'

Yes, he had fucked me good; had fucked me to the stars and back, and had he entered the room at that moment I would have thrown myself at his feet and pleaded for more.

Later I reflected, not a little ruefully I confess, that in reality Philippe's performance could be best described as professional. He had bedded me, and excited me, and set me shuddering with rapture over and over again with the skill and subtlety and knowingness of a true professional. It made me smile deep inside, and warm to him in a different way.

Who, of all people, should know about being professional in the delights of sex but I? I had learnt my skills as the plaything of the Tukanna, it being necessary in what was then my captive state to please them in any and every way they desired. True, I had performed as an enthusiastic amateur after my rescue, seducing Hendrick as a means of getting back to father, and then various officers for sheer fun. But for the last year or more, back in England, had I not myself been a professional?

And, if Amelia and my happily expanding list of regulars were anything to go by, a good one. I was, to put it plain, a good whore. A whore who more than satisfied her punters – and, yes, enjoyed doing it. What a lovely life!

Meanwhile, this whore, relaxed and content, was enjoying a happy chat with the other whore, Natalie. It has often occurred to me that we fallen women, as straight-laced and hypocritical society calls us, have more open and generous natures than our so-called respectable sisters. Natalie was like so many of the other *filles de joie* I have come to know; cheerful, good natured, full of fun, and without an ounce of jealousy in her.

For example, I already guessed, and soon had it confirmed, that she was rather fond of Philippe du Fallier. Indeed she was, if truth be told, actually in love with him. Yet here she was, chatting happily with a girl who was still in his bed, and still glowing from as rapturous a night of sex as she could wish for, and even comparing notes, as it were. Did he, for example, do that lovely thing with his tongue in my ear? And to my breasts?

Indeed he had, and I warmed at the recollection of it. He had spent a long time on my breasts, working me beautifully with his hands and his mouth, kissing and nibbling and sucking, and moulding and pinching and scratching oh, so gently and knowingly, that he'd had me almost coming just from that alone.

And yes, I told Natalie, he had indeed moved down and spread my thighs, and nuzzled and licked and drunk from me, and set me spinning and churning and spasming with what is probably the most wonderful thing a man can do to a girl; his mouth to my quim.

Did he let me suck him too? '*Ah bon!* And does he not feel and taste divine?' Indeed he had!

And did he take me *comme un chien?* I did not understand at first, so Natalie showed what she meant by climbing on to the bed beside me, kneeling on all fours with her back bowed and her knees wide, and pointing to her backside with one hand. For a moment, I thought she meant had he buggered me but she soon made clear very graphically, that she was asking if he had taken me from the rear. Indeed he had, and Natalie made it clear she always enjoyed this immensely.

She shocked me then by asking whether he had spanked me. Natalie actually seemed shocked by my surprise! But it is delicious, she insisted. You made yourself nude, she went on, and he took you across his knee, and he spanked your bottom with his lovely bare hand. Then he lay you face down on his bed, entered you from behind, and reached under you with his hand while he shagged you and teased your clitoris; it was superb. Why, he made you come like a wildcat!

I knew all about that. He had made me come like a wildcat, but with no spanking involved, thank you very much!

On the other hand, I seemed to be encountering more and more often the notion that a certain amount of controlled discomfort – let us not call it pain, though that is what it is I suppose – not only could, but did, add to the pleasures of sex for many people.

Natalie had told me that being spanked by Philippe intensified the delights of the ensuing shag. I remembered how Felicity, back in South Africa, had become more willing to surrender to Jonathan's seduction after he had smacked her bum for her. The image of that girl at the house party in Warlington came to mind, swinging spreadeagled from a frame, her nipples brushing across a strip of coconut matting. And then there were those girls and that young man, responding so ecstatically to the beat of those silk whips at Philippe's demonstration of *ligotage*.

It was all most puzzling.

It became only more puzzling as Philippe continued with my education. He took me to many different places, where I met many different people, and grew astonished at the variety of their pleasures.

Once, I watched through a fine lattice, as a man who must have been in his fifties, but was dressed as a small boy, grovelled to his 'nanny'. He then pulled down his breeches and bent over, evincing every sign of delight as she, a strikingly handsome woman of similar age, beat his bare bum with a bedroom slipper. Such was his delight that as he gasped, '*Merci madame, ah merci!*' his cock reared up and he actually had a come while she was spanking him! And when he had done so, the woman allowed him to kneel between her parted feet and lick her plump cunny.

Another time, I observed another session of *ligotage*, which this time had people, both men and women, playing the parts of slaves, obeying every whim of their owners. Naked men and women moved about on all fours, with leather collars around their necks, being led about on leashes like pet dogs. One man – a prominent member of something called the *Bourse*, Philippe told me – was being led about by his mistress by means of a leash attached to a strap around his genitals.

A girl, naked save for a chain hanging loose from clips on her nipples, carried around a tray of glasses just like a waitress, and waited for each person she served to slap her bottom or give her chain a little tug by way of acknowledgement, at which point she would smile and whisper *merci*. Women clad in black leather, their breasts exposed, carried long straps or riding crops. And every one of them, even the people pretending to be dogs, showed every sign of high excitement. Indeed, every cock and every nipple in the place seemed swollen almost to bursting!

And I can tell you for a truth that when they got down to the actual sex, it was very active and vigorous indeed. There were bodies everywhere. Writhing couples on the floor; a rather beautiful girl up against the wall, supporting her weight by hanging from a gas-mantle while a leather-clad man rutted wildly between her raised thighs; one of the mistresses kneeling astride the face of her slave while he lapped avidly at her; so many sights!

It was only later, much later, that I came to understand that Philippe was not only educating me. At the same time he was, with great subtlety, habituating me to the association of these sights and activities with my own physical pleasure, for he always began to kiss and caress me at some stage in the proceedings, got me worked up, and afterwards shagged me to delirium.

He talked to me, too, philosophising about people's deeper needs, and our work being to satisfy them. He also told me that to truly understand it was necessary to have at least some experience. At the same time, a little calculated roughness began to creep into his love-making. He would squeeze my nipples a little harder than before, or nip them between his teeth. He would dig his fingers hard into the cheeks of my bottom while he fucked me. He even, on several occasions, gave my bum a single smack when he was taking me from behind, in the manner Natalie called *comme un chien*. At the time, it did not matter, even felt pleasant because he would time it for when I was coming. Only much later did I realise its true significance.

He was, in fact, getting me used to the notion of a little pain being an accompaniment to pleasure, and indeed accentuating that pleasure.

The first time he spanked me was in the midst of pleasure, and led to more. We had stolen some time on a free afternoon to go to bed. We had undressed one another in that teasing, lascivious manner we both loved so well, and wallowed in a long, slow, luxurious shag. Afterwards, our conversation led to some sort of silly teasing. I cannot even remember what it was about now, except that it led to giggling and tickling, and then to him chasing me around the room for all the world as though we were a couple of children.

It had been me teasing him, I know that, and he

had begun chasing me with the laughing threat to tan me for being cheeky. And when he caught me, that is exactly what he did!

He caught me by my foot as I tried to evade him by scrambling across the bed, and I fell on to it face down, breathless with laughter. He held me down with his hand on the small of my back and suddenly he was spanking my bottom. It stung, it really did, but strangely it was exciting rather than painful.

He spanked me quite hard with his bare hand, attending to both cheeks of my wriggling bottom, laughing the while as indeed was I, at least at first. Then my emotions changed. From being a giggling girl I became a strangely excited woman, for there was something deeply stirring in being thus mastered by my lover, knowing that soon he would be thrusting his wonderful cock into me and driving me to the heavens.

I could not have expressed it thus clearly at the time, for I resolved the matter in my mind later. All I knew then was that the stinging smacks all over my bottom were stirring me up even more than they were hurting me, and that when he threw himself on to the bed and rolled me on top of him I was already wet with excitement. As you know, I love riding a man from on top, and that time I truly went wild, grinding myself on to him, bursting into a come almost as soon as I got him in me. I groaned with rapture and came more violently still when he reached around with both hands and grasped my burning bottom.

And this was the Lydia who had always been averse even to the idea of violence. Who had always shied away from the very notion of spanking and such as part of sex. How little we know of ourselves.

Do not run away with the idea that I became a devotee of such activities, for of course I did not.

For me, there is enough pleasure in the simple acts of shagging and sucking and so on to keep me satisfied. It did, though, give me a greater understanding of, and indulgence towards, those many people for whom such things are a sexual thrill in themselves.

Even so, Philippe did spank me on several other occasions as part of our love-making. It was good, and if anything it deepened my infatuation with him, for I was indeed in a state of infatuation. I had fancied him strongly from the moment our eyes first locked, and my feeling had only grown stronger during that period when he seemed indifferent to me. Now that we were spending every night in bed together, and often parts of the afternoons as well, I would have crawled naked through a pit of snakes for him. Having my bottom spanked was a tiny price to pay for the rapture he aroused in me!

And I confess that I actually made him spank me several times, by way of those silly, flirty, teasing games lovers play. Afterwards, the shagging was always volcanic! Oh, how clever an educator he was! Even when one evening he set it up, I did not see through it.

We had just finished an early supper when he told me quite calmly to go upstairs and take my knickers off because he wanted to spank me. As I mounted the stairs, all that was in my head, and in the tingling of my nipples and the burgeoning warmth between my legs, was that my lovely Philippe was going to make love to me.

I got up to our bedroom. I hoisted my skirts and pulled off my knickers. I waited. I thought to save time, and to give him a little thrill into the bargain, I would take off everything save my corset and stockings. Again I waited.

To have one's lover's voice ringing in one's head,

to have stripped off ready for his arrival, to be ready in body as well as in mind for the delights of holding and fondling and merging passionate bodies, is very stirring. To be kept waiting, as I was, only makes matters more tense.

By the time he eventually entered the room, I was veritably wilting with frustration. He had found something more important to do, I told myself. Another girl, maybe Natalie, had distracted him. He did not love me. I was not adventurous enough for him. All these thoughts and more had run through my head and lowered my spirits. Thus, when he walked in, I brightened with a sort of nervous hope.

He looked rather stern, his face set, his eyes not meeting mine. Curtly, he told me to stand and bend over the footboard. Confused, but grateful that at last he had come to me, I obeyed. He told me to get my feet apart. I did so. Then, oh glory, his hand descended upon the place that had been so impatient for him.

I gasped and wriggled as his fingers delved about in my vulva. He was not being gentle, but it felt so good. As he explored me, my feet drew further apart as though of their own accord, and my back arched to present my cleft better. And then the first smack arrived, and made me squeal.

They fell very fast, those first smacks, to the inner and under curves of my bottom. They stung. They were too quick to register individually, but they set my bottom on fire. I would have risen up and avoided this punishment had I been the Lydia of old. Philippe was not holding me down. I could have avoided this had I wished. Yet I stayed, bending over obediently, accepting the stinging smacks of his hand on my burning buttocks.

And then it changed somehow. Something

happened inside my head. The stinging of his hand on the tender flesh of my buttocks became a stimulation rather than a pain. I began to register how close or how distant his strokes were from the place at the centre of my being that now gaped for his hand.

My cunny was virtually weeping I was so far gone. He had spanked me pretty severely, and it felt wonderful! When he stopped, and spun me round, pushing me to my knees, I was so stirred up I felt something like adoration for the glorious cock that bumped against my eager lips!

I sucked him slowly, cupping his balls with tender fingers, encircling the base of his shaft, savouring his warm, fresh, slightly musky taste. He stroked my hair as I worshipped him with my mouth, and the touch of his hand and the heat in my bottom in combination with the fullness in my mouth, sent me almost into a come as I knelt there.

He did not reach his climax in my mouth; he seldom did, in fact. Instead, he withdrew from me, and helped me on to the bed. He spread my legs and moved his mouth down on to me. His tongue, his magical tongue, and his soft, warm lips, at once sent bubbles of light bursting in my head, and shivers of hot glory churning through my womb. Oh, he knew so well how to enrapture me!

Eleven

During the several months I was with Philippe in Paris I learnt nearly all there was to know about running a bordello. I learnt how to organise and supervise the catering arrangements, the interviewing of new girls and what to look out for in terms of whether they were likely to be successful or not. And it was certainly more than just looks and apparent willingness that were vital. Naturally I was also taught bookkeeping. Philippe was very keen on the business side of things.

I also observed a wide range of activities and met a good number of punters, though I did not service any. Nearly all the while I was in France, Philippe was my only lover. The single exception to that was also the occasion Philippe persuaded me that, in order to fully appreciate the needs of some of our clients, I should myself engage in *ligotage*.

Philippe was a very persuasive man, and I was infatuated with him. Even though I had reservations, and was not a little nervous, I agreed so as to please him. To see his smile of happiness when I agreed filled my heart with warmth. Our love-making that night was full and gentle, for Philippe understood my nervousness and was, in a sense, rewarding me for my courage.

* * *

I grew, if anything, more nervous as the preparations for my first experience as a participant in *ligotage* got under way. The party was to be held at a mansion near the Porte de Saint-Cloud, which was perhaps half an hour's drive from Philippe's establishment. We were to go there in a closed carriage, myself wrapped in a vast cape, for the costume I was to wear was somewhat bizarre. Had I not been so nervous and worked up, and had Natalie, who prepared me, not been so tense and excited, I might even have found it ridiculous.

After afternoon tea – a custom I had introduced to Philippe's establishment – I took a long, hot bath. I had agreed to Philippe's suggestion that I be shaved, and this task Natalie performed so lovingly, so delicately, that it became almost an act of love-making in itself. She first trimmed me with scissors, then lathered me delicately with a soft, long-haired brush. She used an open razor, of the cut-throat variety, which made me nervous. She was very gentle, though, and kept glancing up at me and smiling, and I became relaxed again.

When she finished me, and rinsed me off, and dusted me with fine, scented powder, I glanced down at myself. I had never realised how pretty my cunny was until then. It was plump and soft, with a straight, narrow crease descending from the quite pronounced triangular swelling of my *mons veneris*, with a sort of little arrowhead of smaller folds at the top, covering my clitoris.

To tell the truth, for several years now it had been the centre of my life, but I had never really looked at it. Half-sitting, half-lying there, with my legs spread, I suddenly felt very proud that my cunny was actually beautiful! Natalie thought so too, for she murmured, '*Oh, c'est jolie, c'est jolie!*' and bent her head to kiss me there.

Then Natalie massaged me with scented oils, and dressed my hair; it was swept back tightly and bound with a ribbon into a mare's tail at the back of my head, but with a thick strand left loose above each ear. These she carefully worked into two tight plaits which hung down almost to my collar bone.

Next, she buffed my finger and toe nails, and painted them with glossy black lacquer. Philippe had not told me quite what to expect, and I found myself staring at my hands, which looked most strange as I held them still, fingers spread, while the lacquer dried.

Natalie now proceeded to make up my face with cosmetics. A triangle of rouge was spread upon each of my cheeks, and smoothed and feathered with a soft pad. Fine, pale powder was next dusted all over my face and neck and brow. Next came my eyes, which Natalie outlined with thick lines of kohl, making me look almost Egyptian.

Lastly, my lips – those of my mouth and, to my surprise though I should perhaps have expected it, those of my quim – were made deep red with a shiny rouge which Natalie painted on with a fine brush such as a water-colour artist might use. Already, I realised when I caught sight of myself in the long mirror, I was being transformed into some exotic creature who was not really Lydia. I had not looked, nor felt, so different from myself since I had been prepared by Farah for my night in the Bey's bedchamber back in M—.

Now came my costume, and as it was put on me I did indeed become different from myself, if you take my meaning. First came the long, black boots Amelia had got for me for the house party in Warlington. I think I must have put on a little flesh in the intervening period, for when Natalie hooked up the last of the dozens of buttons my legs, especially the tops of my thighs, felt very tight. Encased was the word that sprang into my mind.

Next came a strange object, one could hardly call it a garment, which was something between a very wide belt and an abbreviated corset. It was boned and laced like a corset, but reached only from just above my navel to below my breasts. It was of black leather to match my boots. Natalie cinched it very tight, even placing her foot on my back to give her leverage with the laces. It held me very straight, and I could feel my tummy swelling out below the area of constriction. Strangely, it felt rather comfortable, and did not interfere with my breathing at all.

This belt had any number of metal rings fixed to it, both top and bottom, and Natalie busied herself fixing further items to these. Narrow black straps of elasticated satin were stretched down front and back, and buckled to the loops at the top of my boots. From each side, a thin silver chain was passed down across my tummy and between my legs and back up, to be fixed tightly to the ring from which it had started.

These chains were quite tight, and passed on either side of my newly shaven vulva, and had the effect of making me want to keep my legs apart, even though they were not actually uncomfortable. The next set of chains were attached to thick metal rings lined with cushioned satin. Natalie fixed the first ring of each pair to my ankle, and puzzled me by leaving the second lying loose.

Her action was explained when she slid long, black silk gloves over my arms. I call them gloves for want of a better term, for though they reached nearly to my armpits, they had no fingers, but were retained only by a loop over each of my thumbs and my ring fingers.

When she was satisfied that these were on properly, Natalie fixed the second of each pair of metal rings about my wrists. The chains which ran between these ankle and wrist rings were of just sufficient length to allow me to raise my hands an inch or two when I was standing straight, and to move them from side to side a little. Even this freedom was taken from me by what Natalie did next.

To the chains which ran from the belt down between my legs, she fixed further chains, laterally, from front to back just at my hips. To these she linked the chains that ran from my wrist rings. The effect of this was double. First, it tightened the chains between my legs: second, it pinioned my hands entirely.

Something very strange was going on inside me while all this was being done. I had agreed to take part in this because I was infatuated with Philippe, because he had asked me during a moment of loving passion, and because I longed to please and impress him. At the same time, though, I have always looked askance at this kind of ritualised performance. Usually, my strong sense of the ridiculous would have set me giggling at the outfit I was being got up in.

Now though, I felt out of myself, as it were, as if I was observing some strange, exotic woman being prepared for some voluptuous ritual and – I have to confess it – I was already very much stirred up by it. I was, to put it plain, feeling randy.

Now, Natalie approached me with a complicated harness-like affair of straps and buckles. At the top was a wide leather collar, which she fixed around my neck, though not tightly. From each side of this collar, she draped wide straps out to my shoulders, and from these came further, narrower straps which she took round beneath my armpits and buckled at the back. A band was slipped under each of the shoulder straps and buckled tight, so that my shoulders were pulled very square and my breasts thrust forward.

A strange tangle of straps and chains hung down from the front of the collar, and Natalie now began to work with these. She took a central strap from which others hung and fixed it to a ring at the front of my belt, so that it lay between my breasts. Next, she wrapped a chain as thick as my little finger around the fullness of my left breast, and a second around my right. These chains were attached to the central strap, and from them further straps were attached upward to my collar, and around to be buckled tightly across my back.

Frowning with concentration, Natalie carefully adjusted this buckle and that, ensuring that the chains lay close against my ribs. Then, to my astonishment, she tightened the chains so that they squeezed the swells of my breasts and made them stand out even more prominently.

What she did next only served to work me up even more than I already was. I have always been very sensitive in my nipples. Natalie now began to paint them with the same rouge she had used on my mouth and my cunny, and the touch of her brush sent little shocks of excitation through me. By the time she had finished, my nubs were standing out hard and eager.

She took up two short, very fine chains, each with a sort of slip-knot of silk at one end. These she placed over my nipples, tugging them just tight enough to stay on, and to continue to stimulate that part of me. Now I learnt what the purpose of the two thin plaits she had made in my hair was, for Natalie took each chain in turn and fixed it to the end of a plait. They were not fixed tightly, but even so the effect was that whenever I moved my head there was a little tug at one or other of my nipples.

Then she made my situation even more extreme. From the mare's tail hanging down my back she strung two more chains. These she slipped through rings on my belt directly beneath my breasts, then up to fix them to my nipples with two further slip-knots. She adjusted the tension so that unless I kept my head up and straight, these second loops tugged at me. At the same time, if I raised my head too far, the first pair of loops came into action. Only by keeping my head still could I avoid teasing myself!

The whole costume was devilishly cunning, for if I tried to move my hands, chains made themselves felt on each side of my cunny, and if I moved my head more than a very little, I tugged at my nipples. Though ostensibly free to move, I was as much bound as it is possible to be!

Natalie told me to walk to the far wall and back. Never before had I been so amazingly aware of my every action, of every nuance of my movements! The tightness of my boots made me conscious of the freedom of my thighs above their tops. The constriction of my belt-come-corset and the harness about my breasts and shoulders held me very erect. The thin chains passing between my legs made themselves felt at every careful step, and seemed to consciously work to make me part my thighs; an effect made all the more insistent when I inadvertently moved my arms, and thus tugged at the chains. And I had to keep my head very still, for my nipples were throbbing from the stimulation they were experiencing.

Though it may not sound so, this outlandish costume was not in the least uncomfortable, provided I moved carefully. Indeed it actually gave me a strange feeling of security; a security blended with vulnerability though, for while the whole length of my legs and arms, and a good part of my torso, were closely covered, my bottom and my vulva and my breasts were all fully exposed to the eye and anything else.

As I walked with great care back across the room, I was able to watch myself in the full-length looking glass on the wall. Had I not known it to be me, the object reflected in the glass would have startled me she looked so strange. Gleaming expanses of black leather forced the eye to the exposed parts of her body, and emphasised their pale nakedness. Tight straps and chains offered up her breasts and drew attention to her naked, shaven love-lips. And those lips were already swollen and pouting with the excitement she – I – was already feeling. Now I was truly beginning to understand how the people I had seen before, and presumed to judge, could derive sexual excitement from dressing up in their exotic costumes. I understood because I was undeniably feeling it myself as I looked at my reflection.

That Philippe, too, found my appearance exciting was plain almost from the moment he entered the room to see whether I was ready. He was a very sophisticated and experienced man who had seen and done pretty well everything there was in the realm of the flesh, yet he stopped and stared wide eyed when he saw me. As he moved slowly towards me his eyes ran rapidly over every part of me, and a swelling distorted his elegantly cut trousers. The way his eyes shone, and the softness of the kiss he placed upon my lips, were almost all the reward I needed for agreeing to have all this done to me.

He draped my high-collared, floor-length cape about my shoulders with his own hands, and stayed close by me as we went downstairs to the closed carriage which was to transport us to the house at Porte de Saint-Cloud. I had to move quite carefully, and descending the stairs was a bit awkward, but with Philippe taking my arm occasionally it was managed without mishap.

Unfortunately, my cape was only buttoned at the neck and, between the front door and the carriage, a gust of wind caught it and blew it wide open, giving several startled pedestrians an extremely revealing eyeful. Climbing into the carriage was made all the more difficult by the fit of giggles which overtook me!

On the short journey, Philippe kissed me, and told me I looked wonderful, and that I was wholly admirable for agreeing to do that which I had told him I was nervous of. My heart swelled with pride and happiness at his words, and his kisses and glances down at where the open cape showed off my body ensured that, by the time we reached our destination, I was once again thoroughly worked up.

The party was very mixed and quite crowded. Many of the people were in normal evening dress, though there were a number in costumes of *ligotage*, most of them female. I am afraid that I was far too self-conscious to take note of these other costumes, and so cannot describe them very well. I was myself the centre of a great deal of attention. My costume had given me a feeling of unreality, and this was increased as the other people looked me over, and touched and tested parts of my harness, and spoke to Philippe about me as though I were an object incapable of conversation. Mind you, since most of what they said was in rapid French I pretty well was incapable, for although my grasp of the language had come on very well it was not yet that strong.

Bits that I did grasp, the odd word or phrase here and there, made it plain that what was being said was very much to the point. My breasts were remarked on, and the elegance of my posture. Philippe was told that I had a very attractive backside, and several hands smoothed over that part of me as though to emphasise the point. Several people, both men and women, congratulated Philippe upon how inviting my shaven vulva looked, and I think, though I cannot be sure, asked whether I might be available later.

My mind had become detached, as it were, as though I was an observer rather than a participant in all this. The way Philippe led me from group to group, not introducing me but conversing calmly with this person and that, and showing every sign of pride at the attention I was drawing, made me very aware of myself. Being looked at and touched and commented upon was, in a strange, deep way, mentally arousing. Moving about in that costume, feeling the chains between my legs, and the tugging on my nipples, got me stirred up physically. By the time the party moved into the vast dining room I was, without a doubt, very randy indeed, and totally focused upon Philippe.

One moment stands out in my mind, a moment as unlike my normal nature as was appearing in this exotic costume. Moving through the wide double doors leading to the dining room, Philippe espied an acquaintance, and called to him. This man, like Philippe, had with him a girl. She was breathtakingly lovely, with huge, limpid brown eyes and a great shawl of dark hair that swept to her waist. Stark naked save for a pair of high-heeled shoes, her figure was superb, with full, firm breasts rising from a narrow rib cage, long shapely legs and round curvaceous hips. Her wrists were held behind her with a pair of silver manacles. The man who Philippe had hailed was leading her by a slender chain which was attached to a second chain, this one strung between her rouged and swollen nipples, to which it was attached by clips that looked like silver snakeheads, the mouths devouring the nipples.

Philippe chatted with the man, clearly commenting upon the woman. When he laughed, and reached out and ran his hand over her chained breast, I felt a sudden pang of angry jealousy. I never feel jealousy! I regard it as a sad destructive emotion, yet I felt it then! It was my breast he should be touching, not hers! Me he should be fancying, not this brazen thing!

Oh, how silly we can be when we are in a state of exaggerated emotion!

The dinner was an opulent affair by any standards. A table at least twenty feet long, and spread with crisp white linen tablecloths, was gleaming with silver cutlery, crystal glasses, vases of flowers, and decanters of wine. All the people in normal clothes sat, but those of us in costume were obliged to stand beside the chairs of our escorts.

Footmen clad in white knee-breeches and dark blue tail coats glided about, serving the guests. Conversation was light, and there was much laughter. A string quartet played in a gallery, accompanying the chatter. Like me, the other half a dozen people in costume all had their hands pinioned, and all of us had to be fed by our escorts. It was the most unreal situation I had ever been in.

Beneath my feelings of otherness and arousal, had been a sense of helplessness. Harnessed and chained, I was, in a very real sense, dependent upon Philippe, to help me in and out of the carriage, for example, or to put on and take off my cape. Now, I had to be fed by him, spoonful by spoonful.

It had the strangest effect upon me. Being thus dependent, and upon Philippe of all wonderful men, made me feel peculiarly warm towards him, as I suppose a child must feel towards a caring adult. At the same time, the necessity of bending forward to receive the gift of food had an entirely physical effect.

I had to keep my head and my torso straight, else the chains attached to my nipples distracted me. Thus, I perforce had to bend forward from the hips. This caused the chains between my legs to slide across the sensitive flesh of my vulva as I bent, and to slide back again as I straightened. At the same time, they tugged and teased at the constricted folds of my swollen cunny, sending hot chills through me, and making me overwhelmingly conscious of the growing heat in my womb.

I had to bend forward whenever Philippe held up a spoonful of food for me. As course after course came by – consommé, fish, pink mutton, cheese, fruit, pudding – one after the other, and as I was obliged to bend and straighten again and again, the teasing of the chains against my oh, so sensitive nether parts grew and grew until, by the end of the meal, had my knees not been encased in my high boots I am sure they would have buckled. I am sure that, had Philippe even so much as kissed me, let alone touched me between my legs, I would have come instantly.

After the dinner came the main purpose of the evening. Brandy being drunk and cigars smoked, people began to drift away through the double doors by which we had entered. Soon only Philippe and I and one other couple, a middle-aged pair in normal clothing, were left.

Rising from his chair, Philippe gave me a kiss and smiled into my eyes, which set my heart beating afresh, and led me out of the dining room. We went, slowly for I still had to move rather carefully, across a panelled foyer and through another doorway. Here, the scene was very different from that at dinner.

Each of the half a dozen or so people who were in costume was the centre of a group. Each, too, was being used in some way or other.

The woman with only the chain and nipple clips, who had made me jealous when Philippe had admired her, was draped backward over a sofa, her ankles held high and wide by two women as a short, thick-set man shagged her vigorously. He was still fully dressed, which contrasted dramatically with her nakedness, and he was using great handfuls of her glorious, waist-length hair to pull her on as he rutted in her. What was most startling, though, was that she had her chain gripped between her teeth, and was pulling back on it so that her nipples were being tugged up in a most painful-looking manner.

Other girls were being used in various ways in other parts of the room, kneeling with their mouths busy, or bending over while a man worked off his excitement from behind. The one and only male in costume, a very handsome young man with a pale, athletic body, was tied back down on a *chaise longue*, his head and shoulders hidden by the skirts of the woman who knelt astride him, his pale cock straining for the ceiling as another woman alternately stroked and slapped it.

I looked around very nervously. I had agreed to take part in this, but was unsure now about what I had let myself in for. As if on cue, Philippe turned me to face him, looked with deep affection into my eyes, and kissed me on my lips. He told me I was wonderful, and more desirable than anyone else around. I melted again. Was there anything I would not do for this wonderful man?

As he kissed me and whispered his lovely endearments into my ear, he reached down. He ran the flat of his hand over my shaven *mons*, and slipped a fingertip between my pouting body-lips, making me almost stagger with the thrill it sent through me. His eyes and the lips that were kissing me told me that he knew, knew as certainly as did I, that I would do anything for him.

What I did was to surrender to the group that now gathered close around me. As they did so I looked to Philippe, and he nodded and smiled, and kissed me again. He wanted me to go with them and was pleased that I was willing to do so. I let them lead me away.

The two gentlemen and several women who had come for me were murmuring approvingly and though I did not catch much of what they said I did recognise the compliments about my pretty hair, breasts and my *connasse*, which is the French equivalent of a rather crude English name for that place a woman has between her legs.

A hand began to explore the cleft of my bottom. I tried to turn my head to see what Philippe was doing, but the chains tugged my nipples quite harshly. Other hands were on me now, smoothing over my flanks and belly, and testing the smoothness of my shaven, and by now incredibly sensitive quim. Fingers tested the tension of the chains running between my legs, and then slipped between my folds to tease my throbbing clitoris.

I gasped aloud at this, and again as another finger found my entrance and slipped into me. Walking was already awkward, and made even more so by the hands between my legs. Other hands found my breasts, and the touches on my engorged nipples combined with the overwhelming sensations between my legs, made me stagger and almost collapse as a sudden and unexpected orgasm swept over me. I heard a tinkling laugh as I shuddered and groaned aloud. I am sure I would have fallen had not strong hands supported me.

I cannot remember ever having been in such a state as I was in those moments. Many times in my life I had come while just being fingered and fondled. Never, though, had I done so this violently or publicly. My tummy was flexing and spasming uncontrollably and my legs were like water. My head tried to droop and then to roll, which only sent more excruciating stimulation to my poor nipples. I think I was actually sobbing, I was so far gone!

Much of what followed is not clear to me, because at the time everything was a slowly swirling maelstrom of sensation upon sensation.

I know that I was being kissed a lot, mostly I think, by women. I know that I was borne along and found myself lying on a leather upholstered *chaise longue*. I know that the chains to my nipples were released, only to be replaced by avid mouths, one on each breast, which sucked me and flicked their tongues across my unbelievably sensitive nipples, so that I cried out with the ecstatic pain of it.

I know that someone shagged me, slowly and hard, while those mouths ravenned at my breasts. I know that my orgasms were nearly continuous.

At some stage in this whirlwind of sensation my knees were pulled high, and the chains which had been so tormenting my vulva were eased outward. Let me disabuse you if you think this was a relief. All it meant, for they did not undo the chains, was that my knees were now captured high and wide by the chains looped beneath them, and my vulva and bottom were helplessly exposed to whatever might befall me.

Someone began to lick and nuzzle at me. Tongues continued to torment my aching nipples, and now also to lick and kiss my tummy and my neck. A cock nudged against my lips, and I opened to accept it, sucking greedily as my body squirmed and writhed under this overwhelming onslaught of stimulation.

I was lifted and turned, so that I was kneeling on the *chaise longue*, my head turned to the side and my bottom raised high. Hands were on my hips. I was penetrated and used vigorously, as hands toyed with my dangling breasts. Even while whoever it was thrust powerfully into me, fingers sought and found my splayed cunny, entered me, and teased my straining cherry.

I felt something nudging at my rosehole, and opened myself to it. It felt odd, completely unlike the cock I had expected. Woozily, for I was pretty far gone, I strained my head around to see what was happening. A woman was bending over my helplessly spread buttocks, on her face an expression of concentration. Above the curves of my bottom, my unbelieving eyes registered that the woman's hands held the end of what seemed, to me anyway, to be an enormous syringe, and she was pressing the brass plunger.

It was the other end that had penetrated my bottom, and I suddenly felt a strange warmth begin to flood my insides, as though I were being filled with warm oils. I was distracted as somebody thrust some fingers into my cunny, so I did not feel the syringe being removed. By the time I was able to focus again, something else was being eased into my bottom, something that was solid but not stiff. And there was a lot of it, for the woman seemed to take ages easing whatever it was into me, and my bottom began to feel ever so full.

I was distracted again by something being moved close to my foggy eyes. I focused, and was as startled as I was puzzled. It looked somewhat like a model of a cock, and was bigger than any man I could imagine, much thicker and more gnarled along its length. What with the hand rummaging in my cunny, and what was being done to my bottom, it was hard to concentrate on the object in front of my eyes. Then, when a woman's hand smoothed some kind of oil over it, and it was tipped at an angle and moved suggestively, I realised with a shock that it was indeed a dildo. But it was so big! Surely they did not intend to use it on me!

It was removed from my gaze. I felt fingers working between my legs, parting me, and sliding in and out as though to lubricate me. Then I felt it nudging against me, moving up and down along my sopping folds, and pressing against my entrance. It was too big; oh heavens, it was too big!

Twelve

Somebody was kissing me again. Fingers were teasing my nipples. My bottom felt strange. The dildo pressed and pressed, and fingers teased my aching clitoris, and the dildo began to enter me. My body convulsed, I think I cried out, and the dildo slid into me. Deep, so deep, its thickness stretched me, its gnarled surface tormenting my sheath unbelievably.

I buried my face in the leather of the *chaise*, sobbing with the extremity of the stimulation I was suffering. The dildo was filling me to my chest, and whoever was manipulating me with it began to move it insidiously, keeping it deep and rocking it. At the same time fingers were still teasing around my clitoris.

I was as lost as lost could be! I began to come, my sheath convulsing on the ridged carvings around the shaft of the dildo, my belly pulsing, the muscles of my splayed thighs convulsing with the unbelievable spasms that were churning through me.

And then it got worse, more overwhelming than ever! The dildo was pressing and retreating, pressing and retreating. I was gasping and dragging my finger-nails across the leather of the boots by which my wrists were still chained, and then they began to ease whatever was in my bottom out of me.

Later, Philippe told me they were called Chinese love beads. All I knew at the time was that my helplessly trussed position, and the movements of the dildo filling my squirming sheath, and the alternate stretching and relaxing of my rosehole as the device was slowly pulled out of my bottom, all combined to send me into such overwhelming convulsions I felt my body must burst asunder, and my very brain explode.

My head had swirled away from me. All there was of me was my helplessly churning body, and the sensations that were being inflicted upon it; sensations that were at once shattering and voluptuous, devastating and ecstatic.

Then suddenly there was a cessation. I was not being shagged or fondled; there were no cocks thrusting into me, no fingers teasing. I strained my head round to look back. There, standing alongside my raised bottom, was a magnificently handsome woman of middle age, her black hair touched with grey. But it was not her beauty which froze my breath. It was what she held in her hand.

It was a whip. One of those exotic, silken whips I have described before. The long red threads of fine, gleaming silk swung to and fro as she smiled down at me, selecting where the first blow was to fall.

I was absolutely and entirely helpless. I could not have got out of the way of what was about to happen save by rolling myself bodily sideways, and falling off the *chaise longue*. Even then, there would have been many hands to hold me still.

The woman's eyes roamed over my upraised bottom calmly, as though evaluating an item of goods in a display. She reached down and ran a smooth, cool hand over both my buttocks and down along my cleft. As I twitched in scared anticipation, she smiled again, slowly.

At the very moment she raised the whip, its blood-red skein of threads shining in the lamp light, Philippe's face appeared over her shoulder. He was not looking at my blatantly offered bottom, nor at the woman or her whip. Instead, he was staring intensely directly into my eyes; it was a stare which transfixed me, and told me that he loved me for what I was doing to please him.

Hypnotised by Philippe's eyes, I was aware of the red skein of the whip falling. It was not as my imaginings of being beaten had suggested. It did not whistle through the air, rather it sighed. It was not a searing line of agony, but a wide, sharp painless impact. Though it stung a little, I could not have called it actually painful. Indeed, it was not as trying as the several spankings Philippe had already subjected me to.

That first stroke, the first of many I have to say, fell across my left buttock. They began high and to the side, and continued through to encompass my inner curves and the inside of my thigh. More strokes followed almost instantly from the other side, and mirrored the first exactly. There were, though I had not seen it, two people whipping me.

Philippe's eyes continued to hold mine as the silken whips set up a warm stinging over the whole area between my belt and the tops of my boots, even falling vertically to take in my quaking cleft and my vulva. It was, I knew, even in this abject position, swollen and pouting with desire.

Suddenly, Philippe was closer as he knelt beside me, his eyes boring into mine, his breath warm on my neck as he leant in to kiss me. Then, somehow, I was on my back, my knees chained high and tight. Philippe appeared between the angled columns of my thighs, his trousers open, his beloved cock rearing. At the very moment he reached down and parted my folds to enter me, the two women with the whips began to beat me on my breasts. It was unbelievable, and I spasmed again into such a come as nearly bucked me off the *chaise longue*.

The last thing I remember with any clarity at all is wailing with ecstasy as Philippe plunged into me, and the whips fell on my bursting, grateful breasts.

The rest was a hot mist of confused sensation. Hands, mouths, breasts, sexes, were all about and over me. How long it went on I cannot say, only that such extremes of stimulation, such repeated, helpless comings, can become as agonising as they are rapturous, and that I was in such a state that I almost had to be carried to the vehicle which bore us back to Philippe's house on the rue Saint Dominique.

I sorely needed the steaming, scented bath and the tender care with which Natalie treated me the next day. I had been so far gone when we got back home that I simply fell on to my bed as I was, and lapsed into a sleep of exhaustion – exhaustion and strange dreams.

Natalie woke me tenderly in the morning, and helped me out of the remnants of my *ligotage* costume, and along to the bathroom. To my surprise, there were no actual marks on my body to show that I had been trussed up with chains, and even whipped. I felt an incredible sensitivity in my skin, though, and my joints were stiff; my breasts and cunny were in such a condition that the merest touch, even of my bath water, sent shivers of hotness through me.

Natalie understood. She had, she told me, been in just such a case herself more than once, and was it not wonderful. The idea gave me pause, for yes, despite my reservations, it had been in its own way. I had experienced what was probably the most intense and sustained sexual stimulation I would ever know.

I was even now exhausted from it. Philippe's eyes and lips had told me he loved me, and that made the whole thing worthwhile.

How far, oh how far had you come, Lydia!

How far indeed was shown by the way Natalie bathed me, and how my poor, unruly body responded to the sponge she smoothed across me, and the way she tenderly towelled me dry. She then took me on the floor of the bathroom, her lips and tongue and fingers driving me wild as she took her pleasure between my splayed thighs.

Everyone was very soft with me during the two last days I spent with Philippe in Paris. They were still respectful, of course, for I was his protégée. Yet there was a certain tenderness, almost a motherliness, in the way they treated me, even the footmen downstairs. It was as though they were lovingly proud of me for passing some sort of rite of passage.

Philippe himself was especially loving towards me; touching my hand for no reason; kissing me; looking up in shining-eyed welcome when I went into his office; making love to me with slow, gentle, knowing passion on those, my last nights with him.

His eyes when he kissed me goodbye at the railway station at which my journey back to England began were warm and proud. As for myself, I was in a turmoil. If he had asked me to stay, I would have done so with joy.

He did not. Could not, of course, as the sensible part of my brain reminded me. He was a businessman, and I a businesswoman. I had come here at Amelia's suggestion to be educated in the ways of managing a house of pleasure. It had been accomplished. I was educated, and ready to return to Amelia and the *Silken Web*.

That much my head told me. Yet my heart and the very breath of my lungs told me otherwise; told me that if Philippe had so much as raised an eyebrow, I would have spent my life chained up and bound for him, even if the whips had been real ones!

I journeyed home alone, which was in its way a good thing for, though desperately miserable at first, the hours on the train in France, and then on the ferry, and then on the train again from Dover, gave me time to adjust myself. By the time Amelia and Karl, and Emily and Kate, greeted me at London Bridge station, I was in command of myself once more.

Amelia knew, of course, that changes had taken place in me. One glance into each other's eyes told me that. Though Kate and Emily were bubbly and enthusiastic, and wanted at once to hear every detail of Paris and my adventures there, Amelia was quiet and acted like a big sister.

She somehow knew that I needed peace, as it were, and time for the absence of Philippe to cease its dull ache in my spirit. Thus, for many weeks she never suggested, and prevented Emily and Kate from suggesting, that I go to the *Silken Web*. Karl did not arrange any private engagements for me, and did not seek to come to my bed.

Only Albert, Amelia's groom, tried it on, by pressing me against the wall when I was passing the stable one afternoon, and attempting to kiss me while moving his fingers against my cunny through the cloth of my skirt. I was no less stunned than he was when I instantly burst into tears, and ran sobbing to my bedroom, where I threw myself on to the bed and cried and cried.

My outburst had a cathartic effect upon me. I am not the kind of woman to make such a fuss. Indeed, I have always prided myself in being sensible and down to earth. My pining for Philippe was foolish. I was casting a pall over Amelia and my friends, and was certainly not pulling my weight in the business.

In a matter of only a few days after my emotional outburst I had managed to pull myself together. I made a conscious effort one evening, and took myself down to the *Silken Web*. Amelia expressed doubts as to my wisdom, but I argued her down.

I wore the lowest gown I owned, a blue cotton frock, with a full skirt, tight bodice and a square-cut neckline that came hardly above my nipples. Beneath, I wore a black corset with suspenders, black silk stockings, and a pair of the skimpiest knickers I could find.

Perhaps in reaction to my former mood, and the fact that I had remained entirely celibate in the ten weeks or so since I had returned from France, I took on any and every punter who fancied me. Needless to say there were quite a few. More often than not, I did not even wait to gull them into buying the regulation bottle of champagne, but simply concluded the deal for requirements and price, and took them upstairs.

I balked at nothing and no one, performing whatever my punter desired willingly and with enthusiasm; an enthusiasm which was in fact pretended, at least at first. I confess that, early on, my performance was mechanical and I took no real pleasure from the hands which fondled me, and the cocks which thrust so eagerly into me.

It was only quite late, when I had already serviced eight or nine customers, that my senses took flight. The man who achieved this was not particularly prepossessing; he was almost ugly in fact. And he was rather rough to. Perhaps it was the roughness that did the trick.

He wanted me stripped to my corset and stockings, and to take me from behind, whilst I was lying face down on the bed with my arms and legs spread out. He lay full on me, his weight crushing my breath from me. He was big, and he thrust himself into my bottom instead of my cunny. He bucked and rutted hard, pushing his hands beneath me and grasping my breasts as though they were lumps of dough. His breath was hot on my neck, and he actually bit my shoulder as he fucked my bottom harder and faster.

And suddenly I was spiralling up into a come; a come which wracked my body, and made me groan and buck myself against this rough, ugly man who was using me so callously.

He was delighted, and laughed as he pumped his come into me. He slapped my bottom jovially when he got off me, and put a ten-shilling note on the table instead of the five shillings we had agreed on.

I too was pleased, though my bottom was a little sore, and after washing myself went happily back down to the main room. Whatever the barrier inside me had been, it was truly gone, for my next shag, and the one after that was delicious, and I came quite voraciously!

It was as though I had cast off some kind of mask of frigidity, of spiritlessness, and was soon quite back to my old self. Not that I became greedy – though I did enjoy delightful times with the others in the house – for indeed, I now entered a period in my life when I actually had less sex than hitherto. My role in the business began to change.

I still had the occasional private engagement, usually with a regular, but when I went to the *Silken Web* it was rarely to entertain punters. Instead, I now found myself more and more often sitting in Amelia's office, carrying out her erstwhile task of checking off the girls' sales and the fees for their evening's work.

I use the term 'girls' because it was our common parlance, rather than because it was accurate. Some were indeed girls, younger even than my own twenty years. Most, though, were women, and ranged in age up to their early forties at least.

They were, almost without exception, a cheerful and thoroughly likeable bunch; all of them down to earth, generous, and quick to laugh. I have found that such is nearly always the case among we 'ladies of pleasure'. It is as though the very basic nature of our work, during which far more is stripped off than one's clothes, removed totally the very possibility of that pretentiousness which is such a part of normal society. After all, one can hardly put on airs when one's companions know full well that you have just been shagging a total stranger for five bob!

Let Gladys stand as an example. She was a plump, almost matronly woman, who hailed originally from a small town near Stoke-on-Trent. Not wishing to become a drudge in one of the local potteries, she had run away from home quite young, and found herself work at a thriving inn on the London road near Reading.

Inevitably the landlord had demanded services of her, which she had not much choice but to supply. She was, she told me, about sixteen at the time and ripe, and her employer had been pretty demanding. Although she had been a virgin in the beginning, and the innkeeper had demanded to shag her more or less whenever he could get her alone, and often in the most uncomfortable places such as over a barrel in the cellar or up against the wall in the yard, she soon found that she was enjoying it.

It was not a great step from shagging the innkeeper to supplementing her meagre wages by shagging the customers for sixpences. Sadly, she had known little of the realities of nature, and found herself with child. At first she had thought the absence of her monthly show a bonus, for it meant that she could garner more sixpences. Only when her belly began to swell did matters change.

The innkeeper's wife, who must inevitably have known what had been going on with Gladys all those months, sent the poor girl packing amidst a stream of obscene imprecations. Such is the hypocrisy of our world! It was fine for her husband and the customers to fuck the young servant, but as soon as it became inconvenient out she had to go. Is it not always the woman who pays, and the men who get away with it?

Gladys had survived on the handy sum her many sixpences had afforded her and had left her baby, a healthy boy, with the childless wife of a farmer, who had befriended her during her last months. She still saw her son once in a while, now a handsome and lusty young farmer himself, and married with a brood of youngsters by a pretty wife. The only sadness, Gladys told me, was he did not know she was his real mother.

After her delivery, she had made her way to London, where at last lack of funds had obliged her to tout for trade. She had found the area around Covent Garden the most profitable, but had in the end been picked up by a policeman. That was always a risk when a girl plied the streets, of course.

Apparently, in those days there had been a law in existence which permitted the police to stop and examine any female they regarded as suspicious, which meant, as was common knowledge, any presentable female they found alone in a public place after dark.

Ostensibly the law had been designed to curb public prostitution. What in fact it did was to give policemen the right to molest lone females at their will. In Gladys' case, she had been walking between the grocer's shop, where she had bought some bacon, to the house where she rented a room. She had not even been on business!

Even so, a man in a tweed Ulster had accosted her, shown her a warrant card, and challenged her as a common prostitute. She had protested her innocence, of course, and told him what she had been about. He demanded to be shown her room. There, he had stated his right under the law to examine her. In fact, he simply wanted to shag her. It would have been the same had she really been an innocent working class girl.

That particular law has gone now, thank heavens, but I wonder how many pretty girls of modest means – these things were hardly likely to happen to women of the middle or upper classes – were forced to submit to a policeman shoving his hand under their skirts to check whether or not they were virgins. And to give her a thorough fingering in the process, of course.

Anyway, back to Gladys. Young as she was, she had enough wit in the ways of the world to know what this policeman was after. She took him up to her room, pleasured him and from then on had him as a protector, or 'ponce' as the street vernacular calls such men. After several years, and various adventures, Gladys had ended up on Amelia's books, and very popular she was too.

As I said, she was plump, and she had a sweet, matronly way about her. Most of her clientele was made up of regulars, and principally of men of mature years, who found a comfort and easiness in her ample bosom that they might not have in a younger, more nubile girl.

A fascinating sideline was that, from time to time, one of her regulars would hire her services to introduce a young son, nephew, or even grandson to the delights of the bed; an introduction my mind's eye saw her accomplishing with all the tenderness and practicality of a caring nanny or nurse.

She even acted in a matronly way with any of the younger girls who might have a problem, who perhaps had fallen for one of their punters or, worse and more common, had one fall for them. At such times, her open-heartedness and ribald sense of humour was always guaranteed to slice through any illusions!

A side of my work with Amelia which began to develop around then was the interviewing and supervision of what Amelia called 'probationers'. These were girls who by one means or another – usually recommendation by one of our existing girls, but not always of course – had come to the attention of the house as potential employees.

They were of all shapes and sizes, and many backgrounds, for we did not discriminate on superficial grounds such as class or looks. It was personality we looked for, that little spark of uniqueness which would make the punters go for her.

It may seem odd to those less familiar with the real world of sex, but looks had very little to do with whether or not a girl was popular and profitable. She might be tall or short, round or skinny, pretty or plain, but if she had the right sort of personality, and the ability to make a man think himself wonderful, she could be a success. Why we even had one girl, Violet, whose eyes in moments of excitement would roll and look in towards one another – a trick she could perform at will too – and many a punter would proudly boast that he had fucked her cross-eyed.

All these girls had stories to tell of how they came to our line of work, and they nearly all had a similar theme: seduction and betrayal. Kate, Emily and I were rare in coming to this world voluntarily. For most girls, it was a case of needs must.

One of the most important things we looked for at our interviews was the manner in which the girl told her story. She might be hesitant, shy, reluctant or broad humoured; that was not important. If, though, she seemed bitter or cynical or resentful, we sent her elsewhere. We wanted happy girls. Not that we simply cast aside the others, that would have been callous. What we did, in fact, was to recommend them to other houses or, in most cases, find them employment as domestic servants among Amelia's wide acquaintanceship among the middle and upper classes.

Of those we did engage, most had fascinating stories, stories which revealed as much about the selfish hypocrisy of our society as they did about the quality of the girls whose tales they were.

Take Maudie.

Maudie Taylor was a gem. Quite short, and verging on plumpness, she had thick, dark hair, deep brown eyes, and a laugh that could break windows. Bubbly is the first word that would apply when trying to describe her. I first encountered her immediately after I had interviewed a rather crushed young woman who had been made pregnant by a soldier who had now gone off to the war in Africa. This poor thing was not at all the type we were looking for. But she was a good girl, and I managed to find her a place with a very nice family in Lambeth; one where I was sure the master of the house would not take advantage of her.

After this unhappy woman, Maudie lifted the

heart. She bustled into my office looking about her with bright shrewdness. She had, in the colloquial phrase which is so apposite, 'no side'.

She had, she told me, ripened early, and even before she left the local national school she had attended, was starting to attract the local lads' attentions. Thus she began to learn the subtle art of innocent flirtation.

She had known from the beginning that her pert visage and burgeoning figure might be of use to her in avoiding the fates of most of the other girls in her neighbourhood; they either slaved in the local cotton mill, or sorted coal at one of the local pitheads. Thus, using her looks and her quick wits, she had got herself a post helping out the town grocer; he was a single man of mature years, and legendary as a skinflint and woman-hater.

He had not hated Maudie, though. Indeed, the cheeky vixen had teased him quite outrageously, letting him catch sight of her pulling up her hose, or gaze down the neck of her blouse as she bent to sort packets or straighten a sugar sack.

Apparently, it took Mr Forbes, the grocer, several months to pluck up enough courage to feel Maudie's bum, and he had been so red and nervous Maudie nearly laughed. After that, she twisted him around her little finger.

For a while, it was as though he had to steal gropes, and she always squealed and acted shocked – though not too shocked, of course. She did not want to scare him off.

It was a further while before he plucked up the nerve to change the target of his gropes from her bum to her bosoms. After that, though, she allowed him to conquer her. Oh, how many men are taken in by a girl's innocence into believing that it is they who conquer, when any sensible woman knows a man never gets anything a girl is not ready to give him!

Looking at her as she sat there in Amelia's office, grinning naughtily as she recounted her story, I could just see her, in my mind's eye, teasing the poor man, and pretending to be scandalised when he slipped a hand down the neck of her blouse, and found her warm breast. And I could visualise, too, the way she came over all coy and twittering, then breathless and submissive when he groped under her skirts, and got his cock out and put it in her hand.

Oh, she was a sweet and ribald creature! She had supposedly surrendered her innocence to the grocer, and, out of his guilt and fear that she would tell on him, got a rise in wages.

So far as the grocer knew, he took advantage of his poor innocent assistant for several months. In fact, she took advantage of him, weedling gifts out of him, pretending that she was swept away by his passion for her, conning him for extra cash for new clothes and whatever. Mind you, the grocer was not losing on the arrangement, for if Maudie was tasty now, how much more desirable she must have been when she was in her first flush of ripeness, and the tight-fisted, woman-hating grocer was getting to shag her pretty well every day.

It ended sadly. Maudie had developed a genuine affection for him, and had even made plans to settle down with him, but he passed away. The physician said that he had suffered an apoplexy from too much exertion. His will, clearly made out before he met Maudie, left his estate between the local chapel and a charity for orphan boys.

At a loss, and having no claim, Maudie was thrown back upon her wits. She went from her home town to Manchester, and looked for work. Still shunning the factory life that seemed to be the only thing open to a girl of her class, she had used her natural talents to get by. At first she had been an amateur, cleaving to this man and that for a few weeks so as to have a place to rest her head and food in her belly.

Then one chap, a former sailor, had suggested that she might do well on the game, and she became a professional. As a quick study, and being far from shy, she had prospered, but soon found that the life of a streetwalker palled on her. Fun, but too risky, she said.

She decided to move up in the world, and made her way to London for the better pickings she'd heard of. She plied the streets of Soho a little, just to keep in funds, but had all the while been looking to join a quality house, having heard that such a life was both more fun and more profitable.

Looking at Maudie, I knew without doubt that wherever she was, there too would be fun, for she had the look. I took her on, she agreed to our house terms, and proved to be a great success. She built up a long string of regulars, always a good sign with a whore, and caused nary a problem either with punters or other girls.

All in all, I was pretty pleased to find somebody as good as Maudie so early in my career as the assistant madam of the *Silken Web*.

Thirteen

I had not yet, though, truly earned my place. Another trial awaited me. Karl broached it over dinner one evening. There had been a special request. He thought that perhaps I might feel up to taking it on. It would mean being away in the country for a while, and would require thought and discipline, but he reckoned I might manage it if I was willing. My curiosity piqued, I pressed him for more information.

The request had come from a noble source, requiring the strictest discretion. It concerned the education of certain scions of the family; education of the most discrete, most intimate, and most important kind.

I met the twins for the first time upon the lawn behind the mansion to which we had all been directed. They were playing croquet. They were beautiful!

They had black hair and the most brilliant blue eyes you could wish to see, which gave their looks a strange, fey quality. The young man was quite tall, and had a breadth of shoulder and slimness of hip that betokened an excellent figure when he was fully matured.

Roderick's hair was quite long, and parted in the middle to flop down over his ears. It framed a face which, though still retaining some of the softness of adolescence, showed clearly that he would become strikingly handsome as time went by. Like his sister, his complexion was pale and fine, but he had effected a small, downy moustache on his upper lip in order, I supposed, to make him look more mature. It actually only succeeded in emphasising his youth.

Alexandra his sister, younger apparently by half an hour, looked if anything a little older than he. Her glossy hair was done in quite a grown up style, held high at the sides by tortoiseshell combs inlaid with nacre, and falling in a great swag almost to her waist at the back.

She had a heart-shaped face in which those wonderful blue eyes looked almost too big, a small, straight nose, and the prettiest of mouths, with plump pink lips and perfect white teeth.

Though not yet quite eighteen years of age, her figure was already almost that of a woman, with a high bosom, a narrow waist, and hips that promised to swell deliciously in time.

It seemed that their mother had passed away in giving them birth, and they had been brought up by Aunt Emmelina, their father's older sister, and her husband, the nobleman who had contracted with Karl for our services. Their blood was, to coin a phrase, blue, but apparently quite a light blue. Even so, the introductions Karl effected were rather formal and surprisingly so, in view of what we had been contracted to do.

Our contract – Karl's, Ashoko's, Emily's and mine – was to educate Roderick and his sister Alexandra in pleasure. It sounds outrageous I know, but apparently their uncle had spent many years in the east, and was much taken with certain philosophies he had encountered there. Among them was the belief that to become fully aware of the potentialities of the human senses, those senses had to be trained and disciplined. He was himself attending to the realms of food and wine. Our task was to deal with matters more, well, carnal!

That Alexandra and Roderick were aware of this was made clear by the way both of them blushed as we shook hands, and regarded us closely from beneath lowered eyelashes. That their uncle clove strongly to his eastern philosophy was amply demonstrated at dinner, and opened my eyes to aspects of our task I had not yet considered.

The meal was served in an opulently furnished dining room, with heavy chandeliers, great swathes of velvet curtains, a huge mahogany table, sideboards and dressers, elegant ladderback chairs, and brilliantly coloured eastern rugs and carpets. The cutlery was of silver, the glasses and decanters the finest cut crystal, and the crockery of the finest gold-edged bone china I have ever seen. Before each setting was a silver fingerbowl, with a slice of lime and a couple of mint leaves floating in the hot water, and a beautifully folded damask napkin.

Two places had no setting at all.

Of we four only Karl seemed unsurprised at this odd arrangement, though he did not offer any enlightenment. Professional discretion prevents me from naming our contractor and so I shall henceforth refer to him as His Grace. Only when His Grace, Aunt Emmelina and our two charges entered did the thing become clear. His Grace sat, naturally, at the head of the table, and his wife at the foot. Roderick took one of the unset places, Alexandra took the other.

The meal was as rich as the room in which we ate

it. It began with a delicious mushroom consommé. The grilled trout with almonds was, if anything, even better. It was made awkward, however, for me at least, by the fact that the twins ate nothing. No bowls or plates were placed before them. Nothing. They simply sat, hands in their laps, not even joining in the conversation. I felt most uncomfortable.

A crisp salad of lettuce, dandelion leaves, watercress, tomato and radishes, tossed in a piquant vinaigrette sauce was placed before each of us, accompanied by a very dry white wine. I was relieved when the footman serving us approached the twins, bearing a plate in each hand. My relief turned to shock when the servant put the plates in front of the young people, for each of them bore nothing but a single lettuce leaf!

His Grace's philosophy obviously included training the senses by placing the subject in the presence of the source of stimulation, in this case the most delicious food and drink, but forbidding them any indulgence. I see now that such a process has its point: forbidden fruit tastes all the sweeter. At the time, though, it seemed to me to be rather cruel.

Although six of us at the table were served succulent roast quail and partridge, a glorious upside-down pudding with cream, and a surprising variety of cheeses with dry biscuits, and although we drank several superb wines and a most excellent port, the twins were restricted to that single lettuce leaf, one morsel of rather sweaty-looking cheddar cheese and half a dozen dry wafers. For drink, they had water. And all the while the meal progressed, well over two hours in duration, His Grace was seeking to elicit from us comments about its deliciousness.

Questioning Karl later, for I was most concerned about it, I learnt to my relief that Alexandra and

Roderick were not in fact confined to a starvation diet. His Grace's procedure, and a cunning one it was too, was to supply his wards with a good breakfast, but then nothing all day until dinner.

Then, they sat as they had with us, witnessing but not partaking of a delicious meal, savouring the sights and the aromas of a cornucopia of superb dishes, their mouths watering. Afterwards, they would be taken off to a separate room, where they would be given a sample of a single dish from the meal they had witnessed, and a single glass of one of the wines that had been served.

Then, one at a time, they were required to stand before His Grace and comment upon what they had been given, cataloguing the various flavours, aromas, textures, and so on. If their description pleased His Grace in terms of its sensitivity and expertise, they were fed whatsoever they requested. If it did not, they went to bed empty.

It seemed, to me, to be rather a harsh regime, but His Grace swore by it as most effective. We, as contractors were expected to be just as effective in our particular field.

I intended to discuss it with Karl that night. We four had been allocated the whole of the south wing of His Grace's place, but even so only two rooms had been set out for our accommodation, both with very expansive beds which were more treble than double.

Clearly, His Grace's housekeeper, or butler, or whoever it was made the arrangements, had worked on the assumption that, being in the business we were, we would pair off as regards to bed partners. The assumption was correct, of course, but Karl had decided to pair off with Emily. He had done that quite frequently of late, and I had begun to suspect that some kind of association might be developing. If so, it was pleasing, for Karl was a lovely man and Emily deserved an expert lover.

That being the arrangement it, of course, meant that I had perforce to bed down with Ashoko. This was not, let me assure you, an unwelcome necessity. Ashoko was, by any standards, a man good to bed with. Not only was he sweet and understanding, but he was as good a lover as a woman could wish for.

Somehow or other, I had not lain with Ashoko for months. I remembered that delicious night when he had been my present on my eighteenth birthday two years and more ago, and how embarrassed I had been, and how satisfied, nay sated, next morning. I remembered our performance in that private theatre when, for the delectation of an audience, I had pretended to be the innocent daughter of a missionary and Ashoko a savage. He had performed a wild ballet, then cut off my clothes with a machete and pretended to molest me, and oh how voluptuous a shag it had been, made all the more so by the fact that a hundred eyes were boring into us as we shagged.

Now, as we both undressed, no words being passed between us, I became once more excited by his magnificent body, and other considerations left my mind. Ashoko's delicate sensitivity is such that he very carefully did not watch me as I pulled off my gown and my petticoats. It was as though he did not wish to intrude, if you see what I mean.

For myself, though, having glimpsed his glistening, muscular torso as he pulled off his cotton shirt, and warmed in my loins at the sight of his tight buttocks and thighs as he stepped out of his trousers, I wanted more contact. I wanted him to look at me as I undressed, just as I had looked at him.

Men have fewer garments to remove than women,

and simpler ones too. Thus, Ashoko was naked before I had even begun to tussle with my corset. I used it as an opportunity to flirt. What a strange idea, to flirt when we both knew that we were about to get into the same bed. Any woman, though, will know what I mean. We want to enjoy the small details as well as the shagging; to play, and toy and tease, so as to inflate our excitement before the act takes place.

I asked Ashoko to help me unlace my corset. We both knew that I did not really need such help, but both knew, too, that it was an invitation to play. To be attended upon, to be helped to strip off my underwear, by this beautiful, naked man was in itself arousing. To feel his gentle fingers delicately undoing my suspenders; to sense his warm skin so close to my own; to feel my corset loosen and my breasts bounce free; to feel his breath, and then his soft lips, on the curve of my neck and shoulder; all combined to set my nipples perking and to fill my loins with warmth.

I still had on my knickers and stockings. Ashoko moved to kneel in front of me, and proceeded to remove these from me slowly and with many fleeting kisses to the areas of my skin thus revealed. By the time I stepped out of my second stocking and stood naked for him, golden bubbles of arousal and anticipation were swelling and bursting in my vagina.

As Ashoko stood up, his superb cock showed that he was as ready as was I. He was, I already knew, a delicate and sensitive lover, and would not start on me straightaway, despite the fact that as soon as I was on my back he had raised my knees high and wide.

Instead of simply climbing between my legs and thrusting that magnificent cock into the sheath that was already wet for him, he toyed with me. Like butterflies, his knowing hands swept over my tingling skin from knees to neck. He kissed and suckled at my breasts, setting my nipples abuzz and hardening them like little nuts. His fingers parted the petals of my cunny, and gently, oh so gently, caressed my inner folds.

He found my cherry and circled it with his fingertips, tugging softly at its protective little cowl and making it stand proud and eager, and then leap and twitch as he found it with his tongue.

He was on the bed beside me now, the warmth of his hard body close against my own. His loins were level with my head. I reached with my hands to fondle the gleaming shaft and the tightening sack of his balls. I opened my lips and moved my head to him, his hot plum filling my mouth with musky ambrosia as we drifted into that slow, voluptuous joy Philippe told me is called *soixante-neuf*, this being a light-hearted reference to the positions of the lovers' bodies as they nuzzle and suck, and send each other to the stars.

As a professional lover, Ashoko was devilishly good with his mouth, and knew exactly what to do to set a woman throbbing. He also knew how to hold himself back, so that hard as I tried, lasciviously as I sucked and caressed his beautiful cock, he did not allow himself to come in my mouth. I, though, had no such reservations, or perhaps it was just that I had no such self control, for Ashoko soon had me cramping and throbbing towards my first orgasm; the first of any number he gave me that night, and indeed on succeeding nights.

Our work with Roderick and Alexandra began the very next day. His Grace had set out his requirements very clearly, but what methods we would use was left up to us. It was, as you can imagine, quite a delicate task.

We were required to sensualise our charges; to imbue them with dispositions open to all things sensuous; to train them, in fact, in all matters carnal. In Alexandra's case though, she was to remain a virgin. They in their turn were required to be completely obedient to any instruction we might give them.

It was as piquant a challenge as could be imagined, and while one part of me looked at it with some reservation as being perhaps too dissolute, my more libidinous side was rather looking forward to it. After all, I had myself been trained by Talesi and his tribe when I was even younger than these two, and I do not think it harmed me. Unlike Alexandra, though, I had not stayed a virgin for very long.

We began very simply, by taking tea with the twins. Since we had a wing of the mansion to ourselves, and His Grace would not be present, we naturally allowed our charges to enjoy the meal with us; for this indulgence they were pleasantly surprised and grateful.

After the meal we divided into pairs, myself and Ashoko taking Alexandra with us, Roderick going off with Emily and Karl.

'Now, my dear,' I said when we had sat down in the little drawing room that had been put at our disposal. 'I gather that you have been told something about why my colleagues and I are here. Is that not so?'

Alexandra was clearly quite nervous, but her breeding caused her to hide it and to try to appear confident. She could not help blushing, however, and there was a slight catch in her voice when she replied to confirm this. Her voice was very soft, and had a slightly husky quality to it which was decidedly attractive.

There was a considerable pause, and since she was

clearly not going to say more, I asked her, 'Would you tell us, then, what it is that you know?'

The delicious girl cast her eyes down and glanced about the carpet before finally looking up at me through long, curled eyelashes. She blushed more deeply, and a pink tongue ran over her soft lips before she took a breath and said, almost in a whisper, 'You are to help me become a woman, ma'am. To teach me the things I need to know to mix properly in society, and to please the gentlemen I will come to know.'

My first thought was that what we had been contracted to teach her would help her to mix very improperly in society, but I suppressed my smile.

'Anything more?' I asked. 'About, for example, pleasing a gentleman?'

It became a surprising, and surprisingly difficult conversation. Alexandra, and I supposed Roderick too, had been told by their guardian that we would teach them the ways of the flesh, but had given them little idea of what he meant by that cryptic phrase. Alexandra guessed that it meant something to do with her looks and her manner, for she had seen – from a distance, for she had not been permitted to attend adult entertainments, balls or dinner parties – how ladies conducted themselves in the company of gentlemen, and also knew that gaining a husband was important.

Only when I pressed her did she blushingly confess that the reference to flesh rather puzzled her, and she could only think it had something to do with bodies, though she had no idea what. At my prompting, she confessed that yes, she had felt disturbed and confused at certain sensations she had experienced, especially since her breasts had developed and her monthlies had begun.

It seemed, and I confess it irritated me greatly, that

His Grace had told, and allowed others to tell, Alexandra almost nothing of her development, or the facts of life. This was silly, because the real facts of life are money and the ability to control one's own destiny; facts denied to so many young women. Why, even when she went to her aunt, frightened because her first ever monthly was upon her, all she had been told was that it meant she was becoming a woman, and nothing more. How callous! How short sighted!

Now, all the poor girl could think was that we four would enlighten her while we were teaching her to become a woman. It was a daunting task, for as well as the lovely girl's nervousness there was an eagerness that was quite moving.

Taking Ashoko – at whom Alexandra had been constantly casting nervous glances – aside, I whispered my dilemma to him. He agreed with me that the young woman's near-total ignorance made our choice as to our initial approaches absolutely crucial. He agreed with me, too, that a certain question had to be answered before we could proceed at all.

His Grace had indicated at the beginning that his inculcation of his wards into the process of sensitisation dictated by his strange philosophy had been with their open consent. In the light of Alexandra's ignorance of matters carnal, conscience demanded that we test this consent with the girl herself. After all, can consent really be consent when based on ignorance?

I returned to where the sweet girl sat waiting, and questioned her. Had she really agreed to be placed under our tuition? How far had her guardians explained to her what to expect? Had she any idea at all what we might be doing? And most importantly, did she now wish to withdraw? If she did, I would myself undertake to beard her guardian and protect her from any wrath he might express.

At this, her eyes widened in surprise, and then she giggled. Oh, he would not be angry! He was a dear man, and loved both she and her brother. Of course they had agreed to having us as their teachers! She did not know exactly what we would be doing, but she knew it was to do with her body and was eager for it, because she had already felt strange and urgent sensations.

She blushed at a more pointed question, and admitted that, yes, she had touched herself both down there and on her bosoms, and it felt lovely. She was convinced that it would feel lovelier by the time we had finished with her.

She finished by clasping my hands in hers and almost pleaded with me to be her teacher. 'And Ashoko, too,' she added with a blush and another giggle.

My mind at rest about the sweet girl's willingness, I conferred with Ashoko as to how we might best proceed. We could, he suggested, move small step by small step, treading delicately so as not to shock her. That, though, would take a long time and, given her ignorance, might still leave her with a lot to learn when the time allotted for our contract ran out.

Like me Ashoko, who is very sensitive for a man, considered that if handled properly, a more direct approach would be more beneficial to Alexandra. We returned to where she was sitting, the light falling through the window setting her lush hair agleam, and highlighting the nervous twisting of her delicate fingers.

She raised her head when Ashoko and I sat down opposite her and returned our smiles, albeit still somewhat nervously.

'Alexandra, my dear –,' she started a little when it was Ashoko who spoke, his deep voice very soft and kind '– you are entirely correct as to the reason your guardian brought us here. It is indeed so that we can help you to cross the threshold of womanhood. And may I say we feel privileged to be chosen to guide someone as lovely as yourself.'

Alexandra blushed deeply and looked to the floor in shyness, but Ashoko continued as gently as before.

'There is a great deal you must learn, and some of it may at first disturb you. Please trust me, my dear, when I say that howsoever surprising or delicate what we shall require of you may seem, it is for your benefit and most important of all for your pleasure. Will you trust us?'

The lovely maiden looked from Ashoko to me and back again, her fingers twisting in her lap. She took a little breath and her tongue flicked across her sweet lips.

'Yes, sir,' she said almost in a whisper.

'You are a good girl,' I said, taking over. 'Now, we have some questions to begin with. Tell me, have you ever kissed a man, or been kissed?'

She looked startled by my question. 'Well, yes,' she said after a moment's hesitation. 'My uncle, of course, and Roderick when I say goodnight.'

We really had to dig, such was her unworldliness. It turned out that she had indeed been kissed, a couple of years ago, by the son of one of her uncle's visitors, and it had much disturbed her.

'He was so sudden, and all hot and excited for some reason,' she said.

'And how did you feel?' I pressed.

It was surprisingly easy, and a benefit of that very unworldliness we had thought a difficulty. She admitted readily that, after she had run off, she too had felt peculiar and had been much more breathless than mere fright or scampering off ought to have made her.

She had felt a strange tightness in her chest and her 'chubbies', as she delightfully called her breasts, had been all tingly.

Had she felt that same feeling on any other occasion? She had, and yes it was quite nice. Yes, she had touched them, quite often really, but of course nobody else ever had. Her first blush came when she admitted that, yes, she had sometimes wanted someone else to touch her.

She blushed even more deeply when I asked if she would like Ashoko to touch her. She did not reply in words, but those huge blue eyes spoke for her as they stared into mine. Shock was in them, then doubt, and then a limpid expression which confirmed that she did want him to but could not bring out the words.

She was flushed and panting a little when she moved to sit on Ashoko's lap at my suggestion. The weather being warm, she wore only a light cotton frock and, though her breasts were not large, I saw that her nipples were already perking against the thin material. We had hit on the right chord. Alexandra was inwardly as sensuous as any healthy seventeen-year-old girl, and as eager to be brought out, though she did not know how, or to what.

Her nervous, hopeful eyes remained locked on mine as she lowered herself into Ashoko's lap. She stiffened slightly, then relaxed as he put his arm around her waist and pulled her gently closer. Her eyes flicked from mine to Ashoko's as he placed a fingertip on her chin, and turned her face towards his own.

The first kiss, soft as it was, caused her eyes to widen. The second, third and fourth visibly softened her. A girl's first real kiss is a precious thing. I well remembered my own, when dear Jonathan had sent my senses reeling under that tree by the stream in

Africa. Ashoko was as expert as any man could be, and I well knew how seductive were the quick, soft kisses he was brushing Alexandra's sweet lips with.

By the time he gave her a longer kiss she had melted to him, and when his hand slipped softly on to her breast she only sighed, and began to return his kiss. She moved a little, opening herself to his hand, and her own rose to touch his cheek. Her eyes had drifted shut and she was lying against his chest, her head resting on his shoulder when his lips released hers.

Her eyes fluttered open for a moment when Ashoko began to undo her buttons. I suddenly thought that we had proceeded too quickly, but Alexandra's eyes merely drifted shut again. She gave a little gasp as his hand slipped inside her frock, and her face nestled itself into his neck.

We had not planned it, but if we had it would have been a stroke of genius. Ashoko kissed and fondled the lovely, innocent young woman for perhaps half an hour then took his hand from her breasts and eased her off his lap.

The look on her face, and the shining softness in her eyes, eyes which looked enormous in her flushed face, and the regretful little sigh she whispered, like a child deprived of a sweet, all told plain that she did not wish this to stop! And the limpid glances she could not help casting towards Ashoko at dinner that evening told volumes.

The next day, Alexandra was almost unable to contain her impatience for us to take her to that little sitting room again.

The first thing she did when we got there was to gaze up at Ashoko with shining eyes, and ask him if he was going to kiss her again. He did, though it was simply a peck on her lips, which clearly disappointed her just as we had hoped it would. Today's was to be a different kind of lesson.

Alexandra confirmed that, although when very young she and her twin had been bathed together, she had in reality no idea what a man's person looked like. When Ashoko calmly stood, and began to remove his clothes, her pretty lips made a little 'O' of astonishment, and she backed against the wall, her eyes darting back and forth from him to me, her hand to her mouth.

As I have related elsewhere, Ashoko is one of the most impressive men I have ever seen. As well as being disturbingly handsome of face, his body is magnificent. Six feet in height, broad of shoulder and deep of chest, his lovely skin, smooth and dark, gleams tautly over lithe, hard muscles.

Even as familiar as I was with the ravishing sight, I was hard put to it to concentrate my attention on Alexandra rather than Ashoko. Her expression at first had been shocked and a little scared. As Ashoko cast off his jacket then his shirt, her eyes widened even further as they flicked over the revealed torso, and the expression in them began to change.

Ashoko had worn leather pumps and no hose, so there was no awkward preamble to his unbuttoning and stepping out of his trousers. As he stood there naked, save for a pair of short cotton drawers, her hand had moved from her mouth to her bosom, and her eyes were fixed upon the area of Ashoko's loins.

And when he slipped the drawers off and stood before us in his naked glory, the sweet girl's eyes seemed to almost start out of her head. She was by now pressed back against the wall, one hand on her bosom the other hovering close to her tummy.

There are subtle signs of a woman's arousal which

betray her even if she prevaricates. Alexandra was not prevaricating, but simply astounded and confused by what was happening, and she was showing all those signs.

Patches of pink had suffused her cheeks. Her lips had parted and were plump and red. Through her open mouth her breath was quick and shallow. Her lovely head was a little bowed towards where her eyes were fixed, and I could see her small nipples standing against the silk of her blouse. She looked ravishing, and for a moment I wondered how even a professional like Ashoko could avoid getting stiff at the sight of her.

We had planned that he should not, of course, for this was to be Alexandra's first real lesson. Putting on a matter-of-fact manner, and talking dispassionately like a schoolmarm, I began to explain to Alexandra the names and nature of a man's parts. It took great self control, for Alexandra's expression, and the way her eyes flicked with amazing rapidity from me to the parts I was describing, made it difficult to contain my laughter.

My amusement died down when I got to the serious business of the lesson, and indeed was replaced by a sort of sisterliness, for the sweet thing had clearly never even dreamt about what followed.

Talking the while about what I was doing, though quietly now and not at all like a schoolteacher, I cupped Ashoko's tight, heavy balls in one hand, and began to caress his shaft with the other. Alexandra caught her breath when Ashoko began to swell into pride. He was, by any standard, magnificent, and I almost envied Alexandra this, her first sight of a grown man.

Ashoko's belly was flat and corrugated with muscle. His thighs were hard, curved and gleaming.

Above, his sex reared itself arrogantly, a beautiful lance demanding attention. Had I not been in the middle of giving a lesson I would have become greedy for him much quicker than I did. As it was, my contractual duty was to demonstrate to my sweet charge that there was nothing to fear from this magnificent equipment, and that it could be handled, and how it would react to a woman's touch.

This I did, torn between the pleasure I always got from Ashoko's body, and my concern that we encourage, rather than scare, our virgin pupil. That she was herself torn was betokened by the way the signs of arousal in her had increased, and the fact that despite having pressed her back against the wall, there was just the hint of a rocking movement at her thigh-tops, as though her loins were unconsciously seeking some kind of stimulation.

Alexandra started when I said, and then repeated louder when she seemed not to hear, 'Come, dear, it is your turn now.'

She actually looked scared as she stared at me, and I had to encourage her gently while I continued to caress Ashoko. She approached very tentatively, glancing apprehensively from me to what I was stroking. She licked her lips nervously, and reached out with her trembling fingers as though terrified she would get burned.

At her first touch of Ashoko's gorgeous cock, she did indeed snatch her fingers away. When she looked to me in surprise, I smiled and cooed encouragement. Her second touch, with just the tip of her forefinger, was less afraid. She slipped it slowly along Ashoko's glossy length, nearly to his base and then back up again, to circle around his smooth bulb.

On her face was the expression of a child concentrating on some new and strange wonder. When her fingertip brushed across the little eyelet at Ashoko's tip, his cock twitched at the stimulation, and she snatched her hand away as though stung. She needed no more than a smile of encouragement to return her hand this time, and soon she had plucked up the nerve to circle him with her fingers and thumb. Glancing at me, she bowed her head and concentrated on stroking him as she had seen me do. Soon, too, she had reached out her other hand and was cupping his balls.

'Is it not beautiful, my dear?' I whispered, my head close to hers.

'Oh, yes!' she breathed. 'And so, so warm and – and –'

Her voice trailed off as she became lost in what she was doing. Ashoko was a miracle of self control. We had agreed when planning this lesson, that he would not come lest it scare Alexandra. I well remembered how startled I was when I first saw a man come, even though I had already felt it in my mouth and my cunny. The jerking and the suddenness with which the pearly effusions shoot out in gout after gout, can be quite surprising if you are not prepared for it.

Despite Ashoko's near miraculous self control, I stopped Alexandra caressing him after only a few minutes, and was gratified to see her give another little sigh of disappointment. It was time to move on to the next step.

Fourteen

There was, of course, as much talking as doing in those first days of the twins' education. Once Alexandra had experienced the delight of having her breasts caressed, and had seen and touched Ashoko's prick we had something concrete, as it were, to work on.

Her face when I explained to her about making love, and the multifareous delights a woman can derive from her body and from a man, expressed astounded disbelief. Explained clinically, even in the light of the minimal new knowledge Alexandra had gained, matters of sex do, I suppose, sound weird and hard to believe. Even so, we decided to explain matters such that our sweet pupil would be at least a little prepared for what she was to experience.

She was very surprised when, on our third day, we proposed that she was to remain with Ashoko and I overnight, and share our bed. Indeed, so nervous of the proposition was she that she actually asked her guardian about it over dinner that evening. Asked quite boldly, in fact, though she was blushing furiously. His Grace hurrumphed, and looked hard at Ashoko and I.

'The girl remains a virgin, what, and will so remain,' he said firmly.

I was, inwardly, a little irritated at this part of our contract, for it was not specified that Roderick was to remain virginal. It was not another example of that hypocrisy by which society ensures that girls remain ignorant until their wedding night, for were we not teaching Alexandra a great deal. It seemed to me, though, to be a little unfair that Roderick's education was to include the ultimate delight, for it was presumed that he would get to shag both Emily and I, whereas Alexandra was to be denied the glory of being introduced to fucking by such skillful lovers as Karl and Ashoko. However, I nodded acquiescence to His Grace's requirement.

'So be it, then,' he said, causing Alexandra to blush anew, and Roderick to smile at her sympathetically. 'You will share their bed this night, my girl, and any other night they require. Now, where the devil is the roast?'

We encouraged Alexandra by ensuring that there were several dishes from dinner waiting in our rooms for her – for as usual the twins had witnessed, but not partaken of, the meal – as well as some wine. Her pleasure at our gesture eased her nerves, though did not completely calm them. Thus, when her meal was finished and we invited her towards the bedroom, she flushed a little and bit her lip.

Once in the bedroom, there was little we could do to ease her nerves. Who would not be nervous going to a bed for sex, for the first time? And especially with two other people! What we could do was to turn it into some kind of ceremony, and so Ashoko took off his clothes first, taking his time and moving so as to try to stir Alexandra up somewhat. He certainly stirred me up, but then he always did!

When it came to my turn to remove my clothes, it

was I who received a surprise, for Alexandra watched me even more closely than she had Ashoko. At first it was somewhat disconcerting, but when I realised that her fascination must be because she had not seen a woman's body before, it became more than a little arousing.

There is, as you well know, a streak of what I call the exhibitionist in me. I found myself undressing for Alexandra as I would for a lover, and getting just as stirred up by the process.

I had on, apart from my frock of course, only silk stockings and some of Monsieur Delat's lingerie: a fine silk *chemisette*, with pretty lace panels decorating my breasts and forming an inverted 'V' from my navel down, and a pair of his most delicate lacy knickers, loose and short in the leg.

Alexandra's eyes widened when she saw my under-things, and widened further as I pulled them off. Clearly, she had never seen such delicate undergarments, and even more clearly she had never seen a woman naked before. I confess that my breasts warmed and my nipples stood up at the way she looked at them. I felt not a little hot, too, at the way her eyes explored the area revealed when I dropped my knickers. I calmed myself, however, as I climbed on to the bed beside the already recumbent Ashoko, for we had business to conduct.

And then I learnt yet another new thing about how people's minds work. I had assumed that Alexandra would need coaxing if she was to undress, would do it shyly, and would want the lamp turned off. I was wrong. After only a tiny hesitation, her fingers went to the buttons at her neck. She faced us; she did not want the lamp extinguished; she wanted us to see her.

It was almost a performance as she removed first one garment and then another, pausing only to fold each one neatly and place it on a chair. She was the very epitome of loveliness. When she pulled off her *chemise*, her breasts were already flushed and her pink nipples stood erect. When she pulled off her cambric drawers and stood before us naked save for her little pumps, there was a gleam of triumph and excitement in her huge eyes.

She posed for a moment, looking like some gorgeous mythical nymph. Her breasts were on the small side, but firm and tip-tilted. Her skin was white and smooth, her legs long, and her hips slender. The fuzz of curls upon her mount was as glossy black as her hair, and sparse enough for the swell of her slit to be glimpsed below.

I felt my own breasts tensing at the sight of her, and that lovely warm moistness between my legs. Ashoko, too, was very obviously stirred by the sight of her as she moved towards the bed, for his cock was thickening nicely and his eyes were shining.

The revelations about Alexandra continued. The first thing she did when she got on the bed was to lie beside Ashoko and begin to kiss him, pressing her delicious body against his flank and slipping one leg over his. No longer did she show any sign of nervousness. Quite the reverse, in fact, for although inevitably unfamiliar she joined enthusiastically in everything we did. Perhaps more importantly, she showed that she trusted us completely, not once demurring at what we taught her.

She did evince some surprise when, having got her to lie between us, I kissed her as well as Ashoko. She obviously had not expected to be kissed by a woman. She returned my kisses, though, and delicious she was too.

Our intention, Ashoko's and mine, was to show Alexandra how glorious, and how intense, the sensations of her body could be; to get her to receive pleasure before teaching her to give it. To this end, we made her remain passive under our kisses and caresses, not moving save as we moved her.

At first, her glorious eyes were wide, taking in everything. Soon though, under the influence of our caresses, they drifted shut, and her face took on that soft half-smile of arousal. There was a moment of tension when Ashoko first slipped his hand down below her navel, but she soon relaxed again, her lips becoming more urgent on mine as he began to tease the length of her tender crease.

When he moved down, and parted her knees, and began to nuzzle her with his lips, she gave a little mew of surprise and her eyes widened to gaze doubtfully into mine. In moments, the doubt was gone, to be replaced by a flash of surprised delight before her eyelids slowly drifted shut. Her head rolled back, her full lips parted, and she gave a tiny moan of pleasure as Ashoko parted her sweet folds with gentle fingers and began to lick her.

I well know how wonderful that sensation is, and almost envied our lovely pupil, for not only was this the first time she had been touched between her legs, but she was being touched in the most delicate, most loving way a man can touch a woman. In only minutes, her perfect body was beginning to flex and tense, her pelvis moving against Ashoko's mouth, her breath becoming ragged.

I moved to kiss and lick her breasts, increasing her sensations. She gave a soft moan when I took her nipple between my lips, and her hand began to stroke my hair.

Her orgasm, the first of her life, was sudden and surprised us all. One minute she was lying passive, one hand above her head while the other stroked my hair, her tummy and pelvis flexing slowly and rhythmically as her arousal grew. The next, she was giving out little surprised yelps and her body was bucking frantically against Ashoko as her climax swept over her.

It lasted only ten seconds, perhaps, but they were seconds which astonished Alexandra, and even scared her a little, for when I looked up she was staring at me wide eyed. I smiled and kissed her cheek.

'What happened?' she whispered, a little shiver passing over her as Ashoko moved his face away from her pink and swollen cunny.

Alexandra was a sweet and willing pupil, and we gave her several more orgasms before I suggested that we slip beneath the blankets to get some sleep. The last thing she said after we had snuggled down was, 'Please, ma'am, may I hold Ashoko's penis?' I went to sleep with a smile in my heart.

Progress with Roderick had been as smooth as with his sister. He had not been as nervous as she, and indeed Karl and Emily had needed to curb his eagerness somewhat at first. Unlike Alexandra he was not entirely innocent for, like pretty well all growing lads I suppose, he had experienced frequent erections and had indulged in that safety valve called wanking.

Like Ashoko and I, Karl and Emily had adopted the approach of making him experience intense pleasure before requiring him to give it. Emily could not suppress a smile when she told me how extremely he had reacted the first few times she touched him, and let him touch her. 'Why,' she said, a giggle in her voice, 'the first time I rubbed my hand over his cock, the poor boy came in his breeches!'

The image brought back sweet memories of my lovely William, on the sea voyage back to England a couple of years ago, and I too smiled fondly. Was it not natural for a lad not yet quite eighteen to become over-excited when a woman as lovely, and as naughty, as Emily caressed his sex, even through the cloth of his breeches?

They had managed to calm the lad by dint of making him come over and over again – a delectable fate, to my mind – and had now reached the stage where they were training him in holding back. This, said Karl with a grin, was far from easy for Emily was a terrible tease. Mind you, he added, that was in its way a bonus, for they had told Roderick that he would not get to shag her until he could show satisfactory self control. Since it was very clear that he desired, above almost anything, to shag Emily, this was a great spur to his efforts.

I had felt reservations about our contract to educate Roderick and Alexandra both before we began and when we first met our pupils. Their beauty and their eagerness soon swept my reservations aside. Within a few days and nights I felt a sort of loving friendliness towards Alexandra, and I knew from the shine in her eyes that she felt the same for me. Teaching her became a joy.

Her eagerness to learn how to give, as well as receive, pleasure warmed me. We used Ashoko as a sort of living sampler; an aid to her education. It became almost a contest between the two of them, Alexandra trying her best to bring him off (from the very first time she managed it, she delighted in making Ashoko come) and Ashoko holding back with all the professionalism in his power.

So far, we had confined her to kissing us, snuggling her body next to ours, and caressing Ashoko with her hands. Her eyes when I described to her, and then moved to demonstrate, sucking him off were a joy. Those amazingly expressive blue orbs told me without a doubt that Alexandra had wondered about just such a thing, and was excited that it was indeed a possibility. How could one not delight in such a creature?

Fellating Ashoko at any time was delicious; doing it for Alexandra's edification was even more arousing. Watching her approach him for that purpose was entrancing. She glanced rapidly from him to me, her eyes shining as she knelt on our bed. She cupped him in her soft hands, breathed deeply, and licked her sweet lips before bowing her head almost reverently. Her long black hair fell across her face as she bent forward, and she shook it aside as though determined that it should not conceal from my eyes what she was doing.

Ashoko kept perfectly still, his wonderful cock thick and still shining from the juice of my own mouth, which had so recently left it. Alexandra circled his base with her pale fingers. Her lips parted to a perfect 'O' as she lowered her face towards him. At first she took in only his plum, her eyes closed and her cheeks working a little as she began to suck.

Soon, she was moving more deeply, and I thrilled to the signs of her mounting excitement as she squeezed his shaft and balls, and her cheeks bulged and caved; she shuffled her knees apart and worked her hips against the hand Ashoko had slipped up between her thighs.

She was taking fully half his length now, her face and breasts flushed and her movements rapid. I became nervous lest her voluptuous actions should bring Ashoko off too violently and he should scare her. It is a shock when a man comes in your mouth for the first time.

I need not have worried. She did indeed bring Ashoko off, and he did indeed come deep into her sweet mouth, but it was as if she were born to it. She did not pull back, or evince surprise or distaste. Indeed, if anything she sucked harder, more greedily, her cheeks and throat working ravenously to take and swallow all he could give.

Even when she had milked him to the end, she kept licking and sucking, and I actually had to grip her shoulder and tell her to stop before she eased up on him. And when she sat back on her heels her entrancing features, incapable of hiding emotion, radiated joy and triumph.

It may not have been permissible, under the terms her guardian had set, for her to shag Ashoko, but she clearly felt that this was the next best thing. Thereafter, indeed, we had actually to restrain her, for she awoke Ashoko next morning with his cock in her mouth, and importuned him to let her do it so frequently that even Ashoko became quite drained.

Our time with the twins was cut short in the unhappiest of manners. We received a telegram on our sixth day with His Grace, telling us to return to London at once because Amelia was unwell. His Grace was away from home at the time, and the twins' Aunt Emmelina was very gracious about it.

She accepted our assurances that her wards were pretty well fully prepared, and summoned her carriage to take us to the local railway station. As we said our farewells I kept to myself the thought that, though we had handed back Alexandra as a virgin, it would surely not be long before she found a way of ridding herself of that encumbrance.

And why not, I thought. I had myself ceased to be a virgin when I was sixteen, nearly two years younger

235

than she was now. Besides, Roderick had been happily shagging since our third day, and what was sauce for the gander should also be sauce for the goose!

Amelia had caught the influenza. She was in a sorry state indeed when we got to her, very feverish and weak. The rest of the household, too, was in a turmoil of fright and tears, for not only Amelia had contracted this awful scourge. Albert, the groom, was also down with it, and poor Bailey, Amelia's lovely old butler had actually passed away with it.

Unknown to us, buried away in the country as we had been, the influenza had swept London in an epidemic. The newspapers were full of it, proposing as cures such things as sweat baths or breathing the steam from an infusion of oil of cloves.

Everyone with any sense knows, of course, that there is no cure for this dreadful disease. All one can do is to keep the patient warm, nurse them tenderly, and pray that they have the native strength to battle their way through.

To our joy, Albert recovered quite soon, for he was indeed a strong young man. Amelia, though, took longer, and had us very worried at times. Blessedly, recover she did, though she was left very weak. At her doctor's insistence, and over her protests, we sent her off with Paul for a few weeks convalescence in Dorset.

It was a gloomy house we returned to after seeing Amelia off at the railway station. Though there was of course comfort in the fact that Amelia and Albert had both got over their illnesses, we had all loved dear old Bailey, and mourned his loss.

None of us felt at all like business, but fortunately the influenza epidemic, even though it was dying out now, had kept people indoors and so we were not disappointing many punters. After an idle week, though, Karl and I agreed that the *Silken Web* should re-open for business.

Thus, I found myself, much sooner than anyone had expected, assuming Amelia's position. I was, albeit only temporarily, the Madam of the *Silken Web*!

To be entirely frank, while being the Madam of a flourishing brothel has its rewards, in the friendships one finds among the girls and the contacts one makes among well-placed clients, it does militate against certain freedoms one might have enjoyed otherwise.

Although I was free to stroll about the *Silken Web*, and chat with the girls and the punters, my position forbade me from engaging in business. In addition, my opportunities for private engagements became very circumscribed, for I had to attend the bordello every night to look after the girls and collect the fees.

Thus, for the first time in years – since I was sixteen, in fact – I found that I was more often in bed alone than with a lover. At first this did not really matter, for I was busy running the business, and learning about my clients and my suppliers and, most of all, about my girls.

Karl was more often away than not. Ashoko, naturally, was much in demand among the ladies. Kate and Emily were very popular. I took Albert to my bed a couple of times, but it was not entirely satisfactory. He was a strong and energetic man, but lacking in finesse and subtlety. I found myself thinking often of my Philippe.

Lest you think ill of me, I must hasten to insist that this was not simply because of my sleeping so often alone. In running my bordello I had often to think of the things he had taught me while I was with him in

Paris, and one line of thinking runs easily into another.

I had known many lovers. Most I could not even remember. Some – Jonathan, Talesi, Motallo, William Forbes, the Bey, Karl, Ashoko – had found a place in my heart. Even with these dear men, though, I would not describe it as love, at least not in the usual sense. I loved them as friends and for the joy of the sex we shared, but I was never in love with any of them.

I was, I realised, in love with Philippe. I had fallen in love with him that first time he looked so deeply into my eyes, had fallen deeper while we were together at his house in Paris, and was still in love with him now.

This new understanding was forced upon me when I received two letters on the same day.

The first one I opened was from Amelia, and came as a profound surprise. She was well recovered through her convalescence, but was not returning to London. Instead, she had decided out of the blue, to retire from the business, to journey to Spain for the better climate, and to marry Paul!

I, and Karl as her associate, would be contacted by her solicitor to sort out the details of the transfer, but so far as she was concerned the business was now ours, in return for an annuity to be paid into her bank account monthly.

Amelia's news was so staggering that it was two days, two frantic days of sending telegrams, and talking with Karl, and adjusting myself to these daunting changes, before I opened the second letter. It was from Philippe.

I had known it probably would be, of course. Who

else would be writing to me from France? Even so, my heart gave a little lurch of excitement when I saw his signature. The letter contained the wonderful news that Philippe would be coming to London a month hence, and asked if I would receive him.

As if there could have been any doubt!

Since my wonderful time in Paris as Philippe's pupil, I had been in an ambivalent state. I have always prided myself on being in control of my emotions. As you will know, I have met many wonderful people, and loved them in my way. That way had encompassed the most intimate and joyous love-making, and had taken me to the very heights of passion and delight. There was a place in my heart for each and every one of them.

With Philippe it was different. Whereas the others had a place in my heart, Philippe had taken it over completely. Never had I felt such trembling joy at somebody's mere presence. Never had I felt such an aching desire to please, or to feel the thrill of giving pleasure.

And never, in all the meetings and partings of my eventful life, had I been so downcast at leaving somebody. I realised when I read his letter, that in the long, dragging months since I had returned from Paris, I had been merely hiding from myself my feelings for Philippe, and had not killed them off as I had pretended to myself.

I suppose that, had I not seen or heard from him again, I would have been able to bury my love for him; I would have been able to wrap it in some kind of scar tissue until it became inert. I had done it before when Talesi and Motallo, the two men who had loved me and introduced me to the wonders of physical sensation, had disappeared from my life. I had done it again when I left the Bey behind in M—, though with him it was easier for we had only spent a couple of nights together.

I thought I had managed it with Philippe also, until his letter set my fingers trembling and my heart fluttering. He would be here in a month! A whole month. Oh, how could I wait?

It was lucky that I was kept so busy getting myself fully into Amelia's role in the business, else that month would have seen the end of my fingernails, I nibbled them so much. I had to take several essays at replying to Philippe's letter, both because my handwriting was ragged from trembling fingers and because they kept turning themselves into silly outpourings of passion. I managed, in the end, to send something fairly sensible, and buried myself in business to make the time run quicker.

The business Amelia and Karl had run was more varied and extensive than I had imagined. As well as the *Silken Web*, which turned out to be an amazingly profitable enterprise, there was a long list of private clients, a register of events such as house parties, and the two charitable institutions the business supported.

These last were a large mansion in Surrey which served as a sort of almshouse for those of Amelia's girls who had retired from business, but did not have the means to support themselves, and a sort of clinic near Clapham Common for girls who had become unwell, or who had let themselves become pregnant. These establishments were financed from the profits of the *Silken Web* and levies on the takings from events, and I felt both pride and admiration for Amelia in setting them up.

Her care for her girls did not end there, either, for the business retained several medical doctors, and paid for regular medical checks as well as any fees incurred by a girl becoming unwell. As well as that, Amelia had even set up a pension fund with one of the large life assurance companies, towards which the business as well as the girls themselves contributed. All in all, it was a most benevolent organisation when you consider that ours was a business easily open to abuse, and the exploitation of its working girls.

Another side of the business which might well have been abused was the details we held of our private clients. There were scores of these, and some of the names astonished me. Prominent businessmen, members of parliament and of the aristocracy, even high-ranking churchmen. If the ledgers in which these names were held, together with any notable preferences, or even the dates and the names of the girls they had hired, had ever fallen into the wrong hands, the scandal would have rocked society.

Absolute discretion had been the first requirement Amelia had dinned into me, and these ledgers showed that Amelia practised it herself to a high degree.

Mind you, I have to confess that, reading through the ledgers and seeing some of the special preferences and little quirks of the gentlemen named therein, I was often driven to giggle. I still do, in fact, when certain members of parliament or clerics are quoted in the newspapers pontificating upon society's morals!

One of the things that warmed me was the manner in which my new role as the Madam was accepted by all the girls, even though I was much younger than most of them. I neither found nor heard of any resentment among them, and quite a few, including of course Kate and Emily, actually congratulated me.

My new position also meant that I could withdraw from the active side of the business, from the need to service punters. Do not misunderstand me. I had enjoyed almost every aspect of my life as a 'working girl', and had enjoyed many happy experiences shagging any and all comers. I love sex, and have only sympathy for – and doubts as to the sincerity of – any woman who says she does not.

The advent of Philippe in my life, though, had made sex with other men less pleasing. I had thrown myself into work as a means of getting over my loss of Philippe. Indeed, that first night I had made myself go back to the *Silken Web* weeks after returning from Paris, I had gone at it rather frantically. You might even have said that it was me shagging the punters, rather than them shagging me.

I knew now, however, that I had only been working to hide an ache. Now my Philippe was coming back to me, and the thought of making love with any man other than him became anathema to me.

The days dragged past no matter how deep I buried myself in work. At last, though, the magic day arrived. I could not sleep a wink the night before, but wandered about the house hugging myself with excited anticipation. I was dressed and ready hours before it was time to go to the railway terminus. Karl, Kate and Emily were all as eager and happy as I, and teased me light-heartedly for being so excited.

I would not let anybody come with me, save Albert to drive the carriage of course. I got to the station early, and bought my platform ticket, and waited with racing heart.

After a million years, the train pulled in, belching steam but seeming to move oh, so slowly. Carriage doors banged open. Passengers poured off the train. There were so many of them. Philippe was not among them. He was not there!

Then he was, half way along the platform, looking tall and beautiful. My heart bursting with joy, I squealed and ran to him for all the world like some silly child.

He saw me, put down his cases and held wide his arms. I ran into them, panting as much from joy as from running. He folded me into himself as I clung on, looking down at me with shining, loving eyes. He bent to kiss me, a long, soft, loving kiss which ravished my heart and made me near faint with rapture.

Epilogue

My Great Aunt Lydia's manuscript ended there, on that rapturous note. I searched hard for more of the manuscript, almost pulling her old desk apart in my efforts to see whether there might be another secret drawer, but found nothing. Having lived her story with her for so long, though, I could not leave it to lie. I determined to research further, to find out what I could.

There was not much evidence, for many of her papers had been disposed of over the years. There were no diaries, and very few letters. I was, however, able to piece together the skeleton of what happened in her life.

Somerset House revealed that an Amelia Amberson had indeed existed, born in 1847. I could trace no record of a club called the *Silken Web*, nor find out much of what happened to Lydia between the autumn of 1902, when her story ends, and 1916, when she bought the cottage in which I first found her manuscript hidden away in the secret drawer of her desk.

Research in the village told me that she had been widely respected and that, though little was known of her background, the people had assumed her to be a war widow, as so many women were in those days. She had led a quiet, respectable life, and was liked and admired by all who knew her, though she had always kept her distance.

The only evidence I could find concerning Philippe was a single letter, folded and unfolded so often that the creases were almost worn through, as though it had been read many, many times. It was dated August 1914, and the ink was smudged in places as if by tears.

It was signed by Philippe du Fallier himself, and stated that he had taken up a commission in the French army, 'to help the motherland drive out those foul Boche'. There was nothing else. I can only suppose that he, like so many, many others, perished in the trenches, and that Lydia was, in a way, a war widow.

There were two further discoveries which I should tell you about before I close.

Among Lydia's personal papers I discovered a note about a bank security box. Having the correct papers, I found no difficulty in getting the bank to allow me access. I had thought the box might contain more papers, perhaps her diaries, or love letters from Philippe.

Instead, it contained only one item: a small inlaid wooden chest, bound with brass. The key was in the lock. I held my breath as I raised the lid, and then let it out in a gasp of wonder. The chest, too, contained only a single item. It was a gold necklace, the one Lydia had described wearing when she was presented to the Bey for that night as his temporary concubine.

It was as she described it, fixing high at the neck and sweeping down in a great curtain to the tops of the breasts, and with a huge pendant ruby. In fact, it was even more stunning than she described, and I gazed on it with awe.

It is still in its chest in the bank security box. I could not even contemplate selling it, and did not even take it out to have it valued. I like to think that Lydia kept it as a souvenir of that magical night with her Bey, and as such it is priceless.

The final discovery was the most astonishing of all and, in terms of my own life, made all the others pale into insignificance.

By roundabout means, indeed almost by accident, I discovered that in 1912, when she was thirty, Lydia gave birth to a child. So far as I know she never married, and in those days there was a terrible stigma attached to illegitimacy. That her reputation in the village was clear suggested to me that Amelia's benevolent society swung into action when her condition became obvious, and she went to the very clinic Amelia had set up to help her girls in those circumstances.

She was delivered of a healthy boy in the early hours of the morning on 24 October 1912. He was christened Philip and given her own surname, Masters. The rest of the story I know from sources more immediate that Lydia's papers.

The boy was fostered by a married friend of Lydia's called Emily Foster, who I assumed was the Emily of Lydia's bordello days. He was told that his father had perished in the Great War, and that his mother had subsequently died of a broken heart.

There was a considerable estate, which enabled him to be sent to good schools, and subsequently to Oxford University, where he took a degree in history, and became a teacher at his old public school.

During his growing years, he was often taken to visit his Aunt Lydia, who lavished great affection on him, and whom he came to love almost as much as his 'mother', Emily Foster. He continued to visit her in adulthood, with the only long gap in his visits occurring when he was on active service as a naval officer during World War Two.

After the war he married, and a few years later his wife gave birth to a daughter, though tragically she died giving birth. He raised the child himself, with the help of a series of nurses and nannies, and as she grew up often took her to visit his aunt.

By now, you will have guessed what it took my numbed mind ages to encompass.

My father was called Philip Masters. I was named Philippa after him. His birthday was 24 October and he was born in 1912. He served as an officer on a frigate during World War Two, and married my mother in 1947. He frequently took me to visit my Great Aunt Lydia, and I had continued to visit her after he died in a car accident in 1962.

I had often mused about the obvious bond of affection between my father and Great Aunt Lydia, and had been astonished when I had been her sole inheritor after she too passed away. Now, all was clear, though I still found it hard to believe.

That dignified little old lady I had been so in awe of whenever I visited her; that woman who, when young, had lived through such astounding experiences as would have shattered the minds of weaker women; that silvered-haired, lavender-scented lady, who gave never a sign that she had been the captive sex-slave of an African tribe, and the concubine of a Turkish Bey, and later a *fille de joie* and finally the Madam of a thriving brothel; that astonishing woman, in short, was not my Great Aunt Lydia at all.

She was my grandmother!

NEW BOOKS

Coming up from Nexus and Black Lace

Intimate Games by Julia Marlowe

January 1997   Price £4.99   ISBN: 0 352 33138 0

After meeting the enigmatic and persuasive Gilles at a party, the sexually adventurous Arianne Fontaine takes him on board as a partner in the exclusive club she has created at her luxury home in Paris; a place where the rich and ribald can indulge their most daring fantasies. When they meet Fleur – a novice to lascivious behaviour – Gilles and Arianne draw her into a life of bizarre sex and ritual discipline.

Molten Silver by Delaney Silver

January 1997   Price £4.99   ISBN: 0 352 33137 2

This is the first collection of short stories by one of Nexus's bestselling authors. In these stories of fetishism and unusual behaviour, characters live in a world where decadence and depravity are never far away – and naughty behaviour never goes unpunished. Each story is flavoured with a liberal amount of deviance.

Candida's Secret Mission by Virginia Lasalle

February 1997   Price £4.99   ISBN: 0 352 33141 0

Candie has a new job at a secret government establishment high in the Bavarian Alps. However, this is no ordinary employment; topsecret investigations are being conducted to measure female arousal and highly-sexed young women are needed to help research. If all goes well, Candie could be in for a big reward. There are so many tempting distractions: Sister Serena, who performs the intimate medical examinations, and Herr Direktor, who oversees the delectable lovelies in his charge.

New Erotica 3 – Extracts from the Best of Nexus

February 1997   Price £4.99   ISBN: 0 352 33142 9

This is the third volume of extracts from the best-selling and most well-liked Nexus books of the past couple of years. The settings are as eclectic as the sexual peccadilloes of the characters. Emma, for instance, in *Emma's Secret World*, who gives up her life of privilege to become the slave of the cruel lesbian mistress. And Constance, employed as a Cornish Governess, who soon finds herself administering discipline to the local gentlemen – including the vicar! These are just two of the stories featured in this anthology which reflects the diverstiy of the Nexus imprint.

Nadya's Quest by Lisette Allen
January 1997   Price £4.99   ISBN: 0 352 33135 6

Empress Catherine of Imperial Russia was notorious for her sexual appetite and unusual pastimes. In this story, she is on the look-out for a new lover, who must be handsome, virile, and able to satisfy her lust for flesh. When the young Nadya, who comes to St Petersburg in the year of 1788, finds Swedish seafarer, Axel, she wants him as a lover. But so too does everyone else, including the Empress. Against a backdrop of unbridled decadence, the Imperial Court is soon to erupt with jealousy and sedition.

Desire Under Capricorn by Louisa Francis
January 1997   Price £4.99   ISBN: 0 352 33136 4

1870s Australia. The feisty Dita Jones is engaged to Jonathon Grimshaw, the most eligible bachelor in Sydney's polite society. But when the young couple are shipwrecked, they are thrown into a world where survival instincts and natural urges triumph over civilised values. Jonathon is appalled at his fiancée's overtly sexual behaviour and fellow castaway Matt Warrender cannot resist Dita's ample charms. After they're rescued, things will never be the same again and Matt cannot forget the woman who has so inflamed his lust.

The Master of Shilden by Lucinda Carrington
February 1997   Price £4.99   ISBN: 0 352 33140 2

When successful interior designer Elise St John is offered a commission at a remote castle, she isn't prepared for some of the more curious terms of her employment. She has been chosen to create rooms where guests will be able to realise their most erotic fantasies. She soon finds herself indulging in some fantasies of her own – which soon become reality. Max Lannsen – the owner of the castle – is dark and mysterious while Blair Devlin – the riding instructor – is overtly confident. Both have designs on Elise. Designs which manifest themselves in bizarre and very sexual ways.

Modern Love – a Black Lace Anthology
February 1997   Price £4.99   ISBN: 0 352 33158 5
Black Lace is the leading imprint of erotic fiction for women and the publishing sensation of the decade. This is the first anthology of the series with an exclusively comtemporary theme. Seduction and mystery and darkly sensual behaviour are the key words to this unique collection of writings from the female perspective. Worlds of passion collide with unbridled erotic exploration and scintillating characters delight in the thrill of total surrender to pleasure and decadent indulgence.